Choler

Book Three of The Jenny Trilogy

Tabbie Browne

Copyright © 2014 Tabbie Browne

All rights reserved, including the right to reproduce this book, or portions thereof in any form. No part of this text may be reproduced, transmitted, downloaded, decompiled, reverse engineered, or stored, in any form or introduced into any information storage and retrieval system, in any form or by any means, whether electronic or mechanical without the express written permission of the author.

This is a work of fiction. Names and characters are the product of the author's imagination and any resemblance to actual persons, living or dead, is entirely coincidental.

ISBN: 978-1-326-03268-5

PublishNation, London
www.publishnation.co.uk

Other titles by this author

White Noise is Heavenly Blue (Book One of The Jenny Trilogy)
The Spiral (Book Two of The Jenny Trilogy)
The Unforgivable Error
No – Don't!

Visit the author's website at:
www.tabbiebrowneauthor.com

CHOLER definition *n. anger, wrath. Believed to be one of the four elemental humours of medieval physiology.*

Chapter 1

It wasn't the brightest of spring days but the rain that had been forecast hadn't arrived and the air had lost its chill.

"Did you see that garden with the beautiful irises?" Lizzie shared her pleasure with the other mothers waiting for their juniors to come out of school.

"Where?" came a disinterested reply.

"Oh you can't have missed them, on the corner as you turn into Meadow Road, they are so lovely this year." Many of the parents had moved away as they found her constant cheerfulness a bit overwhelming.

"Oh those, yes they are nice." Sharon smiled. She was one of the few who saw the childlike side of Lizzie and in a way felt pity for her when some of the others made snide remarks behind her back. They stood alone as the children came rushing out of the gates.

"Mum, Mum I drew this." There was no mistaking whose child was almost falling over herself trying to get to her mother. Bethany seemed much younger in her ways than the other children and often she too bore the brunt of unkind remarks, but by those who should have been sharing their games with her. The teacher had given them a period to be inventive and make what they liked, and while the others set about constructing various weird looking objects, she sat and lost herself in her artwork. But when she had finished, she refused to part with it so to save any fuss she was allowed to take it home.

"Bethany, let me see." Lizzie took the picture being waved at her by her daughter. "Oh that is very good, did you do it all by yourself?"

"Every bit. Mrs Jones said it was good."

Lizzie turned to Sharon. "Look what Bethany did."

"Um oh yes, very nice." but her attention was on her son. "What did you do Denis?"

He just shrugged and kept looking ahead.

"Well didn't you make anything?"

1

"Course. But you don't bring them home."

There was silence and Lizzie felt uneasy about the way he just stared at Bethany but put it down to boyish embarrassment.

"Well we had better be off, see you tomorrow." Sharon steered Denis away but as he walked his head was turned in Bethany's direction.

"Do you have an admirer?" Lizzie smiled and tried to make light of the moment.

"Who?"

"Well, Denis of course, looks as though he likes you."

"Ugh. Not him."

"Why, what's the matter with him?" Lizzie felt she must know what was on the girl's mind.

"Nobody likes him."

"But why?"

"He's just strange, that's all. What's for tea Mum?"

It was obvious the conversation was over, so Lizzie said "Your favourite."

"Yes!" Bethany almost exploded and skipped along in front singing as she went.

It was only about a ten minute walk to their little house, but enough time for Lizzie to constantly think about how lucky she considered herself. Her mind often went back briefly to the time when she had fully recovered from her injuries. Beth and Robert had married as planned and it was felt it would be best for all if all four moved away to make a fresh start. At first Margaret, Robert's daughter had been all for the idea and they settled in a small town near Lowestoft in Suffolk, but after a while Margaret became very unstable, was unable to hold down a job and was soon under continual psychiatric care. She had many phobias. There was no way anyone could persuade her to walk near the sea, and after a while even the sound of the surf seemed to drive her mad.

After a lot of consideration, Robert suggested to Beth that they move back inland. She agreed immediately and although they could not go back to Burford or anywhere near there, they still loved the Cotswolds and decided to look for a small quiet town that would suit them all and maybe settle Margaret into a calm way of life.

The more this girl needed peace, the more Lizzie's energy seemed to grow, almost as if there was only a certain amount to be shared between them. When a suitable house became available on the outskirts of Banbury they moved hoping this would be the answer to their prayers.

Lizzie soon started going out with a local lad, and it wasn't long before Beth hoped they would get married, they seemed so well matched. Danny Worth was a soft natured caring sort and had respect for his parents as well as Robert and Beth, and was always offering to do little jobs for them as the need arose. He had a steady job in one of the local small supermarkets and was liked by everyone. Not wanting to go back into caring, although it was what she loved, Lizzie didn't want to rake up old memories and decided to have a complete change so when Danny said they needed shelf stackers she applied and got a job at one of the branches.

Margaret didn't seem capable of any kind of work in fact she was finding it difficult to mix with anyone outside the home. Everyone had tried to get her to go shopping or to some event or other but she went into a panic attack and had to be calmed down. She was under the local mental health department who were very good but she seemed to be dropping into irretrievable despair. When Lizzie and Danny got married she refused to be a bridesmaid but Beth explained she wasn't capable of coping with such an ordeal.

After about a year, Bethany was born. Lizzie wanted to give her a name similar to her mother but not quite the same and everyone seemed to like this. As the little girl now skipped along so happily, Lizzie wondered where the last nine years had gone. They would have liked another child but it hadn't happened and they were a very happy little family so she didn't fret about it.

They reached the door of their little house and in seconds were in the kitchen.

"Now where shall we put this picture?" Lizzie held it out at arms length.

"Here, put it here." Bethany pointed to the only spare space on the fridge.

"Alright, get me some magnets please."

They both laughed as the magnets either dropped on the floor or other things had to be moved to make space, but this was how this pair lived. It was the same when Danny was around; life was always a laugh even when there was nothing to laugh about. Their humour was simple and childlike but they saw happiness in everything.

The phone rang and Lizzie gave the girl a playful pat on the head and went to answer it.

"Oh hello Mum, you all right?"

There seemed to be a long pause and Bethany, having finished placing her drawing joined her mum. She looked up into her face to try and glean what was going on for she sensed all wasn't well.

"Oh um – yes I'll just check with Danny when he gets home to make sure he hasn't got anything on but I'm sure that would be fine Mum."

She said her usual goodbye finishing with "Love you" and put her arm round Bethany's waist but before she could speak the child said "What's up Mum?"

"Up sweetheart, nothing's up… exactly." Although she played for time she knew there was little point, almost as if her daughter had an inner sense and knew things without being told.

"Is Gran all right?"

"Yes, she's fine, everybody's fine, it's um just that… um well you see they want us to go over for tea on Sunday."

"Why?"

They never went for a meal as such, they may have a drink and a piece of cake if it was arranged that they would pop in after shopping, but Margaret was never seen, always upstairs in her room. Danny might go over to help Robert with some job that took two people but again he never saw Margaret. It had become a way of life that she couldn't be included in social events due to her illness. Most people had worked out what kind of illness and there were always the sour tongued amongst the community who couldn't speak kindly of those less fortunate than themselves.

Lizzie knew better than to try delaying tactics so she said "It seems that your Auntie Margaret has been feeling a lot better lately and wants to see us." The words came tumbling out followed by silence.

"But I didn't think she liked us."

"Oh that's just because she's got this illness, it makes her seem that way."

"She doesn't like me. She shouted at me the last time I saw her."
"But she didn't mean it, don't you see?"
"But why do people do things if they don't mean it. That's silly."
The conversation wasn't going anywhere so Lizzie explained they would have to talk to Daddy about it later and not to worry for now.

Beth replaced the receiver and stood for a moment. Was she doing the right thing? Margaret certainly seemed to have improved on the new drug she had been prescribed but it was like waiting for a time bomb to go off. Even the slightest thing might be taken in the wrong way and then what would happen? Her motherly instinct was telling her not to involve the child but Margaret had definitely said she would like to see her and seemed sincere about it. Maybe this could be the turning point. At least Robert would be there and he, as always was her tower of strength and if anyone could take control of a difficult situation there was none better.

She went upstairs to Margaret's room and tapped lightly on the door.
"Fancy a cup of tea? I'm having one."
"Yes."
"Do you want it up here, or will you come down, there's just us."
"Can't you bring yours up here?"
This was just what Robert was trying to stop.
"You can't let her make the rules" he would say "she will use her mental state to run this place. Well there are other people besides her. Don't be her servant."
These words ran through Beth's mind as she stood on the landing. She wondered if his anger was directed at Margaret or was it in some way getting back at Madge because she was the cause of it all. She took a deep breathe.
"I think I need to put my feet up before I do the dinner. On second thoughts it would help me if you could fetch yours."
Silence. As Beth turned to go back downstairs the bedroom door opened.
"I know your little game. I'm on to you." The venom in the words was unmistakable.
"Think you can trick me don't you? Bet you've even got Dad thinking how clever you are, well it won't work."

It wasn't like Beth to explode but she had had enough. She spun round to face her and came within inches of her face catching Margaret off guard.

"Listen lady. You aren't the only one with problems round here but you are too self centred to see anything affecting those that care for you."

Margaret looked as if she had been shot and for once couldn't come back with one of her vicious replies.

"Wh..What do you mean?"

The sight of Beth sobbing froze her to the spot. This was something new, something she didn't know how to handle. She started to cry, partly from shock but mostly from insecurity for her rock was disintegrating before her eyes.

"You wouldn't understand. You wouldn't want to even try and understand." Beth turned and almost ran down the stairs and without even thinking Margaret was after her and when they reached the kitchen she guided her to a chair and threw her arms round her crying with her. When she looked at her face it was bright red, and the blotches stretched down her neck to her chest.

"Mama Beth, what is it? Are you sick?" She had never been able to use the word Mother or Mum as it reminded her of Madge and the terrible happenings so she made up her own title.

Beth had calmed but said in a slight panic "Water, please some cold water."

Margaret hurried to the sink and realised she didn't even know where to look for a glass so grabbed a beaker, filled it from the tap and hurried back to Beth who took it as though her life depended upon it, which to her it felt as though it did.

"Oh that's better." After a moment Beth cooled down and realised Margaret was sponging her face with some kitchen towel soaked in water.

"What's the matter?" She was looking into Beth's eyes with a look she hadn't known for many years. "You're ill aren't you? I didn't know."

"No need." Beth patted her cheek smiling. "Oh Margaret that is the best tonic I could have had. Sit down."

They sat at the small kitchen table while Beth explained she was merely going through the change and sometimes it was harder to cope with than others but it was normal. They both laughed when Margaret said she thought it only happened to older people and Beth had to remind her that she was of 'that age'. They got round to talking about the family coming for tea and thankfully it seemed that the younger woman was actually looking forward to it. Maybe the pills had helped but she felt she had reached a turning point and hoped life would have more purpose now. Beth warned her that nothing was easy and had to be worked at and that was where family support was essential.

"We will both have good days and bad days, but we can see each other through." Beth said quietly. "I can't possibly know what you go through, and no one can expect you to know what the menopause is like because you haven't had it, but we can be there, and that's all that matters."

"You know if I go off on one?" Margaret asked tentatively, but before she could ask any more Beth cut in with "I shall spank your bottom!"

"Oh if only this is the turning point. Please let it be so." Beth thought to herself.

Although many years had passed since the traumatic events in Burford, Jenny was still on the alert regarding any retaliation from Zargot as she knew that if he had a score to settle, time was no object and he had often let victims sail along for years thinking they were all right. Then, just when they least expected it, he would strike. From her position in the upper spiral on Eden she had to oversee all events in the area but had to rely on her faithful crew to take over on her behalf. The Burford incident was but a drop in the ocean and could easily have been put to one side in favour of equally threatening happenings, but she always had the feeling that this one was aimed at her and so had to be particularly vigilant, even now.

Matthew and Graham would often pay quick visits to check on the current situation and send their feedback so that Jenny was always ready for the unexpected. It was during one such moment that Matthew witnessed the exchange between Beth and Margaret and did all he could to calm the situation. He drew on all the love and kindness Beth had inside and used it to plant the seed in the other woman to help fight this terrible mental illness which was trapping her and preventing her from leading the normal life which was due to her. Against all his training he cursed Zargot for the evil he had left planted in this person and vowed to protect her all he could.

Jenny received the news and was equally determined to rid her of the 'virus' and restore her to a happier life, although it would take time.

Margaret had felt this powerful wave flow over her and while she didn't understand what it was or from whence it came, she warmed to the feeling, begging it to stay and never leave her.

When Danny came home from work, he walked straight up to Lizzie and gave her his usual big kiss then turned to Bethany, scooped her up in his arms and said "And how's Daddy's big girl today?"

She giggled with delight and said "I drew a picture and we put it on the fridge Daddy, come and look."

She was wriggling so hard, Danny had barely put her feet on the floor when she was off dragging him by the hand. He cast a glance over his shoulder to Lizzie with a shrug as much to say he had better do as he was told as she followed the two enjoying the happiness they all shared.

They all stood looking at the picture as he asked who the people were.

"Well that's you, and that's Mum" Bethany was pointing to each figure as she spoke, "and of course that's me."

"And who are the others?" Lizzie realised she hadn't asked before and thought they must be school friends, but they looked like adults so perhaps they were supposed to be Beth and Robert and possibly Margaret. There was a pause.

"Well that's Mrs Jones."

The parents waited for her to carry on but as she seemed to have finished her explanation Danny asked "And who is that lady?"

"One of the mums."

Rather bewildered Lizzie said she thought it might be Gran.

"Don't be silly Mum, this is at school. Gran doesn't come to school unless it's to watch a play or a concert."

Lizzie was intrigued now, wondering why they would be in the picture if it was supposed to be school time but said casually "So the man is...?"

"Oh he's there too."

"But who is he?" Danny was becoming concerned now. Didn't the chap have a name?

"But you know, why are you asking me Mum?"

Beth and Danny immediately looked at each other equally baffled. Lizzie put her arm round Bethany and said "But there is never a man near me, usually it's only Sharon um - Denis's Mum that stays to talk to me."

She turned again to Danny "I've never seen a man, well occasionally one of the dads collects his child like you have now and again, but not regularly."

"Bethany," Danny stooped down "is this man there in the morning when you go to school?"

She nodded. "Yes."

"And is he there when you come out in the afternoon."

"Yes I told you." She looked worried and her lip started to tremble. "I thought you liked the picture."

Lizzie put her arm round her and said "It's Ok we love it, we only wondered who the people were. You are very clever, isn't she Daddy?"

"Very, and we're very proud of you, in fact I think it deserves a treat." Danny had a way of making things better and the child brightened straight away.

"What is it?" She was bouncing up and down again now.

"Well, we've had some new DVDs in and guess what one of them is."

Her gasp could be heard through the house. "Not the Ice Penguins?"

"That's the one." He turned to his wife. "I can get it Friday when I get paid. They'll put one aside for me."

The happiness returned to the house the little girl went to bed that night only thinking of penguins. Her parents once they were alone thought back to the picture and went to take another look.

"Don't recognise him. Do you?" Danny asked.

"Never seen him. Where did she get that from?"

"You're shaking."

"No, No I'm Ok, it's just the man's hair, it reminded me of.. of…"

Danny grabbed her by the shoulders. "Tell me, who does it remind you of?" Then he dropped his arms with shocked expression on his face. "No. Tell me it isn't that one – you know we said we'd never speak of him but…is it him?"

Suddenly Lizzie said "Wait a minute."

"What?"

"Let me think, just a second."

He watched as her face changed to a softer look.

"This will sound stupid but just listen. The colour of the hair and the hard look is familiar. There is someone who stands near me every day but it isn't a man."

"Then who in Christ's name is it?"

"Denis."

Danny looked almost exasperated "And who is Denis? No wait, didn't you say Denis's Mum just now?"

"Yes, Sharon, she's nice, but Denis is only Bethany's age, he isn't a man."

"Right, so why does she see him as a man and not a little boy?"

"Oh." Her hands went to her face. "Surely she isn't one of those children that see – you know spirits and things."

"I don't know what she sees, but we know what she thinks she sees, it's right there." He pointed to the man staring back at them from the picture on the fridge.

They both stood for a moment then Danny leaned nearer scrutinising every part. He turned to his wife and said quietly "We could be getting our lines crossed."

"In what way. I don't get it."

"Well, we are assuming it's Denis because there are things that are the same, but what if it isn't him at all?"

Lizzie still wasn't grasping what he was driving at. "I – I don't know what you mean Danny."

"If, and I'm only saying if she can see things, perhaps there is someone, like a guardian angel who is looking after someone, say Denis, but it isn't him is it?"

"Oh I don't know, but I'll tell you one thing I don't like the sound of it." She was almost in tears now, with past memories trying to creep back into her locked mind.

"Ok, Ok," Danny was hugging her now, "tell you what, let's not put too much meaning on it. It may just be a simple thing that we needn't worry over."

"I hope you're right."

As if a sudden inspiration had hit him Danny smiled and said "Well there's one thing to be grateful for."

"Oh?"

"Bethany isn't bothered by it is she."

"Oh Danny, I never thought of that. No, come to think of it she just took it as normal didn't she?"

"Feel better now?" He guided her to the sofa and patted the cushion for her to sit down beside him.

"Yes, I do." Lizzie tried to sound convincing but inside something was niggling at her and she would have to find out what it was.

Robert had been flicking through the local newspaper and looked up as Beth came in carrying two beakers of tea. She looked as though a weight had been lifted as she sat down beside him.

"Wasn't it great to have Margaret sit for a whole meal?"

"I couldn't believe it" he answered drawing her close "could this be a good omen?"

"I do hope so for her sake."

"And what about yours? You took on a hell of a task with her. It's kept you from working which is what you would have liked, and the times you've stayed in because of her."

"Oh I didn't mind. It wasn't her fault." Beth smiled the way she did when Robert had first fallen for her. The kind loving look that was special to her but she wasn't one to dwell on any sacrifices she had made.

"Anything good in the paper?" she changed the subject.

"Well I was thinking about going round a garden centre or two. This place could do with a freshen up. Put some new ideas into play. What do you say?"

"Oo Yes. I love spring, best time to get started." Beth thought that without pushing, Margaret may just take and interest in something like this.

"Well," Robert grabbed the paper "there's this one near Chippy or there's one on the Southam road."

"Let's do both." Beth was eager to get going.

"This week-end coming, if the weather's good?"

"Oh yes. I shall really look forward to that." Maybe things were looking up after all this time. It would be the best thing that could happen, then life could start again on a peaceful carefree footing.

"Who could wish for more?" she thought as she sipped her tea, cuddling up to the man she loved.

Another of Jenny's sentinels had been keeping a discreet watch on schools in the area especially the one attended by Bethany, whilst others were rotated so that the whole family were protected at all times. Jenny knew that Zargot or one of his agents would strike at some time but it could take many years because the earthlings were small fry and only a means to an end. He had no real interest in Lizzie or her kin, they were the pathway to lead him to her to take his final revenge. But nothing could be left to chance for that is when the good forces could be at their most vulnerable.

But there was another source that was also in the front of Jenny's thoughts. What had happened to Vedron? He appeared to have gone elsewhere but there was no trace of him in the solar system which only left one answer. He must have changed his form, not the earthly one for the spiritual would still be identifiable. He must have taken on a cloak of a totally different identity which meant he had been free to roam anywhere undetected. He could have been operating amongst them without them suspecting a thing. She set Graham the task of sending out probes to locate anything that that could remotely bear his trademark. Little did she know she would not have long to wait.

The Vexons, an alien race which had inhabited the earth in human form for many centuries were driven purely by sexual gratification and possession of anything that came within their grasp. Vedron, one of these creatures had himself been used by the evil Zargot causing the terrible happenings resulting in Madge's death and leaving her daughter Margaret in an unstable state. Vedron was so proud he thought he had been in complete control and although appeared to have retracted into the background following the Burford events, had made up his mind to return and take what was his. But on a regular sweep of the area, none of Jenny's good forces were able to find him or any of his kind. Graham located a cluster of Vexons in South America and they seemed to be confined to one area alone which seemed strange for these beings as they usually spread themselves, hungry for their next pickings. On getting the report special sentinels were despatched to the area to monitor the habits to determine whether or not these were true Vexons or a similar species.

Always trying to be one step ahead, Jenny was not fooled into believing they were simply positioned as decoys thus drawing attention to themselves whilst the true evil ones were setting up an operation elsewhere. She knew they had to be on the earth planet as that was the only one able to satisfy their hunger for there was nowhere else with such an abundance of life forms suitable to their needs. They knew no love, only lust and spared no feelings in their quest. When one area was spent, they simply moved to another. This made the South America source appear to be out of line with their normal ways. Orders were sent out globally to be on the alert for any abnormal activity of any kind, and from any form, bodily or spiritual.

"Do not dismiss anything because you thought it couldn't be important." Jenny was adamant to her immediate workers who passed the information down the line until every spirit worker was aware of the importance of the task. The questions must be answered.

"Where is he and in what state of existence?"

Chapter 2

It was Friday and Lizzie was walking Bethany to school.

"Do we really have to go to Gran and Grandad's on Sunday?" The child looked up with appealing eyes.

"We do, but you love seeing them, so it will be nice."

"I know, but I'm afraid of Auntie Margaret." She was pouting almost as if that would make her mother change her mind.

"Yes, but Gran says she's much better and she is looking forward to seeing you." Lizzie hoped it sounded genuine. "Perhaps she'll play ball with you in the garden."

"If Daddy gets that DVD today, I'd rather watch that."

This was going nowhere and Lizzie didn't want her mind to be distracted all day and not pay attention to her schoolwork, but just as she was trying to find a suitable reply they neared the school gates and her mind switched to the drawing. She slowed her pace.

"Bethany."

"Yes Mum."

"There's Denis and his mum."

The girl looked baffled. "I know." Her tone was signifying that there was nothing unusual about it.

"Who's with them?"

"What do you mean?"

Lizzie nodded towards Sharon. "Is there anyone else there, like in the picture you drew?"

"Oh, you mean the man don't you? Yes of course he's there, he's always there. Don't be silly Mum."

This was a problem now because Lizzie didn't want to admit she couldn't see him because if she did it could frighten Bethany in two ways. She would either think her mum was strange because she couldn't see him, or she may wonder why she could and her mum couldn't. But was she too young to even grasp that?

"Well he's just brought one of the kids I expect." Lizzie was struggling but tried to sound as casual as possible.

"Why?"

Now she was in a spot. What could she say that wouldn't sound odd?

"Well – um – why else would he be here." Then the idea came to her "You said he wasn't a teacher didn't you?" She couldn't remember if they had asked the question when they were admiring the drawing but it seemed like a good thing to say.

"I wouldn't have."

"Oh."

They had reached the gate and Sharon greeted them with a yawn.

"I'm still half asleep this morning."

"Didn't you sleep well then Sharon?" Lizzie showed concern.

"No Denis had a bad night again. Has these nightmares you know, the doc says he should grow out of it, just his age." Sharon shrugged as if she wasn't too impressed then said "Sees these animals only they aren't there. I'm at my wits end I can tell you."

Lizzie kissed Bethany, told her to be a good girl, and watched her disappear into the throng of nosy children. Sharon shouted "Bye" to Denis who waved without turning round.

The two ladies turned and started to walk away when Lizzie had an idea.

"Do you fancy a cup of coffee?"

Sharon looked at her watch and said "You know what, I would. Got to be at work at ten, but I could use a quick one."

"Then why don't we go back to my house, it'll only take a minute."

"Thanks. Might wake me up a bit."

They were soon in the kitchen and as Lizzie made the coffee she casually pointed to Bethany's drawing.

"Bet you don't recognise who she's drawn" She tried to make it sound light hearted and gave a nervous laugh.

"Um? Oh, yes I didn't get a good look at it when you showed me." She stood in front of it and a frown appeared.

Lizzie stirred the drinks and said "Sugar?"

"Um, No – thanks." Sharon had heard the question but her mind was elsewhere.

"Well? Guess who the grown ups are." Lizzie was getting agitated until she had a reply.

"Don't know, they don't look like anyone in particular."

This needed some pushing.

"Well, she says that is her teacher; that is one of the mums, and that....." she paused hoping her friend would say something but if she wanted answers she was disappointed.

"No sorry, don't know. But you know kids - live in a world of their own most of the time. Take Denis for instance."

Lizzie felt somewhat flattened. She had hoped Sharon would either recognise the man or say she had never seen him, but this was a dead end and she was now pouring out her own problem regarding her son's sleeping problems.

"It's not every night. You never know when it's going to be and I can't ignore him can I?"

"Well of course you can't."

"I envy you with having a good husband, 'cos you've got someone there to share the burden. It's not easy on your own."

"No, it can't be. Have you talked to your Mum?"

"What can she do?" Sharon sniffed. "Just says give it time, he'll grow out of it."

Not knowing quite what to say Lizzie offered "A bit like the doctor then?"

"You've said it. Anyway I'd best be off. Thanks for the coffee and the chat. At least I feel awake now."

As Sharon left, Lizzie closed the door and went again to the drawing.

"Well" she decided "you are just a picture from a child's imagination and you aren't going to bother me." She felt that by saying it out loud it would wash away any strange feelings she was harbouring and everything would be all right from now on. But, although she wouldn't admit it, her inner fears were still niggling at her.

Pulling herself together she decided she would start looking in earnest for that part time job she had been considering. She hadn't wanted to work until Bethany started school and then she had done odd casual work so that she would always be there for her, working round the school times but now the girl was there all day she would be able to do more hours and still be there to pick her up. There was always the supermarket but that would be a bit too far to go in the times allowed so she made up her mind to look nearer home and see what was available, after all they could certainly do with a bit of extra money.

There had been a lot of unusual activity in the Pacific Ocean recently regarding strange objects appearing out of the water, hovering for a while then submerging in the blink of an eye. Not only had Jenny been aware of the events long before they had hit the headlines, but she was always on the look out for Zargot's next move. The papers were full of UFO sightings and now these USOs (unidentified submerged objects) had added to the attention.

The good forces always monitored every space in the solar system but there was a higher concentration on the earth due to the numerous life forms occupying it already. But danger was always somewhere, either in the fabric of space, the air, solid earth and water and even the moons orbiting their own planets. All of these segments had their own special forces in constant touch with the higher spirals, the ultimate control centre, not only in the good realms but also the evil, hence the need for constant alertness.

There was also the danger of decoy happenings, for while all attention was centred on watching the next appearance of some unidentifiable craft, the evil could be planting its seeds undetected.

Graham was checking the Midlands area of England and receiving various random reports which at first seemed to have no consequence, but upon reflection started to have a strange similarity. The guardian caring for Lizzie drew attention to Bethany's picture, whilst another pointed out a similar one at a school a few miles away only to be followed by almost identical descriptions spreading over neighbouring counties. Graham returned to Lizzie's house in an instant and studied the image which seemed to be appearing in all the drawings, then he did an instantaneous visit to all the places that had been reported to him and, taking in the vibrations knew something was wrong.

As he mentally showed Jenny his findings she sprang into action, sending all the personnel she could muster to cover every educational establishment in the British Isles. She extended the net so that those on the south coast could also examine the countries on the other side of the Channel. In the past she had experienced many attacks involving artwork and hoped this would follow a pattern and the source would soon be detected. The less experienced could soon be squashed but the higher evil levels might prove more of a challenge, but the first thing was to find out just what they were up against and then plot a course of action.

"Do you want to come shopping Margaret?" Beth smiled at her. "We need to get the things for Sunday tea."

"I – I haven't been to the shops for ages. Do I have to?" Her lip was trembling and soon her whole body seemed to shake. Beth went over to her and slipped her arm round her shoulder.

"Of course you don't. I only wondered if you wanted to." She gave her a loving pat on the shoulder and went to the side table to get a pen and writing pad.

"Tell you what, help me pick what we need." She settled herself on the sofa, pen poised waiting. After a moment she looked up and Margaret was nearly in tears.

"I – I don't know how, I haven't had to do – I mean - I can't..."

Her voice trailed off and afraid she would drop into her despair mode Beth quickly said with forced light heartedness "That's Ok. My fault dear, I should have realised."

Margaret looked back at her almost like a child that has realised it isn't going to be told off.

"Well, I'll get some things to make a trifle. Bethany always likes trifle." Beth carried on as if everything was normal.

"What if she won't speak to me? She doesn't like me."

Beth put down the pen and pad and looked her straight in the eye. "It's not her fault dear. She's very young and the young expect people to fall into little pigeon holes, you know Dads are all the same, Mums, Aunties and all the rest. They have a picture you see of what they think people are like. They are still learning at her age, so we have to be understanding with them rather than expecting too much."

Margaret seemed deep in thought. "Ok. So what if she ignores me? What should I do?"

"Well," Beth paused wanting to give the right response "you know what I'd do?"

"What?"

"When - no if she ignores you just sound as if you're not bothered and say something like 'Oh I used to be like that at your age'."

"And does that work?" She brightened now realising that Mama Beth could be a good friend to her.

"Used to for me."

"You've said that?"

Beth laughed now. "To both you and Lizzie when you were going through the stage of knowing it all."

Now it was Margaret's turn to laugh "Were we like that?"

"Oh yes. Most children are when they start feeling their feet. Don't forget Bethany is only nine, not a teenager, and she still looks at the world in a purer simpler way than we do, although I would hate to say for how long."

"Why do you say that?"

Beth studied her and realised that for over ten years this poor soul had been locked away in torment following the horrible happenings and the world had carried on without her.

"Well, the things they say and at such a young age too."

"I don't follow. What things?"

Beth gave a nervous cough. She had always been a very polite person and didn't discuss bedroom secrets with all and sundry like some of the wives and she was often shocked at the language used by some young people.

Well dear, I don't repeat some of the things, they're not nice and I'm glad you and Lizzie don't but enough to say that they aren't – well – ladylike, if you know what I mean."

"I think so." Margaret would have liked to have heard more, but at the same time felt Beth was protecting her and so didn't push her further. As she looked across she saw how flustered she looked and remembering the last episode rushed to fetch a glass of cold water. She was in such a hurry she nearly tipped it all over Beth who hardly noticed as she drank it gratefully.

After Beth had returned to normal, she reached out her hand and said "Oh Margaret, I don't know what I'd do without you just now." She knew it would make her feel not only wanted, but needed. She prayed this would be the blessing in disguise to help her step daughter get back on her feet and lead a happier life.

Lizzie had washed up the coffee cups and was sorting out some washing when she heard something come through the front door. Being far too early for the postman, she assumed it would be another load of junk mail which seemed to fill the recycling bin at the moment. She was going to leave it but somehow curiosity got the better of her and she went to see what had dropped on the mat. It appeared to be the normal sort of A5 flyer advertising offers, holidays or telling her she had been selected to win a car but as she picked it up she could see it was nothing of the sort. She slowly made her way back to the living room and sat down to study it.

The words seemed to stand out from the page. "THIS IS JUST FOR YOU". Lizzie had become used to the fake promises the firms appeared to make after Robert had given her quite a lengthy speech about the fact that nobody is giving anything away, there is always a catch. He had done it very kindly knowing she was the sort to believe all she was told. But this was different. As she read on it seemed directed solely at her and without thinking she looked for a contact number to ring.

"That's funny," she thought turning the paper over in her hand "there's nothing to say who it's from." The back was plain but as she flipped it over to look at the front again she noticed an address in very small print at the bottom.

"Must have missed it," she laughed and read out the details. Although she had lived here for a few years and knew all the main streets, there were some smaller older ones that she had never needed to use. She went to the cupboard and got out a street guide.

"Farriers End," she murmured "there's no such place" but then noticed a Farriers Lane. "Oh that must be it" she said to herself thinking there had been a misprint.

Danny would have said that it wasn't very business like to get the address wrong, and why no telephone numbers? Most people put a mobile number if nothing else but this just gave the street. Had he been there he would most likely have told her to ignore it. But he wasn't there. She checked again to see which well known street led to this place, checked the clock and decided she would have time to have a look and see what it was like before she had some lunch.

As she walked she went over the wording in her mind. "Are you looking for a little job to earn enough for that holiday you have dreamed of? Do you feel some of your time is being wasted? Are you unfulfilled? Could you be doing more for your child?" There was nothing unusual or personal in the wording in fact it had probably been used many times by many firms but it wasn't the words that were pulling Lizzie along the street. It was the paper itself, for it seemed to be guiding her almost like a sat nav even to the point of directing her round each corner until she was walking down a narrow alley not wide enough for a single car.

Anyone reaching the entrance to this spooky passage would have stopped in their tracks and wondered if they should go any further but this never occurred to her, almost as if something had taken control of her will. Suddenly she stopped. To her left was a plain wall of Cotswold stone and to her right a small door leading into a pokey little shop. For a moment she almost turned and ran back the way she had come but the door opened slowly and she saw an arm beckoning her in.

"Ah you must be the lady for the job." The voice sounded friendly and as someone appeared she relaxed a little.

"Um, well I was just curious." She moved to the doorway and came face to face with a young man which took her by surprise as, for some reason she expected someone much older.

"Do come in. It's a pleasure to meet you. I'm so glad you came."

Lizzie felt as though something was trying to stop her entering but at the same time he was pulling her in. Before she realised, she was standing in the shop which now seemed much larger than it appeared from the outside. She looked around. This wasn't what she expected although she wasn't quite sure what it was she expected. Her mind was racing.

"I don't think this is quite what I'm looking for." Her voice seemed like a whisper.

"It never is to start with." The owner was staring at her which made her feel very uncomfortable.

"Perhaps I should go. I'm sorry to have wasted your time."

The man had moved between her and the door blocking her exit.

"But you would be so perfect for the job."

"I – I don't know what the job is. Please, I'd like to leave now."

"Before you do, just say Hello to my aunt. This is her place really."

Lizzie could feel her heart thumping in her chest. She didn't want to meet his aunt, uncle or any member of his family. The long silky drapes hanging on the walls seemed to be swaying, while the rows of beads jingled in her ears as though they were all telling her to do as he said.

"Well just for a moment, then I must go." she whispered feeling this was the only way she was every going to get out of this horrible place.

"Just through that curtain, she's in the back." The man pointed.

Lizzie took a couple of steps in the direction he indicated then stopped. Something was preventing her from going any further but the curtain in front of her started to move, swaying, swishing until it was flapping against her, pulling her forward until it had wrapped itself completely around her. She tried to scream but felt the air being pumped out of her lungs. Her mind flashed back to Burford and she summoned every ounce of strength calling on someone to help her. Suddenly she was pulled backwards and lifted bodily until she was back in the alley, alone. The door of the shop was shut and there was no sign of life within.

She had no idea how long it took her to feel strong enough to stumble back to the streets she knew and somehow she was guided back to her little home where she flung herself onto the sofa and gave way to uncontrollable sobbing.

Her guardian had called on the higher powers to assist and it was they who had rescued her from the trap. Jenny was informed and when a scan was done of the alley and the shop, nothing was found. All signs of any activity had gone but Vedron had made the contact he wanted and Lizzie was once again his.

There was great consternation now as it was almost a certainty that Zargot or one of his kind had tried to trap Lizzie but Jenny still had her suspicions regarding Vedron. For one thing the attempt appeared to have been handled in a very amateurish way. Surely Zargot would have had a better result. Immediately Lizzie's guardian was replaced with Amity, a higher angel who could pick up the slightest vibration in the surrounding area quicker than most, and Jenny knew she would soon have soaked up the entire episode into her being and related it back to the upper spiral.

She covered Lizzie with her calming powers as she comforted her into a much calmer state. After a few moments for her to gather herself together, she steered her to the kitchen where she watched her dabbing her face with cold water. Lizzie felt the presence and said aloud "Did you help me?" There were no words in the reply but the feeling entered her mind "One of us did but I am here to stay with you constantly and protect you." A feeling of security swept over her and the words so often used before gushed around her "Think of the love. Only the love." She was whispering it to herself almost like a prayer.

After a few moments she began to feel almost normal again and wondered if she had fallen asleep and had been dreaming. The memories of the alley and the shop were being erased until they became a blur and she shook herself and told herself not to be so silly. The strength being pumped into her spirit was boosting her to fight something she couldn't handle alone and she would need all the help possible if she was the target Jenny suspected.

The phone ringing made Beth jump for a moment and was surprised when Margaret went over and lifted the handset and although she handed it to her without answering, Beth knew this was another step forward because she wouldn't normally go near it.

"Hello." She looked at Margaret and smiled. "It's Dad" she whispered.

"How are you doing my darling?" Robert still spoke as if they were young lovers.

"Oh I'm fine dear, and you?"

"Yes, busy but then that's a good sign. Anyway, any more problems?" He was worried about her during this time of her life and he wasn't too sure what he could do for the best. The doctor had told him to be understanding and patient which was no problem and he loved her so much he would have done anything, but he was only too aware that she had taken on his daughter and looked after her as if she had been her own and the extra burden couldn't be helping the situation.

"Oh just the hotties, but Margaret looked after me."

For a moment Robert wondered if he heard it right.

"You said.."

"Yes I know dear," she didn't want to make too much of it with Margaret only a few feet away "don't know what I'd do without her."

"Right."

"Anyway we're sorting out what to get for Sunday tea so we're fine."

"Good, glad to hear that. See you later. Love you."

"Love you too." She blew him a kiss and gave the handset back to Margaret.

As he put the phone down, Robert mused for a moment. He knew Beth well enough to pick up the fact she couldn't say all she wanted but if Margaret was really as helpful as was suggested, maybe this was the start of better things and if only his daughter could get better albeit slowly, life would hold more hope than it had done for a long time. Granted, progress would be slow and there could be setbacks, but what a joy to be able to close the door on previous trauma and catch up on lost time. He knew there would be a very interesting conversation when he and his beloved were curled up in their love nest together that night.

Sharon was already at the school gates when Lizzie arrived.

"You Ok Sharon?"

"Not really."

"Anything you can tell me." Lizzie never liked to pry but was concerned about her friend who had seemed all right when she left this morning.

"Well you know I work at that shop from ten till three, then I've got that cleaning job in the evenings and me Mam babysits for me?"

"Yes." Lizzie nodded.

"Well, that old cow has had the knife in for me for some time and I've been sacked."

"What, from the shop?"

"That's the one. I hope she rots in hell. She should try bringing up a kid like him on what you can scrape together."

"But can she do that? Just sack you I mean."

"Oh she's clever. Made out I've had warnings and this was the final one."

"But..." Lizzie never liked to hear of injustice and would have pushed her friend to fight but it was obvious from her manner that it wasn't going to happen.

"I'm glad to be shot of her and her stinking shop. Hope it burns down."

"Sharon! You shouldn't say things like that." Lizzie was horrified.

They were both quiet for a minute then Sharon said "Trouble is I've got to work round Denis, can't work full time."

"I know. I was thinking about looking for something, you know like you said round school time."

Sharon eyed her up and down. "What did you do before? Before you were married I mean."

"Oh I worked in care homes. I liked that."

"Not cleaning up the shit and stuff?"

Lizzie laughed "Well sometimes, but giving them their meals, and tea and making the beds. I loved it."

"So you're not afraid of getting your hands dirty?"

"I suppose I'm not when I come to think of it. Why do you ask?"

"Oh nothing in particular. Just had an idea, that's all. Let me think about it but you might just have put your finger on something. Oh There's Denis."

Leaving Lizzie standing utterly bewildered Sharon dashed off, said a quick word to Denis and they both disappeared.

"Mum, Mum." Bethany was pulling at her mother's arm.

"Oh sorry darling, I was miles away."

"Can I have a biscuit when we get home?"

Lizzie put her head on one side with a quizzical look so Bethany repeated the question with the word 'please' on the end."

"I should think so as long as you still eat your dinner."

"Yes" the girl chirped as she skipped along swinging her arms.

The conversation with Sharon together with seeing her child so happy had erased the morning's events from Lizzie's mind as she set about preparing the evening meal. Danny wouldn't leave work until six o'clock and they ate as soon as he got in so that Bethany had time for her meal to go down before she went to bed at eight.

"What's this Mum?" she was holding the flyer in her hand.

Lizzie cast a quick look as she chopped onions, tears streaming down her face so she couldn't see clearly what was being waved at her.

"Don't know dear. What's it look like?"

"Just a piece of paper, I found it on the floor."

"Well just put it on the table it might be something that's slipped out of a magazine."

"Ok." Bethany bounced back into the living room, did as she had been told and settled down to watch the television.

A complete search had been performed on the alley and the deserted shop. Normally after a visitation of any kind there would be traces of some sort. Any entity leaves its impression almost like a footprint in the sand until it is washed away by the tide. That is why it is so important to scan any area immediately before evidence is erased. The special 'sweep' sentinels had combed every speck of dust and all seemed clear but as they were about to depart one of them stopped and hovered again over one particular place. They never looked for physical signs, their special powers could sense out the unseen, or unfelt. But one of their favourite targets was the 'closing space'. Any presence disturbs the surrounding air leaving a gap which slowly closes together as they pass through. Only the very highest levels can perform immediate closure leaving no trace, but the normal spirit has no control over how long it takes for the space to become solid again. This is another reason why there must be no delay in performing a sweep.

The sentinel hovered surrounded by the others. It was there. Exactly where the image of the curtain had been was the suggestion of a gap, closing very slowly. Without delay the information was being fed to the upper spiral on Eden and Jenny was scrutinising the images being transmitted. There was just time to scrape enough of the atmosphere to be able to determine its source, almost like a blood sample being sent for analysis, but with no physical means. They had what they wanted and the team was dismissed, commended for their diligence. It only took seconds to verify the perpetrator for the spiritual DNA was there. Vedron had shown his hand without realising it for he thought there was no way they could trace him as he had cleared his tracks too well. But not well enough for the 'sweepers'.

Jenny's team now had the task of trying to decide, not only from where he had emerged, but where he had scurried back in an attempt to prevent being traced all the way to his present location. But maybe he wasn't operating from one precise point. As usual it was necessary not to put too many power angels on his track as he would become aware straight away, also the higher up the spiral they were, would also alert him, so, as was the practice in such circumstances, they had to be exceedingly covert in their approach.

The latest report on the pictures seemed to provide little help but somehow they had to be connected. The schools had been well scanned but no spiritual presence was noticed that bore any resemblance to the man drawn by the children, so it had to be speculation that this entity had done his work or found what he or she was looking for then departed. The reports all came back that any non earthly spirits were merely checking on their families and there was no suggestion of malice or threat.

It seemed to be coming apparent that Vedron was in some way involved and had been searching for Lizzie's present home. The lower spirits could be forgiven for thinking that with his powers he would have sought her out long ago but he had been forced to keep a low profile, not only by the good forces but Zargot who considered him an even greater threat to his own power and would destroy him without consideration. Also, with time being different in other dimensions, it was not important to him how long it took, merely the success of the outcome. Of course he wanted Lizzie to be in the earth form so that he could fulfil his satisfaction and possess her in every way possible, but he couldn't afford to jeopardise his position with the enemies he had made who were waiting for the kill.

Robert's car pulled into the driveway and gathering his things he was soon in the house. He had hoped Margaret would be there but knew he couldn't expect too much all at once.

"Hello." His wife's voice still made his heart beat quicker and he took her into his arms and kissed her as though he hadn't seen her for ages.

"What man could ask for a better welcome my darling?" He was holding her to him as though he was afraid she would be snatched away and when she pulled back he could see in her face the reason.

"I'm sorry Robert, not another one." She was fanning her face which was bright red now and rushed to the kitchen for a drink.

He followed her and kindly said "Should you see the doctor again?"

"I don't know." She looked so weak as she slumped down onto a chair. "Someone told me if you give into them they go over quicker but if you fight it's worse."

"What about the pills?" Robert felt so helpless and wanted to do all he could but had no experience of this.

"Well the doctor didn't seem to know whether to give me them or not, just told me to see how it goes."

"Want me to come with you, if you go that is?"

"Oh I'm sure I can manage, after all it's not just me is it? Every woman has to cope sometime, and Margaret is more important now."

He stiffened. "Ah, so that's what's holding you back. Not thinking of yourself as usual. You have done everything for her. You can't keep putting her first. You are the most important thing to me."

As he spoke they both heard a sound at the door and just caught a glimpse of Margaret dashing across the room and heard her running up the stairs.

"Oh No!" Beth was on her feet in an instance but Robert held her back.

"Leave her. You can't be there every minute."

Beth was sobbing "But she must have heard you and now she thinks she isn't important and we had been doing so well and…"

"Stop it!"

Robert was sharper than he intended but his beloved was becoming hysterical which was the last thing she should be doing.

"I'll go." he said gently as he guided her back to the chair.

Slowly he went up the stairs and stood at his daughter's bedroom door. He tapped softly.

"Margaret."

There was no reply but as he leaned his head towards the door he thought he could hear muffled crying.

"Margaret, it's Dad, can I come in please?"

Again he listened and thought he could hear a faint word. Not being sure what it was he took a deep breath and gently opened the door.

"Margaret."

She was lying on the bed crying as if all the troubles of the world were on her shoulders. He sat on a chair near the bed and slowly reached out his hand wondering what he could say for the best. After a minute she sniffed and looked at him.

"What is it sweetheart?" he whispered.

"Mama Beth."

Robert was a little taken aback as he was expecting an outburst about how he loved Beth more than her.

"Because she doesn't seem very well?" He ventured hoping she would explain.

"Oh Dad. She's so good to me. I know it now, but I'm being punished having to watch her like this. I've always got to see her suffer just to teach me a lesson." She was crying again and Robert moved to the bed and stroked her hand a little relieved in one way but concerned in another.

"Margaret it isn't like that, now listen to me and I'll explain." He waited until he had got her attention then told her that not only Beth had to go through this but one day she would as well and every other woman living. He also told her that if they worked together as a team they could help her get through it then they would have done all they could for her.

"You mean I would be able to help her?"

"Very much so, then we could talk about it together, especially if she was having a really hard time."

"You and me?"

"Of course who else?" He said it in such a matter of fact way that any thought of her being second best would have been squashed.

After a minute she said "What about Lizzie? She's her Mum too."

"Yes of course she knows about it, but she has her own little family to look after but we are here, and that makes all the difference."

"So if I spoke to her, she'd know what I was on about."

"Of course she would, and I rather think she would be pleased to be able to discuss it with you, after all she probably feels a bit isolated."

"So she'd like it?"

Robert smiled and kissed her on the forehead. "She'd love it."

They both had the biggest hug they had known for a long time and Robert's eyes were wet with emotion as he said "That's my girl."

They went back downstairs and Beth was careful not to let Margaret feel ashamed at running off so she greeted them with "I was just going to call you, dinner's on the table." Then quietly "Sorry I was such a baby."

The other two looked at each other knowingly and Robert said "Don't worry, we won't smack your bottom this time." and giving Margaret a wink and a nudge they all sat down to dinner in a much more light hearted mood than the house had known for a long time.

Chapter 3

Following the events at Burford, Beth and Robert were always worried that Lizzie wouldn't be able to cope with the physical side of marriage but Danny had been told the gist of what had happened and because he loved her so much, took his time and never forced her to make love unless she really wanted to. He may have liked to be a little more adventurous but it was obvious Lizzie would only do it in more or less the usual position and wasn't keen on experimenting. She didn't like too much foreplay but just to get on with it and afterwards that was the end of it until next time. There was certainly no quickie in the kitchen or on the hearth rug and if she had known some of the things that her Mother and new Dad had got up to, she would have been horrified. Danny on the other hand would probably have been exceedingly envious.

Lizzie waited for Danny to climb into bed then told him about the conversation with Sharon saying she wondered what she had meant about a job.

"Well, I'd be a bit careful, I wouldn't go into business with anyone unless you know more about them." He kissed her on the cheek and snuggled down into the bed.

"Oh I don't think she means that. I wouldn't want anything that serious." Lizzie hadn't looked at it from a business point of view. "Just a little job without too many ties, not while Bethany is at juniors."

He turned to face her. "Well if you take my advice you won't arrange anything with her until you've talked it over with me. I know you, you'd trust anyone." And he turned his back and closed his eyes. Knowing he wouldn't say any more now, she too turned on her side and they lay back to back in their own worlds.

After a while as she was drifting in and out of sleep she felt his arm creeping over her waist. He often did this in his sleep and she would have to move as his arm got too heavy but this time it was quite soothing and he seemed to be stroking her back with his other hand until she was becoming very heady and a floating feeling came over her whole body. She had never felt like this and for the first time she was enjoying the caressing and gentle massage not realising the to and fro motion was taking place between her legs gradually inserting itself into her body. She was oozing with moisture and being carried along with this erotic urge that she was moving her pelvis in rhythm to the motion begging for satisfaction. Suddenly she could hold it no more and she almost passed out with the thrust that was being given her as they both climaxed.

She was gasping for air and it took some time before she could move feeling as though every ounce of energy had been spent. Danny had never done this before but she would be only too happy for him to repeat it sometime and she turned to look into his face. Although it was fairly dark she knew he wasn't facing her but still lying with his back to her snoring away. She froze. He couldn't possible have turned over and gone to sleep so quickly unless - had she fallen asleep afterwards, or had she simply dreamt the whole thing? She felt down to the top of her legs and pulled her hand back in shock. She quietly made her way to the bathroom, closed the door and put the light on. No, she hadn't started suddenly, so it wasn't that. She knew only too well what she was now washing off herself.

Not wanting to wake Bethany, she crept back to bed and lay with her back to Danny again. It had to have been a dream, but a very physical one. She had heard that boys had things like that but never really understood what it meant as nobody had ever explained it to her.

Amity, her guardian had done all she could to protect her during the spiritual rape but the force was so strong, she had been powerless and upon receiving the news, Jenny knew who was behind the attack. But things had changed. If indeed it was Vedron himself, he didn't appear to have used Danny's body or there would have been evidence of it, so what means was he employing to possess her? Nothing material had been found or removed from the shop so Amity was sent a helper to search the house so that she could stay as close to Lizzie as possible. The helper did a quick search and returned to the bedroom where he homed in on something lying under the bed on Lizzie's side. Together the angels examined it and knew what had been used. Rolled up into a long phallic shape was the flyer that had led Lizzie to the shop and it was covered in slime. So Vedron was using inanimate objects to satisfy his craving for the woman and thus possessing her by making her hunger for more.

The higher levels of good and evil were well aware that, apart from their expertise in the spirit world, there were many more factors which could affect mortals in their everyday existence and hence carry on into their future states. Although many people still believe that when they die that is the end of everything, the more educated in such matters know that one life can have an ongoing power carried into the next world, be it physical or spiritual. Sometimes the high angels would call on information from the elementals who exist in earth, water, air and fire but sometimes a factor would emerge which seemed to be outside of the natural substances.

In the case of Vedron, Jenny was gradually piecing together the fragments of evidence she had to date. If he had been hiding with the elementals they would know about it but if not she was about to embark on a new aspect of their fight against such as he.

At the moment she had only two items of contact. The first as described by Lizzie's guardian at the time, was of something engulfing her. There was nothing tangible because it was all being fed into her mind and although it felt like some sort of curtain it was purely mental. This meant that nothing material or of natural fibre had been used on that occasion. But with regards to the flyer, that would have been paper which would have been made from natural substances so the possibility that he had used the elementals could not be dismissed. It seemed awful to say that they had to wait for the next attack to find out more but that seemed to be the only avenue at the moment. If Vedron used any man made fibre, that could throw the whole business in another direction. The thought flitted through Jenny that he could have been using metal or similar to hide away until he showed his intentions.

"But is that of importance now?" Matthew voiced what others were thinking.

There was a moment before Jenny replied and he knew by her manner it was something he should have known better than to ask.

"Because we learn all the time and store that knowledge in our existence. That is how we fight future threats and even wars."

"Ah so even though it has little bearing on Lizzie's case, some other fiend could use it in their own way having learnt from him."

"Exactly. But don't forget that the main concern is trying to ascertain his next move, which won't be easy. And he may always retreat to his previous hiding to throw us off his trail, so..."she waited for the first to answer.

Matthew jumped in with "It is important now after all."

The surrounding groups felt somewhat told off but knew why Jenny was driving so hard at this point.

Lizzie was up quite early in the morning and being Saturday she let Bethany have a little lie in. She stood in the kitchen musing on the events of the night and decided to put it all down to a rather hectic dream and say nothing about it. She wasn't sure on what Danny's reaction would be if she told him and at the same time she was overcome with a feeling of guilt, so this had to be her secret. After all it wasn't the thing 'nice' people did and certainly not talk about, so best forgotten. With two beakers of tea in her hands she went upstairs and put one on the bedside table near her husband. He stirred, opened his eyes and smiled at her.

"What time is it?"

"About eight now."

"Oh it's still the middle of the night." And he pulled the covers back over his head and pretended to snore.

"Come on lazy. Didn't you say you've got to go in today?" That woke him up.

"Oh Christ, yes. Got to cover for the sick ones."

"What time you going?" Lizzie sat down on the bed and sipped her tea. Her foot touch something and as she bent down she saw the remains of the well used flyer. For a moment she was bewildered not guessing why it was there so kicked it further out of sight.

"Got to be there for ten. Hope to be off at four though."

Lizzie tried to keep her mind off the offending article at her feet. "Well at least its overtime."

"Hopefully." He was sitting now drinking his tea.

"What do you mean?"

"Well they move the goalposts."

"What goalposts?" she was lost now.

"Well, they get you to work to cover those off sick and that. Then when they are back they try to get you to take the time off then."

"But that's not fair." She was appalled.

"Try telling them that. They're a big company they can do as they like."

They finished their tea in silence. Jenny couldn't understand how workers could be treated like pawns but Danny saw it everyday and to him he was used to the firm's attitude of 'take it or leave it'. Most of the staff had become of the same mind which led to constant animosity and many good workers simply now did as they were told but didn't go the extra mile any more.

Sharon sat with a cup of coffee in her hand and a cigarette in her mouth. She hadn't bothered to get dressed yet and her gown had seen better days. She blew the smoke upwards and said to herself "I really ought to give these damn things up. Can't afford them but what else have I got?" She still felt anger at 'that cow' for sacking her. A glance at the clock reminded her Denis was supposed to be playing football at school this morning. Going to the bottom of the stairs she yelled "Denis."

"Hmm" was all she heard.

"Get up."

After about ten minutes she yelled again and when there was no answer she stormed up, annoyed at having to make this extra journey up the stairs.

"Thought you were playing football." She burst into his room and stopped suddenly.

"What the f...." the word never materialised.

Denis sat bolt upright in bed staring in front of him pointing.

"Don't move or he'll bite you." He ordered.

Sharon looked from her son to the foot of the bed.

"Denis, what can you see?"

"Quiet, you'll frighten him."

Sharon had had enough now and marching to the foot of the bed she waved her arms about saying "Denis. There is n-o-t-h-i-n-g- here."

"Now look what you've done."

"What are you talking about Denis?"

35

The lad slumped back onto his pillow "He's gone. Bet he won't come back now. I liked him."

This was getting a normal occurrence and when she calmed down, Sharon couldn't help feeling sorry for him. It must be hell locked inside your own mind with nobody understanding. But if only she knew what it was she was up against. She tried to stroke his head but he pulled away.

"I'm sorry Denis, but I didn't see him. Tell me what he was like."

"You're not interested."

"Of course I am. Please…Denis…describe him, then I can understand, don't you see?"

Slowly he raised himself on one arm.

"He looks after me."

Sharon waited but that seemed to be it. "But why does he run away if he's supposed to look after you, that's not very good is it?"

"No need."

"Denis, you'll have to help me out here." Sharon didn't understand this sort of thing and although she lived with it, she still didn't know how to handle it.

"Well, you're here now."

"Oh, so you don't need him when I'm here?" she was very tentative wondering if she was asking the right question.

He sighed now. "Well you don't both have to be here do you, not at the same time."

"No just a minute, let me get this. He looks after you when you are on your own?"

"Yep."

"So why then did you tell me off for scaring him away?"

"'Cos I feel safe when he's here. Nothing bad can happen."

Sharon felt a bit useless. "So don't you feel safe when I'm here?"

"Course I do, but you're not here at night, when I'm asleep. That's when he comes to look after me."

"Um do you have a name for this pet of yours?"

"He has his own name."

Sharon tilted her head "Which is?"

"Dog."

"His name is Dog, so he is a dog?"

"If you like."

Sharon stood up. "Well if Dog has gone now, perhaps you would like to get your kit ready for football."

"Not going."

"What? I thought you were looking forward to it."

Denis shrugged. "Not picked."

"Oh Denis, I'm sorry." She went to hug him but he pulled away Also she knew it was better not to make a fuss as that may upset him more. If only she could get her hands on that teacher that had dropped him she would rip his bits off – with one hand!

"Come down when you want then." She had got to the top of the stairs when he called out "Can I have some toast?"

"You certainly can my man, move your bum then."

Denis hadn't been far wrong in his adoption of the name. In fact his guardian was Doag who had been placed with him from birth as the angels were aware this child had unusual insight into the spiritual world and would need special guidance and protection. Learning that the lad had an affinity with animals from a very early age, he knew he could hold his attention more if he appeared as a protective pet. He hadn't needed to form the exact image as Denis did that when he felt Doag's presence and so he had remained in that image ever since. There was nothing wrong with the child mentally, but because none of the authorities could identify anything specific they treated him as 'special needs' although Sharon had never known what those needs were. There were counselling sessions, and various tests which proved nothing so in the end she was told to keep an eye on him and report anything unusual. At the time she described it as "Doing their bloody work for them because they haven't a clue."

Denis had been born a couple of days before Bethany and if the parents had heard the discussions in the spirit world they would have been bewildered but concerned. There was a conflict of where the boy's soul should be placed bearing in mind that higher spirits are sexless and only bear names for mortal identification so the sex of the child was not important because the placement would adapt to whatever it was given. Jenny fought hard to keep Lizzie out of this as she knew she had been through enough and deserved a child which had not been placed for a specific reason. Those against her said it was the ideal placing and would attract Vedron quicker as he would trace Lizzie and the Denis spirit would trap and dispose of him with help from the spiral. However Jenny used her authority to overrule them and so Denis was placed in the area where his life would touch Bethany but without being too close to draw attention.

"Well, what is it to be today ladies?" Robert smiled at Beth then Margaret across the breakfast table with a look that expected an answer immediately. His daughter looked from him to Beth and asked "What's he on about?"

"I think he means where would we like to go?" With a girlish grin she looked at him under her lids. "Am I right?"

"Well it looks like being a nice day, so how do you feel about going to one of the garden centres we mentioned?" Noticing Margaret's slight withdrawal he added quickly "Unless you two had something up your sleeves."

Beth was also aware of Margaret's reaction and said "Well you know we have some baking to do today and I'd like to give the place a good clean."

Robert eyed them both. "You'd think it was dirty. And if it's Lizzie and co you're worried about, they've been here enough times before so I don't think they will be looking for every minute speck of dust." He laughed to keep the tone light.

"I think I should help with the vacuuming," Margaret surprised them both with her offer "only - um - last time – um-…"

"Well spit it out." Robert wondered what she was getting at.

Beth cut in to save further embarrassment "It's because Margaret has seen me when I get a hot one and she knows my energy just goes." She put out her hand and gave her a gentle pat on the arm. "And she makes it easier for me to cope."

"Well I think that's great." Robert was happy to see the relief spread over his daughter's face and said "You know I must be the luckiest man in the world."

"Well as long as you know that." Beth ducked as Robert pretended to throw the marmalade at her.

Robert certainly felt uplifted to think there was possibly an end in sight to his daughter's terrible illness. He knew it couldn't happen in five minutes and there would be setbacks along the way, but after all these years there did seem to be hope for all of them. He prayed now that tomorrow would go without a hitch. It had been a while since they had all been together and although Lizzie and sometimes Bethany would pop in, Margaret was rarely seen. He knew you couldn't blame the little girl for being a bit apprehensive and maybe somewhat scared, but it would be a relief if she could get to know Margaret as her aunt but that would take some time and couldn't be rushed. Danny had often been round to help Robert with something that took two people but again he could count the times on one hand that Margaret had put in an appearance. She wasn't the sort of girl he could have fancied and only tolerated her for his wife's sake, knowing how close they had been.

As they cleared the table Beth said "I'll just nip out and get some fresh salad before it gets too busy."

"Going to the local shop, they're a bit dear" Robert was about to offer her a lift.

"Oh no, It's not so fresh there anyway. No I'll pop down to the supermarket. Fancy coming Margaret?"

Her question was answered by a tremble and a whispered "Um, could I just stay here today?"

"Of course you can, I only asked in case." Beth smiled. She wasn't going to push her but didn't want her to feel left out.

Robert also noticed the reaction and jumped in "Well I'll take you, be back in no time." He didn't want Beth going alone in case she had a 'hottie' and he worried about her, probably too much. "You'll be ok won't you Maggie?" This was a term of endearment he hadn't used for years but it brought a response.

"Course I will Dad." Then in a tone that almost brought tears to their eyes she said "'Spose I've copped for the washing up?"

The couple looked at each other, then as if reading each others thoughts they took it in turns to put a sponge and washing up liquid in her hands and drape a tea towel over her shoulder. The laughter that emitted from that house was noted all the way up the line to Jenny, who had she been in earth form would have punched the air with a resounding shout of "YES!"

The guardians who had been specially placed to work on Margaret had been doing a brilliant job and although in earth years it seemed to have taken time, they knew that once she was on the recovery road, there would be no turning back.

As they drove the short distance to the shops, Robert said "Oh by the way, I was talking to a chap at work who may be glad of my lawn mower,"

"Are you thinking of getting a new one?" Beth's eyes lit up.

"Been saying so. Like to have a lighter one, you know more up to date. The old one doesn't owe us anything."

"Not wishing to be unkind, but who would want the old one, like you say it's seen better days."

"Oh it's not for himself. There's a charity place he's involved with and they like all sorts of stuff. He says they'd be glad of anything. Probably use it."

"Oh that's nice. I like to think of things doing somebody some good." Beth smiled on both counts. She knew Robert would welcome a new one and someone else would gain.

"You always have had a generous streak. That's why I love you so much." He patted her knee.

"Robert! Not while you're driving." She panicked at anything that took his mind off his concentration while at the wheel.

"Sorry my darling. Won't do it again." He knew she was right but made up his mind to do that and more when they were alone, then quickly pushed the thought from his mind, at least until he wasn't driving.

The phone rang. Lizzie picked it up half expecting it to be her mother.

"Hi Liz." Only one person called her that and she wasn't too keen on it.

"Oh Hello Sharon. What's up?"

"You doing anything particular?"

"Well, nothing special, just the usual really. Why?" She wasn't in the mood for company and wanted to mull over her dream which wouldn't get itself out of her mind as though it was prodding her to remember.

"Well, you know I said we both needed a job and I had an idea?" To be honest Lizzie hadn't given it much thought.

"Oh yes, I remember." She didn't want to offend her friend by saying anything else.

"Shall I tell you over the phone or shall we meet?"

Time to think quickly. "Well, we're out tomorrow and I wanted to get all my jobs done today, so perhaps Monday, when the kids are at school?"

Sharon's voice deflated a little "Ok, that should do. Don't want to leave it, now I've got my teeth into something."

Danny's advice came into her mind and Lizzie was glad she hadn't gone without thinking but she wouldn't make any decisions until she had told him about it as he had asked.

"I'll see you Monday then. Do you want to come here again?"

There was silence. Then "Yeah, that would be good. I'm not going back to that shop job so I won't be in a rush."

"Haven't you got to work your notice?" She couldn't remember what Sharon had said about that.

"All I want from that cow is what she owes me, then she can get stuffed!"

"Oh I see. Monday then." Lizzie wanted to end the conversation.

"Monday. Bye." And the phone went down.

She now wondered what Sharon was going to suggest but thought it couldn't be too important so put it from her mind.

"Mummy, I don't feel very well."

Her thoughts were interrupted by Bethany standing at the door still in her nightdress.

"What's the matter?" Lizzie dashed over and hugged her.

"I don't know."

"Do you feel sick? Have you got a headache?" she felt the child's forehead.

"I don't know." She started to cry.

"Come and sit by me." Lizzie guided her to the sofa. She looked alright and didn't appear to have a temperature. She was just going to ask more questions when Bethany said "I won't be able to go to Gran's if I'm sick will I?"

"Aah, so that's it." Lizzie thought to herself but said "Well we don't know if you are sick do we?" Then as a test, "Tell you what, how about some breakfast then we'll talk about it."

"All right. Can I have and egg and soldiers?" Then as an afterthought "please?"

"Sure you feel up to eating it?" Most mothers would probably have not pushed it having got her to agree to eat but Lizzie being Lizzie wanted to make doubly sure.

"I think so." The little face dropped with self pity but there was no doubt in her mind that she would clear the lot.

When she had finished Lizzie tried another tactic.

"If you are poorly we ought to see the doctor but it's Saturday so the surgery is only open for emergencies and that means it will probably be Dr. Naylor." He was the one most people avoided as his bedside manner was anything to be desired and he always treated you as if you were making it all up and wished you wouldn't waste his time. The children hated him and said he smelled of mints.

"Oh No Mum, I don't want to see him. He's horrible."

"Well I can't leave it, not if you're really sick."

"I think I'm feeling a bit better now."

She certainly didn't look ill and Lizzie didn't feel the slightest bit guilty about tricking her. Hadn't her own mum warned her about such antics? The first ploy kids would use would be 'not very well' when they wanted to get out of something.

"Why don't you go and get dressed then we can watch that DVD again."

That had a bigger effect than anything and Bethany was out of the room and running up the stairs at great speed. Lizzie watched her going thinking "Nothing much wrong with her, physically that is." But what would she be like tomorrow? Picking up the phone she rang Beth. No reply.

"Oh they must have gone out" she thought knowing that Margaret wouldn't answer and decided to try later. She thought that if her mother could get Margaret to speak to Bethany on the phone it might make her happier about going, but Lizzie always wished for dreams however unlikely the outcome might be.

Amity had witnessed the exchange and tried to send her calming thoughts to the child, soothing out any apprehension about the visit so that when the time came, she could handle it. Also messages were sent to Margaret's guardians so that everything could go as smoothly as possible for this was vitally important to the future happiness of the family, not just for now but forthcoming generations.

It was always to Jenny's annoyance when they had to wait for any enemy to show its hand. She liked to be ahead of them and have everything ready for their downfall. Since Vedron's last appearance she had been in conflict with many minor and major evil forces but there was usually a trace as to their whereabouts. This was known from both sides, the evil watching the good as much as they themselves were being monitored. One theory was that one of these forces, but not Zargot, had been cloaking Vedron and that he had never left the area but lay dormant. Although this wasn't anything new, the longer a spirit was inactive the less power it could have when it emerged, but, depending on the level it had reached it had been known on some occasions for it to germinate and be stronger than before. This was the aspect that worried Jenny. If Vedron was high enough to be capable of this, and knowing how much the sexual hunger drove him, just what could be the extent of the evil he would unleash this time? Also this must be the last, for any future increase could have devastating results to a wider population. It must be presumed that he was after Lizzie but any future attacks by larger entities of his kind didn't bear considering.

Danny had been on the tills all morning and was due for a break. His replacement stood waiting to take over at the end of serving this customer. It was only when he was out of his seat and making his way to the staff room he noticed a man standing by a notice board. He thought nothing of it at first but realised the person's gaze had followed him from his till to the end of the store. Before opening the staff door he turned and was amazed to see him only a few feet away which meant he had to have been following him.
"Can I help you sir?" he asked without smiling.
"No. You can't." The voice was low with the emphasis on the 'you'. He immediately turned and walked away and Danny was left feeling he had been scanned from head to toe. Shaking himself he blamed the robotic way he had been working and then put it down to a crack pot who had nothing better to do. But his body was tingling

almost as if he had just received a slight electric shock. He got his coffee and a bun and sat with one of his fellow workers.

"You Ok Dan?"

"Sure. Why do you ask?" Danny wondered what he looked like at the moment to make him ask.

"Never seen you so red that's all. Not blushing are you?" and he laughed at the thought.

Danny shrugged. "No. Lots of bugs going around though."

"Tell me about it. My girl friend's sick."

"Oh yes?" Danny replied with a knowing wink.

"Not that, well better not be. Her old man'd have my balls off."

"You'll get caught one day the way you spread it around."

"Hey, mind what you're saying."

They shared a bit of man to man chat then both got up and went back to their stations. As Danny took over he felt something scrunch in his trouser pocket and pulling it out with his hand he found a crumpled voucher which he knew quite well he hadn't put there. Screwing it up, he threw it in the bin and got on with his next customer. But he had made contact with the paper and that was enough.

Lizzie was feeling a bit strange and wondered if she had been too harsh on her daughter. Perhaps there was a bug of some sort going round. They often had them at the home where she worked and when one old dear got it they all had in no time. But this was different. She had felt like this before and she knew this kind of nauseating feeling. She was pregnant.

She could never have explained why, but she dashed upstairs and started to grab the flyer in an attempt to straighten it out, when a thought imprinted itself into her brain. "Got You" Frantically she ripped it into small pieces and went to throw it in the waste bin in the bathroom but something was telling her to get rid of it so she almost ran downstairs and rammed it into the pedal bin. She tied the inner bag and took it out to the wheelie bin and dropped it in, closing the lid with all her might as though it would hold anything bad inside.

"What are you doing Mum?" Bethany's voice made her jump.

"Oh nothing darling, just getting rid of something that had gone off."

She hurried her back indoors as though she needed to keep them both as far away as possible from the bin which is exactly what Amity and the girls guardians were trying to do.

Jenny had learned of the Danny episode at the same time as the thought was sent about Lizzie and she knew there had to be a connection. Vedron was not only using inanimate objects, he was taking over humans then discarding them after his use. So he was constantly on the move, jumping from one form to another and who was to say it was only one at a time. If he had learned the art he may be using several forms at once so there was a hope that by so doing, one of them may be tracked by the constant watching sentinels and in turn would lead to another and eventually Vedron himself. But extreme caution would have to be used as this was now no trivial spirit but the most malevolent kind possible.

Chapter 4

Denis was asleep, but would have been unrecognisable as the timid boy lost in his own world most of the time. It had been decided for safety and security, that when he was awake he would remember nothing of his true self and thus not draw attention from any passing evil look outs. But when he escaped to the realms of the higher spirit angels he conversed with Doag on his own level. Then he could relate anything worthy of further investigation and also be given instructions as to certain tasks. When awake he wouldn't necessarily know why he would be doing particular things or going to designated places, he just thought he wanted to. Such was the power of the high angels to be able to switch on or off a memory or task at will but gather all they needed under cover of an innocent. They could also alert Denis in times of extreme danger so that he could revert to his true self if needed, with full awareness of his position. His current placing was perfect for the present but plans were being put into operation to bring him that bit closer to Bethany even if it meant giving other people's so called 'free will' a helping nudge.

Doag was bringing him up to date now on the movements of Vedron and told him to be conscious of any tiny thing that appeared to be out of the usual, even something slightly different. It may not seem much at first but it was often the smallest scrap of information that led to the demise of a possible threat to all that was good. It may seem to be a bit like marking time for now but he was in such a position he may well be in the thick of it when the time came.

"Well I'll leave you to see your 'dog', that should keep them happy for a while." Doag had a sense of humour but never let it cloud the seriousness of the situation.

"They'd have a shock if they saw you for real."

"Not possible. They don't have the ability."

"Think it would blow Sharon's mind." Denis couldn't resist the thought.

"Don't be disrespectful to your Mother."

With a humorous exchange, they parted until Denis would sleep again, hopefully with some useful item to report.

Sunday morning had a lovely fresh feel to it, the sun was out and the birds were singing enough to raise anyone's spirits. Lizzie woke from a doze. She hadn't really slept well and had existed on cat naps all night, her mind being too full of yesterday's shock. It seemed a good idea not to tell anyone especially Danny at this stage as things could happen and then everything would be different. She had suffered a couple of miscarriages in the very early stages and so thought she would wait and see what the next days or weeks brought and then decide. She wouldn't bother her Mum, although Beth would have been the first to lend a comforting ear as she had before but Lizzie felt she had enough to cope with Margaret without adding further to her worries.

"I could be mistaken." She tried to reassure herself inwardly but she knew the truth if only she admitted it.

"It must be time for a cuppa."

Danny's rousing shook her back to reality and she was out of bed like a shot.

"I was just going, only I didn't want to wake you."

He leaned out to grab her as she passed by his side of the bed.

"Come back to bed first." His eyes were gleaming.

"Not now, got a lot to do."

He grasped her with both arms and pulled her down on top of himself.

"There's only one thing you've got to do right now and that's me."

She had never felt uncomfortable with her husband before, and whether it was because the previous night's episode had left her on edge she didn't know but visions of the rapes flooded back into her mind and she fought for her life to get free.

"Oh no you don't, bitch!"

This brought her protective instinct to the fore and fearing Bethany would hear she brought her arm back and gave him a resounding slap across the face. As she ran from the room she saw the girl on the landing.

"Mum? What's that noise?"

Lizzie didn't always think too quickly but she seemed to pull out the stops when her child was involved and started to laugh.

"It's Ok. Daddy and I were just play fighting, we do sometimes. Sorry. We woke you up didn't we?"

"I was scared."

Lizzie took her into her arms and said "You've got nothing to be scared of. We were being silly. Promise we won't do it again."

That seemed to work and Bethany smiled up to her as she said "Oh, that's all right then, I'll go and tell Daddy off shall I?"

Judging from the familiar noise coming from the bedroom Lizzie knew that was the last thing she should do and said "I've got a better idea, lets go down and make a drink and…how about a crafty biscuit?"

"Really, a biscuit before breakfast. Oh yes Mum, can we?"

As the two of them disappeared down the stairs giggling at the naughty thought, the sounds inside the bedroom were not what a child should hear. After the frantic panting which only lasted a few moments Danny gasped several times as he got his breath, reached for the nearest thing to contain his dispensed fluid and lay back absolutely drained but wondering what had come over him, in the mental sense.

Vedron had gone, feeling cheated. He had wanted to insert a physical body into her and relive the pleasures of before. It wasn't enough to use lifeless objects although he felt he was controlling her from inside, but his ultimate aim was to possess her in the flesh in every reincarnation she would have and judging by her fairly simple mind there should be plenty more. Had she been of high intelligence she may be on her last life so that wouldn't have held any promise of future fulfilment. But the main emotion fuelling the fiend wasn't only lust but anger and revenge. The choler of Vedron was turning him into a ferocious unstoppable beast, but in human form.

There was no comparison between the scene in the Worth bedroom and the one belonging to Robert and Beth Bradley. The air of the latter was filled with unending love, and at the moment of intense satisfaction. Robert always made love to his wife as if she was the only thing that mattered in the world, for to him she was. Of course he loved Margaret and the others but in his mind the love of a husband should be the ultimate expression of respect and affection. After Madge, to have Beth as his wife was more than a man could possibly wish for. As they lay now in each other's arms, he gently stroked her hair and whispered "That was heavenly, just like you."

"I'm so happy Robert, I think I keep falling in love with you every day."

"Keep on doing just that."

She threw the covers off as the warmth of his body seemed to be penetrating her until she was boiling.

"Oh I'm sorry…"she started.

Robert sat up. "Let's be in agreement. You never say 'sorry'. Not to me."

"You are a good man."

He glanced at the clock. "Better be moving I suppose. Margaret will be waking up soon."

They tried to keep their lovemaking to the mornings as his daughter was well asleep then. Her medication helped her to sleep and they felt guilty as they blessed the fact they would not be interrupted. Once in a mad moment they had succumbed to passion one evening, only to have her calling out for something. After Beth had been to settle her, the moment had passed so they tried not to let their feelings get the better of them. In a way it was worse than having small children because the sight of them engrossed would have rekindled her original trauma.

"The things we do for our children." Beth laughed as she lay there waiting to cool down.

Robert turned with a cheeky grin "How's about a shower lady?"

"Get out of here you rampant lion." She laughed and lay back.

He reappeared with a flannel saying "Would madam like sir to wash her?"

"If you don't behave yourself."

Looking from the cloth in his hand to her body he said as if to himself "Hmm this wouldn't cover much anyway."

"Right that's it. You're in for it now." She felt ready to get up and was about to follow him to the en suite when they heard a noise.

"Shh. It's Margaret." Robert was trying not to laugh.

"You all right dear?" Beth opened the bedroom door slightly and called through.

"I guess so." Was the mumbled reply. Alarm bells went off in Beth's mind.

Quickly she grabbed a gown and went onto the landing.

"What… what on earth?" She stopped dead for there in front of her was the most sorry sight she had seen for a long time.

Margaret stood tears running down her face, her hair a mess and her nightshirt torn as if she had been pulling at it. Beth turned her round and led her back to her room. Once they were sitting on the bed she spoke quietly trying not to sound as if she was putting her under interrogation.

"What is it darling? Had a bad dream?"

Shaking uncontrollably Margaret stuttered. "I – I- don't- kn-know."

Robert appeared in the doorway draped in a towel. "What's up?"

Beth looked up and said "Don't know yet." and indicated for him to leave for now.

Trying to make light of it he said "Ah leave you girls to women's things I get it."

Beth was grateful for his understanding and turned her attention back to Margaret.

"I've been wicked."

This came as a surprise and Beth asked "Why on earth do you say that?" but fearing it may be a flashback.

"He said I'm a naughty girl and I've got to be punished."

"Oh did he now? Well I should like to meet him and ask what he meant by that because you're not a naughty girl in any way." Beth hoped her stern attitude would make her feel secure and hopefully tell her who she thought had said this. Deep down she hoped it was just a bad dream, but in the past they had been as bad to deal with as reality.

"I don't know. I heard it."

"When did you hear it?"

"Before I woke up."

"Who do you think said it?"

"I don't know." She started to cry.

"Alright, alright, don't worry. Look" Beth looked straight in her face "I think you've just had a bad dream, I get them sometimes and it takes a while to get them out of my head."

Margaret looked shocked. "You get them? Do people tell you things?"

"Oh worse than that?"

"What? How does that work then?"

"Well, I can be trying to get to you or Dad, or I'm trapped somewhere and I can't get out and sometimes..."she stopped.

"Tell me."

Beth paused then said "Somebody is after me and I fall and I wake up in bed with such a bump."

"You have that as well!" Margaret was astounded but Beth noticed how much life had come back into her eyes. "But you never said anything."

"Well, you just get on with it really."

The two sat on the bed for a moment then Margaret said, much stronger now "Has anyone ever – you know - done that – in your dreams like?"

Beth knew she had to be very careful with her answer but as she seemed to be getting her confidence she didn't want to lose it so she gave an uncomfortable shuffle and said "Well, you could say that."

"Hey tell me all about it." The elation in her voice was obvious.

"I don't speak about it, it wasn't very nice."

"But was he actually doing it?"

"Yes."

"Who was it? Tell me?" She was smiling and getting excited at the thought which took Beth aback somewhat as this was the last reaction she expected.

"I don't know dear, look let's forget it. I tried to and now you must put yours out of your mind. These dreams just clear our brains so it's best to let them go they say"

"Oh I think I feel a bit better now. Didn't like him though, seemed to remind me of someone but I can't think who."

Although Beth knew the psychiatrists would have hammered the point to try and get to the bottom of the problem, she felt it was best to let it all settle and hopefully Margaret would soon forget all about it.

As she went back to her own room Robert looked enquiringly at her and Beth related the conversation as best as she could.

"Do you know what I was wondering?" He pulled on a pair of trousers.

"Hardly." She smiled.

"I thought it might have something to do with nerves."

"Nerves, why now – ah wait a minute, she is churned up because she has to see the family. Is that is?"

"Well it's just a possibility. We'll have to see won't we?"

"Oh I hope it all goes smoothly Robert."

He patted her bottom as he passed "You're not alone there."

The decision had been made. Jenny had been in consultation with her father, the Almighty Power of the good forces who, although still insisting she fight with the power of love, knew this situation called for strong tactics and he had enough faith in her to know she had learned over time the best way to deal with the kind of enemies she was facing. He wasn't consulted over the everyday petty squabbles between the various forms of existence but when something threatened that could have a ripple effect, he liked to be aware of it. They guessed that if Vedron had lain low for this length of time, he was gearing up for another attack and although it may not be Lizzie or her surrounding family the evidence so far pointed that way.

Jenny called a meeting of the high spiral.

"We're not going for the cat and mouse game now. No guessing what the beast might be contemplating."

"Sounds serious." Matthew sensed she knew more about the situation than they had imagined.

"I believe it is."

Graham asked "You're going after him aren't you, instead of letting him show his hand."

"Absolutely."

There was a gasp among the other high angels.

"But not in the obvious sense," Jenny explained "a trap, so that he walks into it."

"Ah getting him to come to you." The thought ran through them as they all understood now.

"Well firstly we are not going to hold back on protection. If we need extra sentinels round Lizzie and all her family, then we will provide it, and if he is targeting her, he'll have to show his hand."

"And if he doesn't, then where do we lay the trap?" Graham was looking at it from all angles.

There was a silence as they waited for Jenny to explain.

"I think he will, because from what we have learned so far, he is already in."

"But nobody has seen him as himself."

"They don't need to," Jenny realised that only a few had ever encountered a spirit with the ability to use both live and inanimate objects simultaneously for their evil purposes and it wasn't always sexually driven.

"But we've seen them invade the elementals in their own habitat."

Jenny was patient and glad they were looking at this from different aspects.

"Yes, but not stray, they stayed in that one commodity. They rarely mix the earthly human state with the elements, in other words they are operating as one or the other."

There was a buzz of agreement as they all remembered past cases and what Jenny was saying was the truth.

"The thing that we don't know is." Jenny paused "where over the last earth years has he learned this particular art? And who taught him?"

Again consternation as they realised there was going to be more to this than they thought. Jenny looked round then added briefly "Like you said Matthew "serious.""

The group was dismissed to await further orders knowing that as soon as they were summoned, everything else would be put on hold or passed to another spirit to deal with.

As Jenny pondered the next move she instructed Doag to move Denis nearer at the first opportunity and have him right in the firing line when the time came, for she was certain it would be soon if she could attract the fly into her web.

Amity and Doag were warned they would have back up, not secretively but very obvious to any watcher, also the guardians of Beth, Robert and Margaret received the same instructions. They were told it was necessary and to work with them at all times. Some guardians can be very possessive of their charges and don't welcome help, but the ones already in place had known this could happen so accepted it as being part of the job. In view of Danny having been used by Vedron it was essential to have him protected against further attacks as the evil one would probably be trying to drive a wedge between them and thus have Lizzie for himself. Also special care was needed for Bethany as no one knew just what Vedron's urges were and all precautions must be taken hence getting Denis into the mix.

No one would have recognised Vedron from the handyman working at the retirement home in Burford. Although there were similarities, his general appearance had changed and had he not been such an evil thing, he could appear quite attractive. He had been well groomed in his skills and was now putting them into practice, starting with the simple things such as making connections through paper such as the flyer and the voucher, then testing out using someone else's physical body. At present he didn't need a human form of his own to home in on his objective but he still longed for one as it gave him more satisfaction to be using his own self instead of a borrowed one. But at the moment it was not possible as he knew he would be traced and that would spoil his nasty little plans. But his weakness as ever was his hunger for his sexual needs which must be fulfilled. Whether he was worse when not satisfied or desperate for his next 'fix', even he didn't know. But he must have his release at all costs regardless of the outcome and this hopefully would be his undoing for in an unguarded moment he would leave himself wide open to being trapped. Jenny knew that his kind had this Achilles heel for just as a human being reaches the exhilaration of physical climax and for that moment loses all control, so do these spirits and that is when she would get him. But she dare not make the others aware of what she was plotting.

Vedron had enjoyed his Vernon body. It was well tuned and when he went out at night for his pursuits he knew he was attractive which was why he admired himself so much in the mirror. Some day he would enjoy those thrills again but for now he had new skills to hone and he would get every ounce of satisfaction in whatever he was doing. But the inner ache was nibbling away and it took every ounce of self control to keep it in check but he was a Vexon and that's how they were and probably always would be until their kind became extinct.

It was nearly three o'clock in the afternoon and Lizzie was trying to tie a bow in Bethany's hair.

"But why can't I wear my headband? I like it, and I don't like this bow it hurts."

"If you'll just hold still and stop wriggling for a minute." Lizzie tried again but somehow she couldn't get the ribbon to sit right.

Danny watched trying not to interfere but in the end said "Why not just let her have what she's comfy in. I'm sure she'd be happier." He didn't like to add that his wife was making the child look old fashioned and like most kids Bethany wanted to be in with the crowd and have whatever was fashionable at the time.

"Oh very well then, but make sure it is a new one, not that tatty thing you like so much, and make sure the colour goes with this dress."

"Thank you Mum." Bethany bounced out of the room and she could be heard running up the stairs humming to herself.

"You're not getting up tight 'cos of going to tea?" Danny asked.

"Of course I'm not, I'm not bothered although I hope she's going to be sociable and not sit clutching my arm all the time."

"Aha, so you are." Danny laughed then added by way of reassurance "She'll be fine, you'll see."

Lizzie was grateful in a way that Danny had reacted this way, as it covered the worry she had about being pregnant and hoped she would feel more settled about it soon. But for now the only important thing was to get this afternoon out of the way without any awkwardness.

They hadn't got a car and Danny used a push bike for work so they either walked or got a bus if they went out. Being quite a nice day they opted to walk and were just sorting out what they had to take when the phone rang. Danny glanced at Lizzie who frowned.

"Bet Margaret's not well." It was her kind way of saying her step sister was playing up, through no fault of her own of course.

"Hello," Danny answered it then put his hand over the receiver. "Robert wants to know if he should pick us up."

With relief Lizzie shook her head "No it's fine thank you."

"It's Ok we'll enjoy the walk Robert, but thanks anyway." Then after a pause "Yes we're leaving now. Bye."

"Strange." Lizzie looked puzzled.

"Why?"

"Well, to leave it to the last minute to ask. Something must be wrong."

"Oh for goodness sake, nothing's wrong, he sounded Ok, just offering that's all."

The tone wasn't meant to be harsh but Lizzie felt a bit deflated and didn't answer.

"Is this one all right Mum, it's my favourite and it goes with my dress, look." Bethany stood in the doorway beaming.

"You look beautiful princess." Danny jumped in before Lizzie could speak.

"Yes that will be nice." she added then "put your jacket on, it's not that warm yet and it may be chilly later on."

When everyone was ready they were about to leave when Bethany said "Have you got my picture that I drew for Auntie Margaret?"

"Yes it's in my bag. "

"I hope she likes it." Bethany looked worried.

"Of course she'll like it and Gran will anyway won't she?"

Danny locked the front door "Well if anybody doesn't like it that's their loss." He said with a cheeky grin and a wink to his daughter who beamed back at him.

There weren't only three people going to visit that afternoon for surrounding them were a host of guardians headed by Amity. In fact the family were encased in a kind of protective bubble with such a force emitting from it that any intruder would be repelled long before they were near the humans or their spirit selves.

Likewise at the Bradley house, the defences were so obvious it should have made any evil presence or scout wonder why such a force was being employed. But that was the plan and Jenny was observing every slightest disturbance in the vicinity.

Beth in her wisdom thought it might be a good idea not to have everyone together which may be overwhelming for Margaret so suggested she might like to be in the garden and meet Bethany on her own. This had met with approval and seemed to have taken the pressure off. Robert had been on the look out and opened the door before they had chance to ring the bell.

"Come in, come in," he welcomed and made a point of saying "Hello Bethany, Margaret's pottering around in the garden if you'd like to go and help her."

Lizzie felt her hand tighten as Bethany pulled closer to her.

"Why don't you take her your picture?"

"Oh what picture's that?" Beth had joined them and given the usual kisses.

"She's drawn a picture specially for Margaret, haven't you?" She pulled her hand from the grip and got it out of the bag.

Bethany nodded but was silent so Danny said "She's afraid she won't like it."

"Of course she'll like it." Beth smiled. "Tell you what, let's go and find out and she reached her hand out. Bethany looked up to her mother.

"Well you won't know if you don't give it to her. Don't be shy." And she put the picture in her hand and gestured her to go.

Robert took the opportunity to take Danny to see something in the front room which left the females alone.

"Can understand her reluctance," he said "not easy for kids."

"No, I suppose not." Danny knew this was the best thing but wished he could have been with Bethany. Robert was quite good at putting people at their leisure and they were soon talking about things men discuss which wouldn't interest the ladies.

Margaret was wandering about and actually enjoying looking at the spring flowers which was no accident as the angels surrounding her were calming her thoughts and showing her the beauty of nature.

"Margaret." The voice was soft. She turned and saw Lizzie smiling at her. Something was pushing her gently towards her and for no reason she could explain was hugging her as if her life depended on it. Beth stood holding Bethany's hand and smiled down at her as if to prove everything was going to be all right. Gently she pushed her forward and whispered "I'd give it to her now if I were you."

As the two separated, Margaret's head was turned by her angels and she saw Bethany holding her picture out towards her.

"Is that for me to see?" She asked gently.

Bethany nodded. "I did it for you."

There was silence for a moment then Margaret held out her hand tears running down her cheeks. "You did it just for me?"

Lizzie beckoned her forward as she said to Margaret "She really hopes you like it."

Slowly Bethany handed her the picture and Margaret took it, looked at it then said to Bethany "It's the most beautiful thing in the world" where upon the child beamed and said "You really do like it Auntie Margaret?" then turned back to her mother and gran who both had tears of relief in their eyes.

"I love it and thank you so much for doing it for me." As she held out her arms Bethany seemed to have lost any inhibitions she had harboured and returned her embrace.

"Hey, is this a private party or can anyone join in?" Robert's voice broke the moment as he and Danny joined them.

"Daddy, Daddy, Auntie Margaret likes my picture."

"Well what did I tell you?" then addressing Margaret said "Never has confidence in what she draws. Now perhaps she'll believe us."

Not wanting to spoil the moment by overcrowding, the men went off to look at something in the garage and Lizzie joined Beth to help her get the tea ready, not that there was much to do but it left the two to get acquainted.

"You know where I'm going to put this?" Margaret waved the paper in front of her.

"No, where?"

"In my bedroom, then I can see it all the time."

"Not when you're asleep."

Margaret actually laughed at the innocence of the remark. She was warming to the presence of her niece because she was no threat; she wouldn't be expecting anything from her, she could be herself.

"No but if I wake up in the night I shall see it."

"Even when it's dark?"

"Yes."

Bethany put her head on one side. "How?"

"I put the light on." They both laughed together at what now seemed so obvious and Bethany relaxed for the first time.

Children often don't look for complications and say things as it is and if the mothers could have heard the chat going on in the garden they may have been a little on edge.

"Will you come and see us, then I could show you my bedroom?" Bethany was looking at a snail.

"Well, I don't go out much."

"'Cos you're sick?"

"Yes."

"You don't look sick."

"Don't I? Well there's different kinds of sickness."

"What kind is yours?"

Margaret thought for a moment. This young person seemed to be doing her more good than any of the so call therapists and councillors.

"It's one you can't see."

"Oh." Bethany was musing on this one. "Will I get it?"

"I hope not."

Again a pause then Bethany chirped "I've had chicken pox. Have you had chicken pox?"

"When I was little, and the measles."

"I don't think I've had measles. But I get tummy ache sometimes." Then after a moment said "You can't see that can you, or a headache."

"That's right," Margaret had not felt so calm in a long time and put it all down to this little ray of sunshine who was busy now trying to catch a butterfly. Although she was partly responsible, much of the credit had to go to her guardians who were sending calming waves over her, primarily for her to cope with the family visit, but now because the aura surrounding these two was making a strong bond which all added to the protection. In turn Bethany's guardians were telling her mind that there was nothing to fear and this was her friend. After a while things were taking their own course and their help was partly withdrawn to see how things worked out on their own accord.

"I've found an ant." Bethany was beckoning her aunt to come and look. The simple experience of watching an ant in the garden was something she hadn't seen for a long time, not because it wasn't there but because she didn't look for it. She had been locked up within herself so long, this was all a new world.

"Where? Let me see."

"There look," and Bethany's little finger pointed to the spot.

"Oh yes, but look there's load of them."

"Bet they've got a nest. They lay eggs you know, they told us that at school."

The slight strain of this new feeling was getting the better of Margaret and she said weakly "Bethany, I am very tired, would you mind if I went in for a while, and I want to put my picture safe."

"Can I come?"

"Yes, I'll show you where I'm going to put it if you like, then I might have a lie down. I have to rest a lot you see."

"All right." Without thinking Bethany took her hand and walked with her to the house.

"Oh just look at that." Beth pulled Lizzie to the window. They couldn't believe their eyes.

"I'd never have thought it." Lizzie whispered. "Hope it lasts, nothing spoils it I mean."

"I know just what you mean. Margaret looks worn out. She'd better have a moment to rest before tea."

Beth met them at the back door. "Bethany, I expect Margaret needs a rest now, so do you want to come and help?"

She was surprised when Margaret answered. "Its Ok, she's just going to help me put this up" and she held the picture high "then I may have a little nap. I am a bit tired."

Lizzie piped up with "I'm not surprised, she wears me out. Don't know where she gets her energy from, I don't."

As they disappeared she called after Bethany "Now don't go getting in the way and come down when Auntie says for you to."

"I will." was called down the stairs.

"Well what do you make of that?" Lizzie asked her mum.

"Just hoping. Knowing Margaret I think we had better take it one step at a time. I just don't want the child getting hurt, that's all."

The men arrived back from the garage and Robert lifted his eyes to question how things were. Beth just nodded in return and Danny gave Lizzie a quick hug and said "Told you."

Symphony was fairly young in spiritual terms but had already been used many times when acute alertness was required. It was obvious as she progressed she would enter the high realms even reaching the lower spiral quicker than some of the existing powers.

Only certain ones ever achieved such status but now and again the odd one stood out as a certainty. Jenny had allocated her to the group now protecting Margaret knowing that if there was anything at all unusual this spirit would pick it up.

As instructed she had been in presence continually and now she hovered by the picture carefully stuck to the wardrobe with 'sticky gum' as the girls called the popular way of attaching things. Her attention was still on her charge but she was able to concentrate on at least three or four things at one time and not miss anything.

She studied the piece of paper and was subconsciously drawn to one tiny area. At first it appeared Bethany had signed the artwork but it was too small for that and it didn't match the residue left by the materials used to create the work. There was definitely a deposit but it wasn't still, it seemed to be moving very slightly. Without alerting the others in the team she immediately sent a vision to Jenny who homed in on the substance. If it was moving, it was alive in whatever form but as soon as it had been observed by the high angels it disappeared and left no trace of ever having been there. Jenny commended Symphony and told her to keep observing although she guessed that knowing it had been traced, it would not return. There was nothing to prove it had been Vedron so an open mind was essential but the possibility couldn't be ruled out.

In spiritual terms, Jenny now replayed the events from the meeting, the handing over of the picture up to the positioning on the wardrobe. She tried to find a moment when both Bethany and Margaret had handled the same part of the paper but dismissed the thought as it was too tiny to allow them both to touch it. But what if that didn't matter? Maybe if Bethany had come into contact with it then Margaret, it may have a transfer effect if that was what Vedron was trying to achieve. But why would he need to do that? As Lizzie seemed to be the target, why would he need to bother with the rest of the family? But that was exactly what he seemed to be doing.

The table was laid with a tempting array of food and Lizzie said quietly, "Mum, do you think we should ask them to come down now?" her eyes lifted to the direction of the stairs.

Beth glanced at the clock. "I think we might try, but don't be disappointed if Margaret says she wants to stay in her room."

"Shall I go, or will you?" Although she wanted confirmation that her daughter was still happy and relaxed, she hoped her mother would offer to go as she knew Margaret's ways better and would cope if she didn't co-operate.

"I will if you like, do you want to get the men to the table." And she left to go upstairs.

With a sigh of relief Lizzie interrupted the flow of conversation and shepherded Danny and Robert to sit down.

"This looks good." Danny smiled with appreciation.

"Oh you know Beth, only happy when she's feeding us. Always loved baking you know."

"I do. Guess that's where Lizzie gets it from," then smiled at her thinking "but not as good as your Mum" but wouldn't have dreamt of saying it.

Beth tapped on the door. "Any room for a little one?" There was silence. "Ah you're playing a game, I know, waiting for me to come in then jumping out at me. Well here I come ready or not." Although Beth put a laugh in her voice she felt a little apprehensive at what she might find when she actually opened the door. Gently she pressed the handle down and crept in not expecting the sight before her. Margaret was flat out on the bed apparently fast asleep and Bethany was standing by her side holding her hand and singing very softly, although it was barely audible.

"Is she all right?" Beth was at a loss for words and didn't want to frighten the child but something seemed strange in the atmosphere.

"She was tired so I said I would sing to her. I think she's gone to sleep."

Beth slipped her arm round her and gently took Margaret's hand from her and laid it on the bed.

"Well, perhaps we had better leave her for now, I expect she needs her sleep. So we will go and have tea and you can see her later."

"But she will miss her tea Gran" Bethany whispered.

If only she knew how many times her aunt had missed meals over the years but that was something she didn't need to worry about so Beth said quietly "That's all right she can have it when she wakes up. We'll save some for her."

That seemed to settle Bethany and with a glance at the bed they both went back downstairs.

"Here's my girl." Danny greeted them. "Hope she didn't wear her out."

Robert gave a searching look towards his wife.

Beth smiled "No everything's fine, she's just having one of her naps. Sorry we'll have to start tea without her."

"But we're going to save her the best bits." Bethany's statement produced a round of laughter which was much needed but Robert knew he would go and check at the first opportunity.

Denis had been told to make a move and although he thought it was his own idea went ahead, carefully watched by Doag.

"Mum, what are you going to do with Bethany's mum?"

Sharon wasn't aware that her son had even heard her talking to Lizzie let alone be interested in anything she was planning.

"Well, I don't know that I'm doing anything yet. Nothing's decided."

He stared her straight in the face. "But what would it be if you did?"

She started to feel uncomfortable but couldn't explain why. "So why are you so interested all of a sudden?"

He shrugged "Oh no reason."

"Then why ask? I don't understand how your brain works sometimes, really I don't."

"When will you know?"

"Look Denis, I don't know what you're driving at, but when I know, you'll know and that's an end of it Ok?"

He stared at her for a moment then turned his attention back to the game he was playing.

Sharon's usual guardian had recently been joined by two more and knew there had to be a special reason for this but knew they would be told in due course and didn't question such actions. They were also aware of the higher ranking of Doag and wondered why he should be in situ with such an unimportant child, for Denis's real status was being cloaked from all at this stage. But in their world they knew better than to delve into the unknown.

Following the news about the deposit on Margaret's picture, Graham decided to have another check on the children's drawings starting with the one on Lizzie's fridge. He homed in until he was examining every particle as if looking through a microscope but there was nothing different or anything that hadn't already been noted. It was the same with all the others. On sharing this with Jenny she suddenly said "But there is one difference."

"Of course," Graham had been concentrating on the previous drawings looking for something specific, and it was only when Jenny pointed it out he realised.

"There's no man in this one."

"Exactly" she said. "So you would think this isn't connected to the others."

There was general agreement from the listening angels.

"But consider this." There is no deposit mark on Margaret's picture now, but there was. So maybe there was on the others but it was removed when not needed any more so let us not jump to any conclusion."

She always had a way of sifting all the facts into order and laying them out so that they were reminded that in everything, anything was possible.

The meeting was interrupted by the news that there had been more sightings in the Pacific, both strange lights and USOs but when people had tried to take photos or videos, nothing had come out at all. The whole frames were blank. Some of the assembled company wanted to concentrate on the Vedron matter and not be side tracked but Jenny pondered now and wondered if one of the pieces was slipping into place. If he had been using elements to conceal his presence the happenings could not be discounted and there was always the possibility they were being used as a distraction, and if so there must be a very important reason.

The angels in Jenny's realm were of the air and had their own way of existence but the water angels and demons performed very differently. It would be possible for Vedron to split himself into many drops with the intention of reassembling himself later thus hiding away for as long as he wished from the air spirits. But it was thought that he was of the air so would not be able to exist for extended periods in another element unless he had found a time pause.

There are many parts on the earth planet which are unexplainable resulting in legend and conjecture but always surrounded by mystery. He would only have had to hook onto such an area where he could maybe flit through time and return at will. The only problem is that he may not have control over his movements and not be able to choose his location or his target. This raised the possibility that he had somehow remained in the area in his normal spiritual state undetected.

Graham raised a question which had often been discussed. "But what ever happened to Vedron, or rather Vernon's body? He seems to be only in spirit form, if indeed it is him." he felt forced to add.

"It served its purpose." was all Jenny would offer. The others always felt she knew more than she would impart but her tone implied that the matter was closed.

Chapter 5

Although the tea had gone well at the Bradley household and much relief was felt by most, including Bethany, Lizzie awoke next morning with a heavy weight in the pit of her stomach. Although she was relieved that Margaret appeared to have taken a major step forward to recovery, the nagging thought that she was expecting wasn't filling her with joy. Normally she would have been over the moon and sharing her delight with Danny, but this was different. She kept reliving the scene in the bedroom and although Danny was lying beside her, knew he had taken no part in it, so how could she tell him. Maybe he would put it down to it being another occasion, not even querying exactly when she had 'copped out' as he would say. But Lizzie knew almost the exact moment and couldn't think of anything else. For now she would have to pretend everything was normal until she had worked out what to do.

Her guardian Amity, had been in close contact with her superiors all this time and an intense scan had been performed on Lizzie's inner parts. Jenny was the first to get the results.

"There is no other spirit form awaiting birth."

Jenny, in conference with Matthew and Graham mulled over all possibilities.

"Could it be too soon to have placed one?" Matthew knew this was very rare but had to voice it.

"For what reason?" Jenny was puzzled. "It's only in extreme circumstances that happens and there is nothing here to warrant it."

Graham stated "But let us say that Vedron had in some way impregnated her, he isn't experienced enough and doesn't have the power to withhold a placement."

"Wait, we are concentrating on purely the spirit." She checked again. "Can they confirm whether or not there is a foetus present please."

In the minutest fraction of a second the reply was received.

"None."

"So there we have it, as simple as that. Lizzie is having a phantom pregnancy." Jenny was a little relieved to know there was no physical result, but the fact remained that Lizzie felt she was and what could she do about it. Also, had the fiend had enough power to produce this certain feeling in her?

Matthew had been deep in thought. "My next question is 'Why?' Does he feel he has control over her in this way?"

"To what end?" Graham added.

Jenny stopped their thoughts. "Because as we know, the spiritual power is often much stronger than the earthly one. That is why people do things but can't explain afterwards why they did them." To force her point she said "I don't know what came over me."

She gave them a moment to digest this then added "Of course we know this can often be an excuse to get out of something they know quite well they've done, but not always, as you have experienced. Why are we always fighting to ward off the evil powers? Most people are never aware of what is going on around them, and those that do are dubbed crackpots."

They agreed this had to be the work of Vedron, or someone like him. They couldn't afford to assume anything just because facts appeared to be so. They must keep open thoughts until something certain was proved.

"Come on lad, you'll be late for school." Sharon called to Denis and was surprised when he emerged from his bedroom fully dressed.

"I thought you were still in bed as usual. What's got you up so early?" she smiled as she went back to the kitchen to butter his toast. He didn't reply but went into the living room to get his school bag.

"Talk to yourself woman," Sharon muttered. She wished Denis would be more communicative but perhaps that was what boys were like. It wasn't easy to talk to the other boys' mums as they seemed to be in a clique of their own and didn't get into conversation. Lizzie was the only one who spoke to her but she only had a girl so she wasn't likely to have much idea about boys. She was such a friendly person and Sharon wondered why the women shunned her so much, only speaking when they wanted something like a sponsor, or help at a school sale. They never included her in social events which seemed unkind and hard to understand.

"Sod 'em all" She thought as she took the egg out of the saucepan. If her little idea worked, they could all take a running jump. Then they would see.

"Here's your breakfast." She called out and Denis slowly came into the kitchen and sat at the table. She watched him start to eat then packed his bag with his lunch.

"Are you talking to Bethany's mum today?" The question took her by surprise.

"I always talk to her." Her mind was on what was going in his bag then she remembered his question from the day before. For some reason it seemed important for him to know what and when she was discussing with Lizzie.

He got on with his breakfast and seemed in a hurry to get to school which was most unusual but it made a pleasant change so she said nothing.

"Right" she looked him up and down, "have you got your PE kit?"

"I have, and I've been to the toilet and yes, I've washed my hands."

"All right clever clogs, no need for cheek." But she couldn't help but notice the change in his manner.

"Must be growing up early" she thought as they left the house. "Shall have to watch him or I'll have some parent banging on my door saying he's got their girl into trouble." Then pulled her thoughts to a halt. "Hang on he's only ten!"

"There they are." Denis pointed and hurried forward until he was standing near Bethany who instinctively pulled away from him.

Sharon joined Lizzie. "Don't know what's got into him this morning, Monday as well, you'd think he'd still want to be in bed."

"Why what's up?" Lizzie was still in her own dream world.

"Couldn't wait to get here and keeps asking what I am seeing you about."

"Um, Oh what's that then?"

"Lizzie!" Sharon looked disappointed. "We're going to talk about that thing I had in mind for earning money." She lowered her voice on the last few words in case of nosey listeners.

"Oh. Yes, sorry it had gone out of my mind."

It was obvious this meant more to Sharon than her friend and she hoped she could instil some enthusiasm before the end of their chat, if indeed there was ever going to be a chat.

Denis moved nearer to Bethany. "Have you got a dog?" he asked but she ignored him and turned away.

"Bethany, don't be rude." Lizzie was sharper than usual "Denis has asked you a question, now answer him politely."

"No." was the reply.

Lizzie was shocked. "Don't answer me like that."

"I wasn't. I was telling Denis we haven't got a dog."

"Oh, well look at him when you speak. Where are your manners?" If there was one thing Lizzie was strict about it was good manners.

Bethany didn't really want to talk to Denis but she turned round and for the first time it occurred to her that he perhaps wasn't as bad as she had thought. He was a loner which made him an outcast with the other children and she started to feel pity for him.

"Why, have you?" she looked him straight in the face and noticed he was smiling at her.

"Not really. But I make one up. Perhaps one day I'll be able to have one."

"That's funny." She almost laughed. "But I like cats best."

"Well make one up then my dog can chase it."

They both laughed and the two mothers stopped in amazement. It was time for them to go into school and they walked away together, accompanied by Doag and the group of protective sentinels.

"Well, what do you make of that?" Lizzie was the first to voice her surprise.

"Oh that's kids for you," Sharon shrugged. They can be enemies one week and best friends the next or the other way round. Don't try to understand them, I gave that up a long time ago."

They walked away from the gates and Sharon said "Sure you want to hear more about this idea then?"

"Yes, I think I do Sharon, let's go and talk about it."

They were soon sitting in Lizzie's house drinking coffee and Sharon produced her notebook and started making notes as she described her plan.

"We've both had experience with cleaning. God knows we do enough, so nobody can tell us how to do it."

"Well that's right enough," Lizzie cast her eye around to make sure there were no specks of dust anywhere.

"Right. Well I do this cleaning job in the evenings as you know and I sat there and thought – I do sometimes you know" she gave a knowing nudge as she spoke "why don't I do it for myself, not other people."

"Um – I'm not quite sure what you mean." It often took her a while to grasp what was being said.

Sharon couldn't understand why she wasn't getting the gist of it. "We work for ourselves."

"I'm sorry, I still don't know just what you're saying."

"Christ Almighty Lizzie, we go out cleaning for people on hours to suit ourselves, but we charge them for it. It would be our own little business."

"Oh." Lizzie was visibly shocked. Anyone else would have guessed from previous questions what her friend had in mind but what with the thought of being pregnant and the visit to the family yesterday, it seemed to have gone to the back of her mind.

Sharon looked at her closely. "Hey, you ok?"

"Of course, why shouldn't I be?" she snapped then burst into tears.

"What's up?" Sharon put her arm round her shoulder, "if something's wrong you can tell me."

"I can't. I don't know, oh everything's such a mess."

"Oh God, you're not up the duff are you, not that that's a bad thing" she added quickly for fear of upsetting her even more.

"I don't know."

"Well, have you missed yet?"

"No. But I'm not due yet."

"Well if you take my advice, you'll wait and see. Anyway, you'd want it wouldn't you?"

"Well yes, of course I would."

"Then what's all the fuss about? Oh your hormones playing up I expect." She gave her an extra hug and said "Don't worry, I know it's been a gap since Bethany, but lots of women do start again you know. I'd love to have had more but not with that bastard. Best thing when he cleared off. Never trusted a man since though so I haven't exactly put myself in the firing line if you get my meaning."

Sharon's bluntness had a soothing effect on Lizzie and soon she said "You're right of course. Best wait and see and then – well – take it from there."

"You could get one of the preggy testing kits but they're too bloody expensive I think. Anyway you'll know soon enough."

They drank their coffee and both decided to have a good talk about the possibilities of the cleaning idea. Sharon needed to get work soon, and Lizzie welcomed the thought of extra cash. She had forgotten Danny's warning for now but, as was her way would want to explain it all to him later. It did seem to be a possibility but a few questions crossed her mind.

"We'd need the cleaning materials."

Sharon slapped the notebook. "Not straight away."

"Oh?"

"To start with we'd use theirs and just charge for the actual cleaning, then we would have the money to get stuff and charge more."

"But who would want us?"

"Just about everyone. Folks who go to work, those who can't do it, older folk."

"But how would they know about us?"

"Aha. Advertise." Again she slapped her book.

Lizzie laughed now. "You do seem to have thought of everything."

"We will learn as we go along. You know things like, when we get them to pay, we don't want to be giving credit. And it will have to be near. Neither of us have a car, but we could use bikes if we had to."

"Well I like the sound of it. But I would have to talk it over with Danny first." Only then did Danny's words come into her mind and she was glad she hadn't made a hasty decision.

"Sure, but tell you what, he'd be the first bloke to turn his nose up at a bit of extra dosh. I know that for sure."

After a while Sharon left hoping her friend would see the sense of her plans, and if she didn't, she would jolly well go ahead and do it on her own. Lizzie did like the sound of it and knew it was something she could do, but the thought of working in someone's home seemed a bit daunting. It had been different working in a care home because that wasn't the resident's own property. She would have to think about this very carefully.

If Vedron's frustration was simmering, then his anger would be classed as near boiling point. He had spent, what to him was a long time preparing himself for his return. He was desperate to possess what was his and absolutely nothing was going to stop him, and when he had achieved his goal, no one in any form or existence would we able to touch him for he would be invincible. Zargot had observed his 'training period' with some degree of mirth, but disregarded him as the scrap of rubbish that he was. The Vexons had often gone through periods of trying to usurp the higher evil powers but had been crushed every time but there were always some who thought themselves way above their station, but would come tumbling down just like the ones before them. This one was a mere nuisance and not worthy of much attention, unless it interfered with their own plans, so Zargot and his followers simply watched the fun and waited.

Vedron had felt he was making good progress as he made physical contact with Lizzie but hadn't bargained for the fact she would be a wife and mother by the time he came to claim her. Of course she had resisted before but he had easily overcome that, not realising that it was Zargot who was calling the shots. Now he was acting alone and wondering why he wasn't getting the same results. He had tried to take over Danny's body but the forces protecting the man had pushed him out. He didn't even realise that this was to his advantage, for had he stayed Jenny would have located him, captured his being and all would be lost. But he was already conscious of the fact that he must not be in one place or form for any length of time, or he could be trapped.

In desperation he had entered the Bradley house and considered Margaret as a stop gap, but on seeing her present state decided to concentrate on his main objective. The task now was to get a body of his own, not borrow someone else's. In his world it wouldn't be as difficult as those in human form would imagine. Bodies are made up of cells and it is just a case of getting the right amount together and there was no shortage of material on earth. It had often been known for a spirit who had unfinished business to return in a similar form, carry out the job then return, discarding the unwanted shell for it to filter back into the earth as though it had never been. He had been studying this art during his absence but was yet to put it into practice for real. Of course he'd had dummy runs which had seemed to work but this was in an area where there was a concentration of guardians who were not just protecting their charges, they, or rather the one at the top would be out to get him. But the urge to get satisfaction was driving a force within him that could blind his strategy or awareness. He hovered now some distance away from Banbury, planning his next move.

Robert and Beth had decided to reorganise their garden to give it a fresh look but not be too drastic and keep some of the natural look which they loved. As he had a couple of days off to use holiday leave due to him, it seemed a good time to tackle it

"How about modernising the back just outside the house and it would be nice to sit there in the summer evenings?" Robert looked up from the sketches he had been making.

"You're being hopeful." Beth laughed then said show me what you mean.

"Well, where we've got this little bit of paving, we could extend it or have it done in that decking they use now."

"Oh yes, would there be room for a table and a couple of chairs?" She liked this idea.

"As many as you like. I was thinking of – well – if all goes as good as it did yesterday, we could all sit out there for tea or something."

"I like that. And we could get one of those umbrella things that stand in the middle of the table."

She waited for a reply and he smiled mischievously.

"Or..." he was playing for effect now "we could have a cover over that bit, or even the length of the house."

"Oh Robert, um – what sort of cover had you in mind." She liked this very much but couldn't quite work out what he was thinking.

"Well, they build them out from the house, like a car port so you'd still get the light in and they don't always use glass, there's a new kind of stuff, sort of double plastic but very strong. Anyway it was just a thought."

"I love the thought. Could we afford it?"

He flicked through a magazine and stopped at one page. "There, something like that. We could ask for a quote, it's free." Then laughed and said "The quote I mean."

"Go on. What about the rest, or hadn't you got that far?" She had snuggled up to him now and was enjoying the closeness which seemed to increase each day.

"Well, not a lot. Maybe kick out some of the old plants, you know those we said were getting a bit tired, and pop some fresh ones in, but the bottom part I'd leave much as it is."

"Oh yes, it's so natural and the plants attract the butterflies." Then laughed and said "When Bethany was trying to catch that one yesterday. What a picture!"

Robert hugged her "And did you see the look on Margaret's face. It was pure joy. I reckon she could soon be chasing them herself."

"Oh Robert, do you think so?"

"Why not?" Then looking at his watch he said "Oh Bill's coming round at dinner time to look at that mower. "Made up my mind, we are getting a more modern one."

"This gets better." She slipped her arm across his waist and he grabbed it and pulled it down further.

"You're right, this is better." He held her hand in his crotch while he kissed her as though they had been apart for ages.

"Robert" she giggled "you naughty man."

"Tell me it doesn't feel good."

A slight noise made them jump back to their sitting positions and Robert grabbed the magazine and held it over the obvious lump which had appeared making his wife nearly choke with laughter.

"Morning," A very tired voice called from the hall and Margaret crept in as though she had been out all night.

Beth jumped up. "Did you sleep well dear? You went out like a light."

"Can't remember." Margaret flopped down in the armchair.

Both parents were quite relieved. Usually she could remember her dreams especially the horrid ones and so she must have been relaxed.

"Cup of tea dear?" Beth was almost out of the door.

"Oh yes please, my mouth feels like a wrestler's jock strap."

Beth stopped in amazement and Robert suddenly felt no need to use the magazine as a cover any more.

"What was that?" he laughed.

Margaret looked from one to the other.

"What'd I say?" her voice was still sleepy.

"Oh nothing much but it was funny." Beth was still grinning then added "glad you've had a good night anyway."

"Have we got any marmalade?" Again this was unexpected. She normally had to be urged to eat anything first thing.

"Yes, would you like it on toast." Beth couldn't hide her pleasure, then suddenly she felt her mouth go dry and she panicked for a drink and rushed into the kitchen.

"I'll go and help." Margaret got up and shuffled out leaving Robert with his mouth open in wonderment.

"Got another one Mama Beth?"

Beth downed a glass of water in one go. "Oh I feel such a fool."

"Don't." Margaret had sidled up to her. "I'll help you."

The change in her, combined with all that she had been through affected Beth so much she broke down and hugged her "You shouldn't have to be worrying about me."

"Why not? Don't you want me to?" Margaret was crying as well now mostly from relief that she wasn't the only one who had a problem.

"It's something we have to cope with we women, if its not one age it's another. They always blame your age you know."

"They can't blame my age." Margaret sniffed and reached for a piece of kitchen towel to blow her nose.

"They might try." Beth was getting back to normal. "Anyway I'm fine now. Thank you. Now you go and sit down and I'll bring you some breakfast."

"Can I make the tea?"

"Course you can. I'll put the kettle on. Oh by the way," she looked at Margaret "there's a man coming today to take the old mower away we hope."

"Why?" Coming out of the blue Margaret wondered what this was about.

"Well, your dad and I have been talking and we are thinking of doing up this end of the garden with some decking or something."

"Oh, just this end." She looked worried.

"Well," Beth continued "we'll freshen up the plants but you know where you and Bethany were, at the bottom bit, we thought we'd leave that more or less as it is because we like the natural look. What do you think?"

Margaret was never asked what she thought as she could never give an answer or make a decision.

"Oh, I like it, especially the bottom bit. There are butterflies and all sorts of things there and Bethany was so happy looking at them, I wouldn't like them to go."

"Oh I meant to tell you. When you nodded off, Bethany stood by your bed and sang to you."

Margaret's eyes filled with tears. "She did?"

"Yes, we had to pull her away and she asked could she come and see you again."

"She asked to see me?" the tears were running down her cheeks and Beth was close to joining her so she grabbed a tissue from the drawer and dabbed both their faces.

"Just look at us, two grown women bawling all over the place. I feel sorry for your Dad."

Margaret had to smile. "She will come though won't she?"

"You try and stop her. Now where's that kettle?"

The guardian angels had observed this scene with satisfaction and a report was relayed to the upper realms where it was received gratefully. Every good vibration, every loving thought added to the protection of these people and the stronger it got, the harder it would be for any evil doer to enter their area. Checks were being constantly recorded in the Worth household and plans were in place to put Lizzie out of the misery the fiend had forced on her.

"Get her started, I don't care if she is due or not, and what's a few days anyway?" Jenny issued the order and Amity immediately put Lizzie's body into a mode that would obey instructions. Within minutes the urge to go to the toilet and check the moistness made her almost sob with relief. She reached into the bathroom cupboard for her towels and whispered "Thank God" to herself. Now she needn't worry about having to tell Danny and what a good job she hadn't told anyone else. She jumped.

"Sharon."

Quickly she went to the phone. Although she liked her friend, she wasn't a hundred percent sure she wouldn't have mentioned it to someone else as her mouth ran away with her sometimes. The familiar ringing out tone went on and she was just about to put it down when Sharon answered.

"Oh Sharon, I just wanted to tell you."

"You've decided, that's great. Tell you what, I'll try and design some sort of flyer and..."

"Sharon!" Lizzie was almost shouting. "It's not that."

"Well, what is it then?" She sounded a bit deflated.

"Oh nothing much, I just wanted to tell you that ...well I'm not pregnant after all."

"Well then, that's even better news. Told you. That means we can get on and sort out the business. Nothing to stop us now."

"Sharon. Listen. I've haven't talked it over with Danny yet." There was a hush. "I said I would have to do that and I must. Then I will let you know." Then added, "Tomorrow."

Knowing this was going no further Sharon said a quick "Ok. Bye" and was gone.

Lizzie knew she had been expecting her to agree to the job but even more than ever she knew she must talk to Danny and would go on whatever he said. He knew more about such things and she would then decide.

Chapter 6

A lone man walked along one of the little back streets of Banbury. There were no cars and the array of little shops made it a very popular area. Being narrow it meant that any shoppers were fairly close to each other and often had to let someone else pass if it got busy near one particular place. It would be hard to estimate his age, he didn't stand out as particularly attractive, was of average height and build and would pass by without drawing any attention to himself.

He made his way to the end of the street and down a cobbled passage to a small tea shop. There were a few people inside and he chose a table in the corner where he could watch the other customers. With the pretence of reading the menu as he drank his tea he was taking in every movement of all the people including the young waitress. He was mentally noting how they conversed, moved and even how they ate and drank. And if anyone had bothered to look would have guessed that he was either a newspaper reporter or a private detective.

After a while he left, and walked round some of the busier streets getting acclimatised to the hustle and bustle of a busy market town. Nobody gave him a second glance which suited him and after a while he decided to change his surroundings and made his way to the supermarket where Danny worked. Taking a small basket he picked up a few items and wandered around until he saw Danny at one of the tills. Timing his movements he got there just as the person in front had finished and noticing what others had done, put his things on the belt. Danny looked up briefly and smiled then got on with passing the produce through the scanner.

"Would you like a bag?" he asked.

"A bag?" the man asked.

"Yes sir, a carrier bag," and he lifted one up for him to see.

"Oh yes, thank you."

Danny told him how much the shopping had come to and the man felt in his pocket for a ten pound note. As he handed it over Danny went to take it from him and froze although he couldn't have explained why. Shaking himself he took the note and got the change from the drawer. As soon as the money had entered the note section of the till, the feeling left him, but as soon as he handed the receipt with the change to the customer he felt drawn to look at him, straight in the face as though he was being guided to remember him.

Alarm bells had gone up from Danny's guardians, and immediately higher sentinels were in place to seek out the whereabouts of the customer. They soon located him in the car park and watched him from a distance. He made his way to the bus stop and joined the queue waiting for the shoppers' shuttle, a local service for people without cars. As they didn't want him to be aware that he was being observed they held back until the bus arrived but as they checked the passengers getting on, he wasn't among them. Quickly, one angel mingled with the people but their target had gone. They checked around the bus shelter and extended the search out into the car park but it was as if he had completely vanished. When the report reached Jenny, she couldn't be positive that it was Vedron, but the facts certainly seemed that way, and if it wasn't him, then who had stirred this reaction in Danny? The guardians on duty at the time said they sensed a familiarity but didn't recognise the current visitor. There was no option but to leave this for now but it proved that something was working the area for some reason.

A similar looking man was, at this moment unlocking the door to his flat, a simple place in a small boarding house on the other side of the town. The house was let to single men or women who needed to hide away unnoticed from society for a while. No questions were asked and as long as they paid their rent on time, the landlord didn't bother them and they didn't communicate with each other. It seemed to be an unwritten rule which suited them all. Although classed as single, they could be still married, divorced or just loners.

The man now sat in the sparse room which was merely a bed sit with means of making a drink, and a small fridge. The only other room was the bathroom so it barely met with the description of 'flat' but nobody queried it, and it sounded better. He had bought a sandwich but put it in the fridge for later as he needed to concentrate now. He lay flat on his bed and after a few moments' deep meditation, felt himself floating as though he had no body. He mentally drifted out into the hall and along the landing until he was outside the room on the opposite side to his. He paused for a moment soaking up the vibes and when he was satisfied the room was empty, slowly floated inside turning himself upright. Quickly he examined every part of the place, slightly smaller than his own, looking for spiritual traces rather than physical ones. A sound wave disturbed the air and he instantly returned to his own room but now with his bodily senses alerted. He heard the man come up the stairs and go along to his room, close and lock the door.

The watcher was disappointed not to have spent longer searching, but he had hit upon something extremely important and knew that he was on the right trail and must see it through to the bitter end, whatever that may be.

Vedron had seen the net closing and quickly managed to escape. No people had seen him go because they were too busy thinking of their own tasks and getting on the bus was taking their concentration at the time he chose to leave. He was quite pleased at this first attempt to mingle with the human race but knew he would have to be very careful from now on as his nemesis would be out to crush him permanently. He knew Danny hadn't recognised him on his own so the protective force had alerted something in him to make him look again. But Danny had never seen him in his new form so there was no reason for him to even be the slightest suspicious. The next test would be very interesting. Then he would see what the angels were made of and they in turn would know he was capable of taking what was his. Feeling very smug and self satisfied he returned to his lair, but his sexual frustration had not been vented so time was against him. He observed his bodily image and would like to have made it irresistible but he knew that would draw attention, so for the time being he would have to manage with this insignificant scrap of a man who at this precise moment must satisfy his lustful urges. He lay down with the image of Lizzie on top of him and within a short time had given in to his addiction.

"There's the door bell." Beth called out to Robert.

"Already there," he answered. "It's Ok. It's Bill. We'll go round the back."

"Is that the man for the mower?" Margaret was looking out of the back window.

"Certainly is. I don't know! When your Dad makes up his mind to do something...."

"I don't like the look of him." Margaret interrupted and ran out of the room.

"Now what was all that about?" Beth thought as she followed her. "Margaret dear, what is it?" She caught up with her in her room.

"Tell me when he's gone." She was trembling from top to toe.

Beth had an idea. "You wait here." She got up and went to the door.

"What are you going to do?"

"Back in a minute." Beth called over her shoulder and was making her way down the stairs and into the back garden.

The two men were chatting about the pros and cons of decking and the mower stood ready to be taken away. As Robert saw her he said "Oh Bill this is my wife" and extended his arm to draw her nearer. He still loved saying 'my wife' and used it whenever the opportunity arose.

"Hello Mrs Bradley."

"Oh, Beth please." They shook hands and Beth noticed the firmness of his grip. In fact it was so firm she had to pull her hand away. Bearing in mind Margaret's reaction when she saw him, she now studied him intently although trying not to be too obvious about it. Then making her excuses said that it had been a pleasure to meet him and excused herself.

"Well?" Margaret greeted her. "What did you make of him?"

Beth had to be very careful. She knew the other woman had picked up some sort of rejection when she had seen him but Beth didn't want to cause any setbacks at this stage when things seemed to be looking up.

"Hmm, not sure." She sat on the bed.

"So you did feel something. I knew it." Margaret's reaction was a surprise as she didn't seem so upset, but welcomed someone else agreeing with her.

Beth breathed a sigh of relief and decided to try the 'confiding' tactic. They were sitting side by side now.

"Well, it's hard to say, because he seemed very nice, when your Dad introduced us, but…"

"Yes?"

Beth looked at her. "You'd probably understand. He shook my hand but….um…"

"You got a strange feeling when he touched you." Margaret announced it with pride. That's right isn't it?"

"I think you've hit the nail on the head."

"Go on."

"Like I said, he seemed alright then he squeezed my hand and I felt it was going dead and I had to pull away." Beth felt rather silly explaining this but it brought out Margaret's old self.

"Horrible man. I knew he was bad. Hurting you like that."

"Oh, I'm fine now, but thank you for warning me Margaret. You have a talent you know."

"Do you really think so? Nobody's ever told me that before." And she sat like a child who's just received a good school report.

"Well I think he's gone now. Probably best not say anything to your Dad eh?"

"No. Wouldn't understand. But we do." With that she gave a very knowing look to Beth and they both went downstairs as if nothing had happened, but Beth still wondered just what vibe they had both picked up from this Bill.

Denis made a point of speaking to Bethany at playtime but making it appear to be casual and not forced. She warmed to him now especially as he liked animals and she realised he had a nice voice. Although still very young, she didn't like people with harsh tones and often Sharon grated on her as she spoke far too loudly whereas her Mum and Gran had softer voices.

"It's my birthday soon." Denis smiled at her.

"That's funny, its mine too."

"My mum wondered if I wanted one or two friends round for tea, but not a lot 'cos she's just lost her job, but I'm not supposed to say that." Denis was very clever at letting her think she was in on a secret.

She almost whispered "Yes I know, but I haven't said anything."

"Well," he looked her straight in the eye "I don't suppose you'd like to come, only I don't mix with the boys much."

She already knew that, in fact everyone knew what a loner he was. "I'd have to ask my Mum."

"Will you?"

"Yes, when she picks me up."

Denis cut in "I'd rather you asked her at home."

"Why?" Bethany put her head on one side which was a cute little way of hers.

"Well, the others are nosey and they'd probably tease me, and you of course."

Bethany beamed and took a sharp breath "So it's a secret. Oh I love secrets."

As one or two children were noticing them talking he moved away and was soon lost in the playground.

Some of the girls were in a group that seemed to think themselves above everyone else and if they spoke it was only because they wanted information or to mock.

"Got a new boyfriend then Bethany?" The leader shouted for all to hear but fortunately the noise in the playground dulled her sarcasm.

"No. Why should I?" Bethany was on the defensive. She never liked this girl who had often tried to make her look silly and turn others against her.

"Hey, Bethany and Denis are sweethearts. Has he kissed you yet?" A roar of laughter went up from her followers.

Bethany's back went up, but before she could respond a strange thing happened. Doag hadn't wanted too much attention drawn to them but knew Denis had to be as close as possible in order to do his job. Surveying the scene he had moved Denis away and selected the most unkempt lad in the school, whose body odour preceded him and his finger nails almost had livestock living under them and moved him close to the leader of the pack. Just as the girls were chanting "Bethany and Denis sitting in a tree..." Doag pushed the smelly urchin forward, made him grab the leader and plant the filthiest smacker on her cheek.

The scream that emitted from her sent the lad packing but Bethany could hardly hide her mirth. Denis observed it from a distance but later when he was asleep and in his own form would learn from his partner just what he had done.

It wasn't the usual practice of the higher realms to have the main guardian in human form, especially a child's body, but Jenny was using this ploy to ward off any suspicion. She had left lower level sentinels as obvious protectors as someone had to appear to be in presence but Denis was placed to have him on hand. Although his mind was blocked during his waking hours, that action could be switched off at a given moment and he would become his true self, but that was for later and he must go about almost unnoticed for now.

"Your friend has a tight handshake." Beth joined Robert in the garden as he was measuring the ground outside the house.

"What friend dear?" He was still jotting down notes and hadn't really taken in what she said.

"Bill." She waited for him to look up.

"Oh I wouldn't call him a friend. We just work together. He does a lot for charity though. Seems a kind sort of bloke." He picked up the tape measure and realised she looked concerned. "Why, what's bothering you?"

"Oh don't take any notice of me, I'm probably just being silly."

"No, No, come on, I know you. Something's eating at you."

Beth wondered how she could explain what had only been a feeling albeit unpleasant, but there didn't seem to be anything in particular she could say and she didn't want to bring Margaret into it.

"It's just... Oh I don't know, he gripped my hand so tightly and it didn't feel right."

He smiled, put down the things in his hand and took her in his arms.

"You aren't one given to fantasy my darling, and I'm just wondering, now don't take this the wrong way but you know, well—just now with the change and everything, perhaps that had something to do with it."

Some women would have slapped him for a remark like that but in a way it was a relief as it let her off the hook about explaining something she couldn't. And she had Margaret she could talk to about it so it seemed the best thing to agree with him.

"You're right as always." She kissed him gently and saw the satisfaction on his face thinking he had sorted the problem.

"Sorry to interrupt but if you must carry on for all to see." Margaret's voice made them jump but they all laughed and the relaxed atmosphere was noted by their protective forces.

"We'll leave you to your measuring," Beth took Margaret's arm and said "how about we go and look for those butterflies Bethany found."

When they got to the bottom of the garden Margaret said "Ok, why did you drag me off like that?"

"Oh, silly me I tried to tell your Dad about Bill's hand and..."

"And he laughed I suppose." Margaret finished the sentence a little relieved as this strengthened the bond between them. They understood what no one else could.

"Not exactly, he just put it down to the change."

"Hmm. Well that doesn't matter. We know." And she gave a little toss of the head with her nose in the air that made Beth laugh. They spent a while watching nature and relaxing as if nothing in the world could hurt them and Margaret pointed to a bird floating on a thermal and whispered "I wish this could go on for ever, and nothing change."

For a guardian to relay a message to higher powers, it had to go through various levels in order to prevent it being intercepted by evil sources. It was often due to incompetence in the lower evil that allowed the angels to receive information of their plans in this way. Although a message could be with Jenny within a split second, it may have been 'decoded' many times before she actually received it. But if a special force was operating undercover, they may not be able to divulge their whereabouts by sending even the most innocent communication.

The watcher positioned in the boarding house was in this situation and could not even have a decoy guardian in place, such was the necessary secrecy demanded. To avoid suspicion he created an image of a protector to make it appear that everything was normal. He knew where Vedron was hiding but could not divulge it yet or all could be lost for the fiend would simply disappear again and it could be decades before he re-emerged.

He had been tracing him using his own special talents and monitoring all the new skills Vedron had learned, but he knew the Vexon was still a novice in many ways and it would only be a matter of time before he overstretched himself. Now the watcher was about to enter the arena completely alone against his foe, but only one of them would survive.

For Vedron to have been undetected by all but his watcher, meant that he had been either changing his identity or using different substances but it hadn't taken long for the experienced watcher to work out just how. He knew he had started like most students with simple things then worked on to more intricate items but he was far from mastering the more complicated things. Also he hadn't always perfected one skill before moving on to another, such was his haste to get back and claim the spoils.

As he was being monitored, his watcher had been disgusted by his methods and wanted to put an end to his ways as soon as he could but knew that was not how it had to be. This creature had to be disposed of once and for all, never to return.

On his visit to Vedrons's room he had found a small item in one of the drawers and knew he had to examine it again. He didn't need to follow his prey now every time he left the building, for he had placed a spiritual tracker on him and could follow his movements but home in on him if anything needed close observation.

His senses told him the man had gone out so he immediately returned to the drawer in the room and found what he was looking for. It would have been unnoticed by the human eye as it was so small but the watcher knew it was what he suspected. Careful not to disturb the air around it he studied the fragment and identified it as a spiritual cloaking device. Although Vedron could switch his identities between humans, as he had done when he entered Danny, and likewise with materials such as paper etc, he couldn't always be on the move. Apart from risking being traced it was something he was incapable of doing for a length of time so he had to have some means of going to ground quite often.

The main question in the watcher's mind was how and where he got it. These things weren't something that were widely used and in the wrong hands they had proved destructive. Someone or something had supplied him, but at what price? It was most likely that, in exchange for this privilege he had to repay in some way, maybe even with his own soul. Making sure he erased every trace of his visit in the atmosphere of the room, he went off in the direction of his quarry.

Doag was sharing with Denis the happenings of the day and they agreed that it would be safe to let Denis carry on with the plan for now as it didn't seem to be attracting any attention from evil sources. He was getting closer to Bethany at just the right speed and she was returning the friendship, so he was sitting in the wings as far as Lizzie was concerned and would pick up any warning signs from Amity without her knowledge. It was necessary to have spirits at different levels working independently at this stage, as too much obvious attention in one area had often ruined an outcome.

It was noticed by all concerned that Lizzie seemed to have been left alone recently, but as Vedron was in the area she was most likely to still be his main target so all diligence was required from every source. The event at the supermarket could not have been random and so there must have been some reason for it. Although the events in the Pacific were still very active, Jenny knew that essential resources must not be drawn from Banbury as that could be just what they wanted.

Symphony, Margaret's guard had noted Bill's strange presence before anyone and was especially observant when he made contact with Beth, and her obvious rejection. A message had gone back to the high levels even before Margaret was aware of him, that he was hosting another being without his knowledge. Whoever it may be was using him for that short time to make contact with another member of the family, and as soon as that had been achieved, it was thought that he had made his exit. He was so well hidden, that although it was observed that Bill had a passenger, it was impossible to say who it could be and therefore no action dare be taken. Sometimes it was common for a family member to try to get through to someone they had left in the bodily form by using this method and you couldn't just go about flushing them all out every time it took place.

But the watcher knew. Taking cover himself, he had seen every second in slow motion so that he didn't miss a single detail, and he was now piecing together Vedron's evil sadistic plan. His aim now was to try and stay one move ahead so that he could be ready for him and observe every thing, not just what he was doing, but the way he was doing it, and thereby build up a picture of his weaknesses and strengths. Many would have been inpatient and taken him out at the first chance, but the highly experienced watcher knew better, for that wouldn't end his wave of possession, only delay it. It had happened many times in the past, that, in order to save living souls, fiends had supposedly been disposed of and the humans left to live their lives in peace, only to find that many years later the same events took place again in other parts of the world proving the evil had not been overcome entirely.

Lizzie had mixed feelings about telling Danny of Sharon's cleaning idea, and although she had to admit it could be a good thing, felt a slight twinge of hesitation about it. But it went from her mind as he walked in the door because he seemed a bit quiet for him. He kissed her and Bethany as usual, washed his hand and sat down for his dinner.

"You all right?" Lizzie put the plate down in front of him.

"Yes fine ta." He ate his meal in almost silence and if it hadn't been for Bethany chatting on about the drama in the playground, it could have been a very awkward mealtime. They finished eating and Lizzie cleared away with Bethany in tow asking if she could go to Denis's birthday party.

"Who else is going?" Lizzie thought it strange that Sharon hadn't mentioned it, although her mind seemed full of the business idea.

"Don't know, praps only me."

"Perhaps dear, not praps. Well it doesn't sound like much of a party. Maybe we should wait until his mummy invites you."

"But Denis said…"

Lizzie was still worried about Danny and wanted the washing up out of the way so that she could talk to him and so answered her daughter in a harsher way than she meant.

"I don't care what Denis said, it's what I say, and I say wait until you are invited."

She felt guilty as Bethany's lip trembled and she disappeared into the living room, so as soon as she had dried her hands she went to join her. It was obvious the child had been crying and she put a comforting arm around her and gave her a big cuddle. Danny watched from the armchair but said nothing.

It wasn't until Bethany was tucked up in bed that Lizzie felt she could ask him what was wrong, for something obviously was eating at him.

"So come on what's the matter?" she patted his shoulder as she went by and sat down.

"Nothing."

There can't be anything worse to a spouse than when their loved one is harbouring a problem but answers with that one simple word.

Lizzie wasn't amused. "Well something is. I can see it."

"I told you, there's nothing the matter."

"Oh have it your own way. If you don't want to tell me."

"Look, there's some things you can't understand."

"What, you mean just I can't understand?" she was getting a little angry now.

"No, I don't mean that, oh I don't know how to put it."

She took a deep breath, not sure if she wanted to hear any more. "I think you had better tell me, whatever it is."

"I can't."

Now her heart sank. "There's someone else isn't there?"

His head shot up in surprise. "No, nothing like that. There could never be anyone else."

She breathed a sigh of relief. "Well then, nothing can be that bad." She waited for him to answer but all she got was a shake of the head. Then something hit her in the pit of her stomach.

"Oh no. You're not ill? Tell me you're not ill."

He shuffled uneasily then put his head in his hands. She flew to him, knelt on the floor and cupped his hands in hers. There was a muffled noise and she couldn't make out the words.

"Tell me again Danny."

"I think I'm going mad." He was almost crying as he looked up into her eyes. "I know you went through a lot and we don't talk about it, and I didn't want to bother you with this but it's driving me crazy."

Gently she stroked his head and said "Come and sit with me on the sofa and we will talk about it."

She didn't know what to expect but knew she had to be strong enough to cope with whatever he was feeling. When they had settled he looked straight ahead because he couldn't face her.

"Things have happened I didn't understand, and I couldn't have told anyone."

"What kind of things?" her voice was soft and soothing.

He gave her a quick glance then looked around the room as if gathering the courage to speak.

"Well, yesterday morning, I was doing things, but it was though I wasn't. I mean, I grabbed you didn't I and I was rough with you, only I didn't feel as though it was me that was doing it." He kept repeating himself as though he was going round in a loop and couldn't get out. Lizzie let him ramble for a moment then held up her hand.

"It isn't as strange as you might think."

"What!" he never expected this reply, but then wondered if it had any bearing on her previous problems.

"Go on, anything else." she prompted.

"I called you a bitch I think. I'd never call you that. I've called other women worse things, but not you."

"Forget it." Lizzie was beginning to realise that something strange was going on and perhaps he had been the one inside her but not remembered it. But worse, he could have been used to enter her. She shuddered as memories started to flood back.

"Lizzie" she jumped as Danny was shaking her to get her to escape from her thoughts.

He looked at her closely now. "What have I done Lizzie?"

"You've done nothing. Somebody or some thing did it to you, or through you."

"What are you talking about," He was getting a bit uneasy now. He could cope with her not wanting to recall her rapes, but when it got a bit spooky he didn't like the idea. He wasn't much into the spiritual side and had mocked people when they had said they'd received messages.

"Well you said it. You didn't feel as though it was you. And that's it."

"No. That isn't it. You're saying I'm possessed now."

"Well you said you were going crazy, not me."

It was quiet for a moment then Lizzie asked "And was that all?"

"Sort of." He didn't know whether to leave it at that and that be the end of it, in fact he wished he had never mentioned it.

"What's sort of?"

He looked almost annoyed with her now. "Well if I tell you anything, you'll make out I need exorcising."

"Oh well if you're going to be silly about it." and she grabbed a magazine and pretended the matter was over.

"Ok, Ok, don't go off on one." He hadn't expected this exchange but in a way it was nice to get it off his chest as he couldn't tell anyone else his feelings.

She put the paper down. "I'm listening." she said quietly, "and I won't call the vicar if that's what's bothering you."

"Well, today at work, this bloke came in. Didn't pay much attention to him, he was just another customer at first."

"Go on."

"I am. He gave me a note and I got a strange feeling and I looked at him and I felt something was wrong, that's all I can say."

"Did the feeling go when he went?"

"I suppose it did, couldn't say just when. Not nice I can tell you."

"And that was it, nothing else?"

"No. Well go on you can laugh now." He looked huffed folded his arms and sighed.

"I'm not laughing Danny." She gave him a pat on the leg. "And you've been worrying about these things ever since they happened haven't you."

"Well of course I bloody have, enough to scare the shit out of you."

Lizzie gave him a disapproving look. She didn't allow swearing in their home, especially in front of Bethany and if he wanted to use that kind of language at work or with his mates, there wasn't much she could do about it, but not here. However she would overlook it this time as long as he didn't make a habit of it. She'd heard plenty from the old men at the home so wasn't shocked, but she just didn't think it was nice.

They sat in silence for a moment then she said "Danny, you are not crazy or anything like that."

"Well, it's not normal. Bet there's a good explanation for all of it. In bed I'd probably woken up from a dream and wasn't properly awake, and at the store it was just one of those people. Hey did you know, one of the old timers there says that you can have thousands of people go through, then one stands out as suspicious or strange or something but you don't know why. That's what it was, I had one of those." He slapped his thigh in satisfaction because he had worked it all out.

"Feel better now?" Lizzie was relieved at the outcome although deep down she knew full well there was much more to it than he realised and she must be on her guard. First thing in the morning she would talk to her mother and Robert.

She was just about to go and make a cup of tea when she remembered Sharon's plan. Trying to recall everything that had been said she then asked him his opinion, glad that it would take his mind off other things.

"What about the tax and insurance?" was the first thing on his mind then added "but I don't expect you'd earn enough for that yet, but you'd have to keep a note of what you did get."

"What, like bookkeeping you mean?"

"Sort of."

"Oh, I didn't think of that. Perhaps Sharon would do it."

"No you need to keep your own records." He realised this hadn't been thought through and he didn't want to see her get into trouble like he'd seen others do by not declaring earnings.

"Oh."

"Another thing, how are you going to get about?" He knew this would be a stumbling block.

"Sharon says on the bus or we could get a bike each."

He frowned at that. His ride to the supermarket was nothing like the traffic she would have to contend with if the jobs came in at the other side of the town.

"And you'd have to carry your cleaning stuff?"

"Well, Sharon says, we'd use the customer's at first then get our own." She realised now that having to carry enough bottles and cloths either on a bus or on a bike wouldn't be so good after all.

"And who would be dishing out the jobs?"

"Pardon?"

He knew he had hit the trump card now. "Who would decide which of you had which job?"

"Well, um I suppose, um ….." she was at a loss.

"I'll tell you" he paused, then almost shouted "Sharon says."

"What do you mean?" she was staggered at his outburst.

He turned her to face him. "I see it this way. She will get the calls, if there are any. She will pick the jobs to suit her, maybe the best paid. She will send you the furthest away. Maybe all the money will go to her then she will pay you yours. Now, what has Sharon said about all that?"

Lizzie was stunned. They had never gone into all those details, and come to think of it Sharon had only put the good points forward and left out the rest. Lizzie had said something about people not owing them but her mind was in a whirl now and she couldn't remember anything specific. What if she didn't get all she had worked for? Danny had put the doubt in her mind, for much as he loved his wife, he knew she could be very vulnerable at times and be the target for the users of this world. It saddened him to see her so low now and so he said "If you really want to earn some money why not go to the hospital, they're always wanting domestics and the like and it wouldn't be the same as going back to a home?"

"Oh Danny I'd never thought of that." she brightened immediately.

"I know that's the other side of town, but there is a bus that stops outside the entrance and you wouldn't be lugging your cleaning gear."

"And they would take care of my tax and stuff?"

"So no worries."

"Oh Danny," she hugged him now "I'll ring them in the morning."

He smiled mischievously "And don't forget to see what Sharon says."

Although this was in Lizzie's favour, Doag's attempt to bring Denis closer to Lizzie through Bethany meant that it was a setback. Had Sharon and Lizzie been working together the two children would have had ample time to be in each other's company, but Sharon could now be peeved at being turned down and not be keen on her son's friendship with the girl. This was something he would have to overcome and find new ways for it to work. Danny was a sensible lad, pity he had been too sensible just now.

Vedron was weighing up his progress on the planned possession of his beloved. His aim was to plant 'connects' as he called them in all people close to Lizzie, so that when he moved in he could control them so that they didn't interfere and try to keep her from his grasp. He needed a clear run when the time came and was hoping his speed would outwit the hovering angels which he knew would be in presence. Firstly he had put Lizzie's in place, Danny had been a pushover, and although he didn't consider Margaret a threat had made contact through the drawing to cover all angles. He knew he mustn't leave anything to chance however innocent it may seem. Now he had Beth. Bill had served his purpose and as he wasn't closely connected to the family he would be of no further use so he could be ignored.

If only he had realised this went against his ruling but he thought they would never be in contact again so he wasn't important. Robert too had been connected as he handed over the lawnmower, as Vedron considered that he was one that was very close and should not be missed. He would have to watch this man as he was of a very strong character and could inhibit the final moves.

So who did that leave now? Her friend Sharon. He weighed up the situation. She seemed to be the closest friend Lizzie had, so he had better 'connect' her and that wouldn't be too difficult. That seemed to take care of everyone. Lizzie didn't mix much and stayed home most of the time as far as he knew and so if she did get close to anyone else he would fix them as well.

He now considered Bethany, a mere child but the one who could influence her mother more than anyone.

"Best to be on the safe side," he thought and made plans to plant his evil cell in her and her belongings. He gave a hasty thought to her school chums but there seemed no one there who would be involved except that boy she spoke to. And he was Sharon's son so if his mother had a 'connect', so should he, not that it would be needed.

He was enjoying this new feeling of control and although it had worked in small ways during his training, he didn't always fully master the complete knowledge of one particular area, feeling he knew as much as he needed. Any expert will tell you that nobody ever knows it all and those that acquire the most knowledge are the first to admit how little they actually do know. This is not to say that Vedron hadn't perfected certain abilities, but for a plan as elaborate as this to succeed it may take many skills to pull it off.

Although he must own Lizzie in the flesh, for his human form must enjoy full satisfaction of his own kind, it wasn't possible in their lives as they were at the moment. So Lizzie must die. Then they would both be together in the spiritual world only to be reborn into physical bodies where they could give themselves to each other in continual fulfilment. Obviously, being in human form, they would ultimately die again, to be reborn and thus continue the process forever. The simpler option would mean he would have to be in body now but Lizzie was recognisable and they would live a life being hunted continually. But with his plan, they would appear as new people and therefore safe.

If the 'watcher' had been privy to this reasoning, he would have blown holes right through it. For a start Vedron didn't have a say in where a new placement would be. He couldn't just pick on two foetuses in wombs and decide they would be the ones he would chose, even on one occasions let alone several. There was also the fact that there are only so many returns permitted, so there would be no way he could carry on this method for eternity.

But the main stumbling block that the watcher would have taken as a certainty was that Vedron was relying on Lizzie's co-operation, whereas she would never succumb to his advances whatever form they may take. But this offensive being was a predator, a sick stalker who would not rest until he had fulfilled his mission. The Vexons were bad enough in their normal hunt for sexual gratification but when one turned into something this corrupt, the good forces tackled it as a major incident because the outcome could have long lasting effects on many. This was why the watchers were used due to their particularly highly honed skills. They had often brought a situation to a satisfactory result, then simply disappeared until required again. Jenny had guessed they were in presence but the thought had to be cleared from her thinking, for the slightest indication of what method was in force could ruin a whole operation and the chance would be gone.

Lizzie took Bethany to school with mixed feelings. She had a spring in her step following her conversation with Danny, but knew she would have to disappoint Sharon by turning down her idea. As they approached the school gates Bethany pointed and said "Look Mum, there's that man you were asking me about."

"Don't point dear, I've told you it's rude." She pulled the child's arm down and asked "Where? Which man?"

"Oh he's gone now." She didn't like being told off in public and felt a twinge of satisfaction that she couldn't show her mother the man as he seemed to have moved away somewhere. Lizzie had forgotten the person in the picture, but her motherly instinct wanted to know if a man was hanging about.

"Well never mind that, what man did you mean?"

Bethany did a little shrug and a sign which normally would have been funny but Lizzie wasn't leaving it there. "You said there was a man."

"I know I did. He was over there only now he's gone. Can I go now?"

"In a minute. Just tell me what man you saw."

"The one in my drawing, he was standing behind Denis."

That shook Lizzie back to reality. She scanned the playground and the area outside the gates but only saw teachers she knew.

"Hey, you with your head in the clouds." Sharon's voice broke into her thoughts.

Lizzie jumped. "Oh Hello Sharon." Then turned to Bethany, kissed her and told her to be a good girl.

"Bye Mum." with a wave she had gone.

"Well?" Sharon was by Lizzie's side in an instant. "Have you thought about it? Good idea isn't it? We could start right away if you want."

"Um…Sharon, well…I've talked it over with Danny and…"

"God. Bet he was bloody chuffed eh?"

"It's not as simple as that."

Sharon wasn't going to be put off "Well, nothing ever is, is it? But we can sort it out. Now…"

"Sharon." Lizzie almost had to shout to break the flow of words.

"What?" Sharon looked puzzled now.

It seemed there was only one way to tackle this and Lizzie blurted out "I can't do it."

They had turned and were walking away from the school now.

"Now let me just get this straight," Sharon's mood had changed somewhat. "One minute you like the idea, then all of a sudden you don't. S'pose your old man's put the knockers on it."

"Don't you mean mockers?"

"I know what I mean. What's he got against it anyway? I'm telling you this could be a little gold mine before long."

Lizzie was about to tell her about the hospital job but something stopped her and she couldn't voice Danny's concerns about Sharon wanting to run it to her advantage.

Fortunately for her the change in her friend's attitude somehow made it easier to come up with an answer.

"Well to be honest Sharon, I'm not that good on bikes, so I'd have to use the bus all the time, and there are reasons why I'm not supposed to carry heavy weights for long."

"Oh and when did all this come into things? You never said anything about that before."

"Well I had to think it over, from every angle like."

"Yes, with Danny making up your mind for you." Sharon was quiet for a moment then said "Well you do what you like, but I'm going ahead with it, then I bet you'll wish you'd gone with it."

Doag had been monitoring this and knew he had to keep these two in touch for the sake of keeping Denis close to Bethany, so he took over Sharon's mind as she said "Anyway, it's no big deal. By the way Denis wants Bethany to come for tea on his birthday if that's ok with you."

This took Lizzie quite by surprise but she welcomed the change of manner.

"Oh, she'd like that, they get on quite well now."

They had reached the road where they parted and Sharon said quite quietly "Not a party you understand, only you know - with my job gone and that - and anyway he doesn't want any fuss and doesn't mix much with the lads."

"Oh I understand Sharon, really I do" then after a thought "but it's Bethany's two days after, would you like me to do a joint tea for them both?"

Sharon's mouth dropped open. "Oh, that would be great..."she stopped "but would there be many there, like I say he isn't a mixer."

"Well family mostly, you know us, and her Gran and Grandad and possibly her Auntie Margaret." She saw the doubt in Sharon's face so quickly said "Tell you what, let her come to you on Denis's birthday, then you and him can come the next day and we'll have a little tea, just us, then she can have the family on the day itself. What do you think?"

"Oh that sounds great Lizzie." She had softened a little, most of the hardness going out of her voice.

"One rule though." Lizzie was quick to pick up when anyone wasn't too well off.

"Oh what's that?"

"No presents."

"But..."

"Look, it's a job finding the right things these days, I mean the stuff most of the kids rave about is so expensive. Bethany's always coming home saying what so and so has got. So let's just enjoy ourselves. There's games, and they can watch a DVD or something."

Sharon looked at her. "You have the most annoying habit of making everything seem all right, even when it isn't. But yes, I'm for that. You'll come won't you, to Denis's I mean."

"You try stopping me. Anyway, somebody's got to help you with the washing up."

"Too right. Not got a dishwasher, not likely to have one neither."

Lizzie laughed now. "I have, but his name's Danny."

"What?"

"Oh only now and then, I do it mostly, but we only have what we can afford, and I'm not ashamed to say it."

"D'you know Lizzie, there should be more like you about." and she gave her a quick hug and had turned before her friend could see the tears welling up in her eyes.

Doag watched with satisfaction. Instead of them parting on a bad note, they had cemented their friendship further for Sharon knew she didn't have to keep up with Lizzie but could just be herself.

Vedron still had to plant the 'connect' in Denis but he wasn't worrying about it, but he wanted to get Sharon covered as her vibrations told him she was close to his target, and just as important was the daughter so these two females must be 'connected' as soon as possible for the longer he took the more he could draw attention and his plan could fail. He had no intention of letting this happen so he set about planning his next move. As the flyer had worked so well with Lizzie, it seemed the best option to use on her friend. As long as she touched it would be all that was needed in her case.

Taking on a similar appearance to the one used in the supermarket, he armed himself with a wad of flyers and started to push them through the letter boxes in her street. He made sure any information on them was untraceable, the telephone numbers were bogus and there was no address. As he approached her door he noticed there was something already sticking in the flap which meant someone had already left some junk. Did that mean she wasn't in? If there was too much to pick up there was the chance she may not even come into contact with his paper, so the less the better. Carefully pulling the original one out, he then pushed his right in and waited for it to drop on the floor. Good. Now she would have to pick it up and the' connect' would be in place.

He had checked the lad was at school so she would be sure to get it. He knew it wouldn't have mattered if Denis had touched it, but then it would be on him and not transferrable and so the attempt would have to be made again, so best get Sharon first then worry about the scrap of a lad. She was the most important and he praised himself for being so orderly. Just as he was leaving the property a small boy came flying down the pavement on a peddle bike nearly colliding with him.

"Watch where you're going." he said in a voice quieter than the boy expected. "Why aren't you at school?"

"Sick." The lad looked him in the eye for a moment then peddled off giving him the V sign over his shoulder.

If the high sentinels had witnessed the episode, Vedron could have been identified, not by his body but his spiritual presence, without him being aware of it. While he was so busy setting his trap, he could be walking straight into one of much higher power, but for now he must float on his air of satisfaction. The watcher left the area assured that his quarry had not penetrated his mask. He guessed the next victim would be Bethany and planned his moves.

Jenny was informed of what her team could tell her but she still had no proof that it was actually Vedron, but there was no other explanation, so every angel was on alert. She hoped the watchers were involved but knew she daren't enquire from her Father, the Almighty One. She was receiving an update from the various guardians and her senses told her something big was being planned but dare not do anything that would impede Vedron, harsh as it may sound. There were those who thought she was risking with the spiritual safety of the key players but she couldn't just banish Vedron, or his kind because they would be back. They had to be terminated or despatched for good, and this may be her best chance, so regardless of any disapproval she had to act as she saw fit. Summoning the upper spiral she made this point very clear and ordered that it be passed down to the lower spiral and beyond with the message not to judge if they were not in possession of the full facts. She had to admit to herself that even she wasn't at this moment.

Chapter 7

Beth had been looking through a magazine while Robert was outside still deciding how big to make the patio area. She glanced at her watch and thought it strange that Margaret had gone up to her room after lunch and hadn't come down again.

"I expect she just wanted a rest," she smiled to herself. Her step daughter, although apparently much improved recently, still had moments where she needed to retreat and be on her own for a while. Nobody bothered her and she reappeared when she was ready.

"Hmm, must ring Lizzie" she thought and took the handset over to the window seat where she could watch her beloved as he made notes.

"Hello dear, how are you?"

"I'm fine Mum, and you?"

"Yes we're all alright here thank you. We wondered what we should get Bethany for her birthday, it's only next week isn't it."

Lizzie smiled as she thought of how much her daughter was growing.

"I know. Where does the time go? Well it may sound boring but we're getting her a dress she wanted. It will do for her birthday tea then she should get plenty of wear out of it."

"Oh that sounds a good idea. Should we get her clothes do you think? I don't like giving money, it's too impersonal. Not like a present."

"Well," Lizzie said "she is really into that jewellery now. You know she was making some the other day."

Beth laughed "Oh yes and the bits kept falling on the floor."

"That's the stuff." Lizzie laughed too at the memory of them all chasing round after beads and such.

"Well that's settled if you think she'd like it."

"Like it? All the kids are going mad for it. It's the 'in thing' I've been informed."

"Lovely. I'll look round the shops for some."

Lizzie thought for a moment. "Tell you what, why don't we go together, and Margaret if she wants, then I could tell you what Bethany likes best. They're very particular you know."

"How about tomorrow? Or is that too soon?"

"No, that would be lovely. What time?"

"Let me just check with Robert." She opened the window. "I'm going into town with Lizzie tomorrow to get Bethany's present. Is the morning alright with you?"

"Any time" he smiled "as long as you are here to do my lunch." He loved teasing her but it often ended up going further than they had planned.

"Behave yourself." Her laughter rang out like music. "Shall I say ten o'clock?"

He nodded and grinned at her with the mischievous look that still melted her heart.

"'Bout ten?" she asked Lizzie.

"Fine. What were you two up to just then?" she asked very poignantly.

"Mind your business." Beth laughed and they said their good byes just as Margaret appeared in the doorway.

"Ah, had a nice rest dear?" Beth put the phone down and beckoned her to sit on the sofa with her.

"Not bad. Who was that?"

Beth told her of the plans to go shopping and asked if she felt she'd like to go.

"In town. With all those people. No, I couldn't. Not yet." She seemed to be getting quite wound up.

"That's alright, we just thought you could come if you wanted. Shall we get something for Bethany from you then?"

The change in Margaret was noticeable. "Oh yes, would you? I'd like to give her something. You choose." Then after a moment "Mama Beth where will she have her birthday tea?"

"Well at home of course. You are coming aren't you? It isn't far and we won't be long away. And don't forget the one on her birthday is just us, nobody else. I think Lizzie might let a couple of her school friends go round on another day, but she doesn't have a lot."

"Oh. They won't be coming here then?" As Margaret spoke Beth noticed her almost pulling back as though she felt trapped. It must be the thought of going away from the house that was bothering her.

"I shouldn't think so. I think they would want to have it at home."

Nothing would have given Beth more pleasure than to host a birthday party at their house but she felt it wasn't helping Margaret to adjust if she was wrapped in cotton wool all the time. She had shown signs of improvement and although it would be slow, there had to be times when maybe firmness was needed. Also there was her own daughter to consider. She remembered when Lizzie was small and how much fun they had had at home and she wouldn't expect her not to feel the same when it came to Bethany.

"Oh the problems of keeping everyone happy" she mused to herself. Thank goodness for Robert. He was what kept her going and she often felt guilty at the tremendous love they shared which grew day by day. She didn't want anything to ruin their acquired happiness but little did she know what was festering ready to erupt in the near future.

Jenny was still receiving several messages via the various spiritual levels but many questions were being asked in the lower ones and she knew she had to calm the situation or Vedron could be scared off and that was the last thing she needed.

Answers are not always given as a spirit progresses, as it is left to them to work things out, and those that do then ascend to the higher realms, while the rest are left to the more mundane tasks which are essential to the continual existence of both body and spirit forms. It would only be a matter of time before the spirits hovering around the boarding house may tie up the situation at the bus station when, Vedron had seemed to disappear, with either him or the watcher. But everyone in the establishment was a non descript loner so it may not draw attention to them alone which would be an advantage. Many spirits gather in places most humans would find offensive, but that is where much knowledge is obtained.

The watcher was banking on Vedron not being traced yet, as a sudden move would force him to relocate his own base in order to keep tabs on him. Also in order to protect his true identity, Watcher would have to assume a different image.

If Matthew and Graham got to learn of this boarding house hideaway, they would have been the first to query Vedron's reasoning. It was obvious he had been well hidden all this time, but by taking on temporary human form for a short period he could easily disappear from view and then retreat to his own spiritual hide away. So what was the purpose of having a physical abode? Being of the upper spiral they would soon hit upon the answer but the watcher knew. For some reason, whoever or whatever had provided Vedron with the spiritual cloaking device, had to have it positioned on the earth in a specific place for it to work. Also it seemed that Vedron had to be in bodily form to be able to use it, not that it hadn't happened before, but it was unusual. So this presented Watcher with another problem. What was the provider getting out of it? That kind of being wouldn't do favours and everything would come at a very high price which proved that it wasn't only Vedron who was the risk but some unknown force who was using Vedron's dogged determination for its own ends. In other words he was just a pawn in a much larger game.

Watcher now had to regroup his plans. Although the special watchers work alone, there are certain events which call for even greater force and they can combine in twos or threes but rarely more. This one dare not risk losing his connection with his prey but more attention must now be placed on the greater threat, whatever it was.

If people going about their everyday lives, sorting out their problems which to them are worse than anything can be, only knew of what was living unseen in their midst, most of them wouldn't be able to cope with it. Likewise when they are in spirit, some never get to learn of the major happenings which are way above their understanding, so they are kept on the lower levels in ignorance.

Another visit to check the cloaking device was needed but this time, knowing Vedron was out, Watcher did an instant survey and was gone before anyone would know. He had wondered if the device was on permanent entry, meaning was it always open for use or was it closed at certain times? He now had his answer. This was one that was in constant use which was good news and yet bad. If it had been select use it meant the provider was controlling Vedron's movements and only allowing him to use the device when he permitted it. The fact it was set on constant meant that Vedron had not only paid a higher price, whatever that was, but it could give a two way access to the evil force behind it. But Vedron wouldn't have worked that out and thought he had the upper hand now.

But these devices are never totally owned. Once discarded by one holder for whatever reason, they are immediately taken into use by another and depending upon their ability can be used for good or bad, so any force can make use of them which is why people appear to vanish without trace, either bodily or spiritually.

This alerted Watcher to the events in the Pacific and again alarm bells went off. He dare not send a message of his own but there were ways in an emergency only known to the select few. He employed one of these now and within seconds Jenny was in possession of it. "VVB + VVD"

She knew they had to move attracting as little attention as possible but immediately scouts were deployed to the areas with instructions to report even the smallest detail as this had the feel of something very big and possibly threatening which was simmering without their knowledge. She momentarily thanked the unknown source of the message then put it away from her. This could answer many questions which had plagued the earth dwellers for years and national security was at risk. She didn't make any connection to the Vedron problem and for now had to rely on the guardians on that case to carry on but report back if it was considered vital.

The majority of experienced sentinels on duty in the Pacific were transferred to the Atlantic leaving a sparse crew to observe the sightings which still appeared enough to keep avid UFO and USO groups interested, unaware they themselves were being observed by both the good and bad forces.

Vedron considered Sharon would have been tagged by now and his main aim had to be Bethany. He would put a stronger connect in her as she could be the problem when it came time to claim his prey. For now he had retreated to his cloaking while he planned his moves as there could be no margin for error on this one. There was still the boy but if he couldn't be done, then it didn't really matter. Time was running out. His urges were growing to an unbearable level and he was using his temporary body to help release some of the pressure but it wasn't enough. It was like showing a chocoholic a big box of chocolates, letting them have one then taking the rest away. He had to have her, possess her, inject his whole being into her and it had to be soon. It was getting so bad that he was making more visits to his body to relieve himself but he overlooked the fact that at the climax, when he was floating in ecstasy and virtually unaware of anything else, he was at his most vulnerable and was prey, not to any watcher or scout, but to the many evil entities that thrive on such habits, and there are plenty. He was like an animal and not the handsome desirable man he thought he was.

He was just coming round after one of these bodily functions when he had the impression of a face watching him. It sneered, its red eyes aflame with desire, yellow bile dripping from its mouth its tongue licking round the lips, but the whole head was covered in matted hair, the ears back as if it was going to pounce. Terror filled him and the cry "Get away" froze in his throat. A sinister blood curling laugh rang round the room and Vedron lay in a state of shock as he heard its departing words. "I'm you."

He didn't know how long it took him to move, but slowly he made his way to the mirror. The sight that hit him made his blood run cold. No longer was the face of the non descript man facing him but the most hideous being he had ever seen. His hands were still wet with his discharge but he held them to his face in horror. Slowly the image faded and he was looking at the normal face he had been using. When he could move, he rushed to the sink and washed his hands and face as if he was removing all traces of the visitor.

"It wasn't me. It wasn't me." he kept repeating as if that would make it untrue. Whatever the cause of the experience, it left him completely drained and he knew he must get back to the cloak until he had recovered.

The sadistic fiends had thoroughly enjoyed the show and knew they had a place to come for their future entertainment. Some of them had been assisting him in his enjoyment, so no wonder he had been on cloud nine, but they weren't doing it for his satisfaction but their own. The group departed in high spirits, most of them were of the female kind but there were a few males amongst them that knew they had to come back for more at the first opportunity. But for now they would seek out the next victim, and that wouldn't be difficult.

It had been arranged. Bethany would go to Denis's for tea on Saturday. His birthday was Friday but it suited Sharon better as she wasn't doing her evening job that day. She asked Lizzie to go as well so they could leave the children to watch a DVD or something and they would have a chat.

"My Mum's offered to make him a cake, if that's alright with you." Lizzie was talking to Sharon on the phone. Beth knew the circumstances and didn't want to seem patronising but knew the single mum would find it a bit hard to manage.

"Oh yes please. I was looking at them in the shop, but have you seen the price of them?"

"I know. She wanted to send him something but thought lads liked cake so that's why she said it."

"Oh. He's a lucky lad. Hey, guess what? The old cow is paying me up to the day I walked out. Says I've got to go in for it Friday. Well I'd like to tell her to stuff it but what with Denis's birthday and that, I thought sod it, I'll have it."

Lizzie laughed. "Bet she'll be sorry you left though. Perhaps she'll ask you back, that's why she wants you to go in."

"Bloody hell. I never thought of that."

"Anyway, Sharon, what would you like to me bring?"

"In what way?"

"Well, for tea, we could do it together."

"Nah – that's Ok, I'll have enough and with your mam's cake, that should do it."

Lizzie was desperate to help and Beth had given her an idea to bring in if needed.

"Oh. That's a shame."

"Why?" Sharon was curious.

"Oh nothing. It's just I've been trying out some of these biscuity things with faces on and I wanted to see if they were all right."

"Oh I see, well, why not, bring 'em along, the more the merrier eh?"

Beth could come up with some good ideas when trying to help but not hurt peoples' feelings and Lizzie would be glad to tell her the ruse had worked.

"What time should we come?"

Sharon thought then said "What about four?"

"That's fine. Danny isn't working so we'll have had dinner at lunchtime so he can manage for once."

"Great. Denis is looking forward to it."

"Oh and by the way, you know it's Bethany's birthday on Sunday, well would it be Ok if Denis comes for tea on Monday, only it would be dinner really."

"Sure."

"Can you come? Oh no you'll be working won't you?"

"Do you know, I could go in later to that woman. What time do you have dinner?"

"Well it has to be soon after six when Danny comes in."

Sharon couldn't refuse the offer of a meal for them both, so said "Yes, go on. Sure Danny won't mind?"

"Course not." She hoped he wouldn't but knowing she was turning down the cleaning idea would help and he would probably get out of the way anyway.

"Well that's that settled then. See you tomorrow Liz." Sharon certainly seemed on high spirits and Lizzie wondered if she had taken the steps to work on her own, but wasn't going to ask.

Lizzie had enquired at the hospital and had been told to go in and see them giving her a lady to ask for. She wasn't going to mention this to her friend until she knew something more definite, and as Danny had pointed out, Sharon might like the idea and tag along, so only tell her when she had to. Then if she got on the band wagon it was up to her.

It was time for school to finish for the day and as the parents gathered in their usual spots a couple of performers arrived to advertise the circus which would be coming to the town soon. The juggler started his routine as the children started to filter out and soon a small crowd had formed. Fortunately there was a small grassed area in front of the gates so nobody had to spill out onto the road. The other visitor could hardly be described as a performer as he merely stood with a huge bunch of balloons in his hand which he began to give to the eager children. As Bethany joined her mum he handed her a pink one and said "I thought you'd like that one" and she took the string from him but as she looked up at it, it seemed to be pulled through her fingers and floated away up into the sky. She looked disappointed but the man said "Oh never mind, here is another for you, and it's much better than the other one."

This time Lizzie tied the string around Bethany's wrist and said "We're not going to lose this one."

When the man spied Denis, who was hanging back from the others, he beckoned to him and said "How about you sonny? Blue for you I think." And he held a vivid blue balloon at arms length. Denis moved forward a couple of steps until he knew the man would hear what he said.

"They're for girls, not me." There was no smile and he turned away so that his gaze didn't hold the performer's attention.

The man just shrugged and let the balloon drift skywards, then carried on giving them out to the eager forest of waving hands begging for theirs.

The two departed quickly but the group would have been astounded had they witnessed what happened as soon as the men were out of sight. They turned down an entry between two houses and disintegrated into the earth. One little trick Vedron had mastered was to produce another form as well as his own that could be disposed of whenever he wished, and it suited him to melt the juggler at the same time as his own form. The balloons would last for a while, then they too would seem to have evaporated. But the 'connect' had been made. Bethany had been given two as an insurance through the strings as she handled them, and although Denis had refused his as not being a 'boy thing', he was unimportant so it didn't matter that much.

But Doag had observed the most important thing from this visit. Neither of the performers had a guardian in presence which meant that either they were both of such a high standing as himself and could operate alone, or the beings were not as they seemed. The message was sent to the high spiral with the suspicion that Vedron had been in presence.

Graham was piecing together the various events, but without the knowledge of the boarding house happenings. Although there was a high alert surrounding the USOs and the coded areas, he had been left in charge of the Banbury case for now, and had to report any suggestion that Vedron could be on the move. On receiving Doag's message, Graham did a quick scan of the area and noticed there were still noticeable disturbances in the area surrounding the school, which he traced to the entry. There, coming out of the earth he could feel certain vibrations and called upon one of the earth spirits to check it for him.

"Definitely two forms have been used, but only one source, so it had regrouped after both had gone to ground."

Graham double checked. "So only one was controlling all the images?"

"Just one. But not highly experienced."

"Because?"

"The 'wake' lines were too noticeable. In high levels they would have been erased quicker leaving no trace. But these haven't completely gone yet."

He thanked the spirit for the details and asked if a tracker could follow the trail to source. Within seconds he had his reply. It had been traced to the area under a boarding house in the poorer area of a neighbouring town. Obviously, this wasn't only a novice operator but a very careless one.

Graham immediately scanned the location but there was no sign of any spirit in presence. If the trail had led there as he had been told, the evil one hadn't surfaced and was confined to the ground. Again he asked for a check and received the reply that the trail had ended there but no one was in presence now. This was odd. There was no spirit either in the ground or in the air sector above it. The boarding house offered no clues as there were only a few vagrant spirits there and none of them recognisable to him. They were a sad bunch, just existing or serving out a penance.

He returned to Eden and called Matthew to go over the facts in case there was something he had missed. The watcher returned to his room undetected, grateful that he could stay in place a bit longer hoping it would be soon that Vedron was forced to act.

"Why didn't you want a balloon Denis?" Sharon hurried him along as she had to get him to her mother's house earlier today.

"They're not for boys. It's not cool." He shuffled along with his head down.

"Oooh, so we're cool now are we?" She had to smile at his comment as he always seemed to let current expressions pass him by and didn't care about being in with the crowd. He just shrugged and seemed more interested in what was on the ground in front of him judging by his manner.

"I want you to behave for Grandma as you're there longer. D'you hear me?"

"I hear you."

"I've got to do more work tonight and I can't afford to turn it down so be a good boy. I'll be back for you as soon as I get off and then its straight home to bed."

He only shrugged but Sharon knew he was no trouble. Her mum let him watch the telly, fed him and didn't bother him too much so he seemed quite content. Also it didn't cost Sharon anything which was a bit of a blessing.

Her mind was fixed on starting this cleaning venture of hers and it didn't matter if Liz wasn't going to do it, so it was time to put feelers out and make contact with any possible customers. She and Liz were still friends and would be in close contact through the children, who seemed to be bonding nicely so everything may be looking up for her.

Vedron had completed the 'connect' stage of his plan and was ready to move on to the next, the taking of Lizzie from this world to claim her for eternity. He was so sure of himself now that he believed nothing could prevent him. He had laid his plans and could control those who may prove a threat, but the 'connects' placed in Lizzie would mean that she would obey him and give herself to him without question. Whether she loved him at that stage was immaterial, for after a short time with him, he was certain she would want nobody else.

Watcher sent another urgent message by the secret route. "VVA". Jenny sent another contingent to that area and a picture was beginning to form so she immediately sent teams to two other points on the Tropic of Cancer. These areas, along with five on the Tropic of Capricorn were all vortices where strange unexplainable things happened, that is to say, unexplainable to the human race. Although they were shrouded in mystery concerning ships and planes that had either disappeared or been found later in a totally different area, the spiritual levels were well aware of their capabilities.

It was becoming clear now that Vedron had mastered the use of these triangles, but seemed to be confined to the northern hemisphere. As well as the ten positioned on the tropics, the North and South Poles are also vortices and Jenny knew she must also cover the North one and not leave anywhere unguarded. It was strongly felt in the upper spiral that things were on the move and somehow everything was globally connected in some way, but only to the north of the equator.

This begged the question as to Vedron's skills. It seemed likely that he had a limited power in whatever form he chose to operate. He hadn't had time to perfect one thing properly, so to dabble could be dangerous. For one thing, anything he attempted could go wrong, but also he could experience interference from good forces and also the evil ones who could hitch a ride on his behalf then mess things up for the sheer delight of it. Zargot had watched him many times with amusement and had booked a front row seat to watch his downfall. For now he was letting him fall deeper into his own self adoration and enjoying watching him being ruled by the increasing sexual frustration which was forcing him to play his hand before the time was right. There was also quite a little army of hideous fiends following him whenever they could and wallowing in the entertainment when he was in view but then having to wait when he went into cloaking mode. There were always plenty on the watch, and as soon as he reappeared they homed in like a load of chattering monkeys waiting for the next filthy episode.

As far as the earthly folk were concerned, the next two days went without anything out of the ordinary taking place. Robert had gone back to work, and Beth and Margaret had decided to clear some of the weeds and old plants in the garden to do some of the groundwork for the improvements. Bill had been so grateful for the lawn mower, that he volunteered to help Robert if he decided to do the patio area himself. This was an offer that may just be taken. Beth and Lizzie had got Bethany's presents and were looking forward to Sunday, although they knew Margaret wouldn't be going, but nobody was going to make an issue of it. They were just glad that she seemed to be on the mend and understood it would take time. Lizzie had been in to the hospital and they had given her an appointment for an interview on Friday morning as she seemed a capable sort of person and very likeable.

Sharon had already chatted someone up regarding the cleaning and they had said they would give her a try, and if they liked the way she worked, there was the possibility she could go every day. It wasn't much but it was a start, and who knew where it could lead? She'd managed to get Denis a small present and her mum had given her a voucher so he could get something he liked and she seemed to be coping with her financial situation. She was glad her son liked Bethany because it meant she would see more of Liz, and she didn't get on too well with the other mothers. They were a boring lot with the main topic of conversation being the price of everything and how many times their old man had wanted his oats that week. Liz may not have quite their quick wit, but she was a likeable person and she was straight forward. She didn't talk about you behind your back or gossip about everyone else and she felt she could trust her.

Bethany could talk of nothing else but her birthday. It was a becoming a joke and all of the adults would say in front of her "Did you know its Bethany's birthday on Sunday?" and someone else would say "No? It isn't is it?" Quite different to Denis who was glad his mum loved him, but sometimes wished she didn't show it so much. His thoughts seemed to be constantly on Bethany, not that he knew why in his waking time, but when with Doag she was the obvious subject.

If everything was sailing along on a calm sea on earth, it was just the opposite in the spiritual areas. Everything in the air was like a tightly coiled spring begging to be released. At the top, Jenny knew that Vedron was using the triangle areas to disappear and reappear at will, but was confused that there was no trace of him by other users. When one was in a time tunnel, although not still in their complete form, they would be recognisable by means only known to those with the power to use them but they would be known. The accidental travellers in these areas would seem to emerge in another area or time with no knowledge of their journey, hence the mystery surrounding the triangles. There are many things known to the spiritual travellers which cannot be divulged to those in bodily form as they are far beyond human comprehension but may be understood in time to come by some. Also if the knowledge was imparted, the person concerned could be at risk of ridicule, or worse, insanity.

As Jenny had received her messages from Watcher by a certain filtered route, she guessed there was even more to this than even she was aware of, but knew she couldn't jeopardise the operation by trying to find out, plus the fact she wasn't sure of the exact entity that had fed her the information.

Watcher on the other hand, now had almost a complete picture. Vedron had been honing his skills under an unscrupulous tutor in return for the cloaking device. But it was obvious the teacher had only given him so much education, purposely omitting important facts, so that the pupil would never be totally adept at any part. He would only be able to use limited resources in whatever he did, but he hadn't realised this. When he left the school, although he and his partner had disappeared from view, they had left a wake that could have been created by a battleship instead of a rowing boat. That should never happen. Vedron's kind never saw through the purpose of their schooling, which was always used for future control over them by their teachers, so instead of having their own free will and power, they were nothing more than puppets being trained for future use.

But there was one thing Watcher must find out. Who was the tutor or tutors? He had an idea but never left anything to conjecture and would prove beyond all doubt before exposing them, after which he would disappear completely until his next watch.

Doag and Denis knew something was about to blow. They'd seen it before and could tell it was time for them to be on high alert, almost like a storm that is hovering when you can feel it in the air, waiting. Denis had to be as close to Bethany as he could and that wasn't too much of a problem at school but he would have to go to bed as early as he could in order to protect her at night. The temporary guardians would warn their higher angels of anything unusual but it was up to him to be vigilant. Doag could also help from his vantage point but nothing must be left to chance. It was almost inevitable that Denis's cover would be blown soon and that meant that all surrounding angels would realise that he and Doag were of very high levels, but that was one of the risks in something this dangerous. However if it could be avoided so be it, but that couldn't stand in the way of the success of the operation.

Having covered the vortices, Jenny took a moment to update regarding the Banbury area. The 'connects' had been discovered by diligent high levels who were requesting permission to remove them. Jenny knew that at first glance this seemed to be the obvious thing to do, but that would mean that Vedron would be aware of it and they didn't know what he would employ next in his anger. The high spiral guessed the devices had to be some sort of control which must be connected with Lizzie and whatever he had planned for her. Again Jenny was criticized as she ordered them to be left in place.

"This may be our only chance to dispose of him for good." She knew this sounded harsh but they were up against an evil driven monster who would keep reappearing until he had his way, so there was only one thing to do and all the angels must do as she bid for it to work.

Sentinels were placed in all the triangles along the Tropic of Cancer and also at the North Pole with specific instructions what to look for. As with night vision lenses that allow us to see in the dark, so the high spiritual beings have a special sense which shows up things the lower ones will never see and will never be encountered by the human race. Thanks to Watcher's diligence, he had managed to plant a tracker on Vedron, but the way he did it is classified to the elite few of his kind. This would go off like a sonar as he passed into or out of the vortices and could be picked up by the high guards, so from now on his movements could be traced wherever he was without his knowledge, but there would be a time limit. If the good forces could track him, the evil ones would also pick up the signal and know he had been bugged.

Time was now of the essence, not only to the high angels but Vedron who could hardly contain his desire to take his love object. He must have her now.

Denis wasn't going to tell anyone at school that it was his birthday. His waking form didn't want any special attention drawn to him and he had asked Bethany not to say anything. Once or twice she nearly let it slip but managed to cover it by saying it was hers.

"Well it's Sunday really but it's almost my birthday." Fortunately the girls had become so bored with her chirping on about it they were taking little notice of her and so her mistakes were overlooked.

"I'll be glad when she's had it." one said to her friend.

"Don't know. Perhaps she'll be going on about what's she's had."

"Then we'll just ignore her."

"Oh right. 'Cos everything will be better than ours."

"Thinks she's better than us."

"I know."

Most children would have been looking forward to going home but Denis just took it in his stride. What was special about it? Friday was good, no school for two whole days and it was his birthday. They'd have dinner then his Mum would dash him round to her Mum then go to her evening job, He'd got his present from his mum and knew he'd have something from his Gran, but that was about it so there was nothing to get excited about. His low profile was going exactly as it had been planned.

Sharon couldn't hide her excitement when she went to collect him and grabbed Lizzie and pulled her to one side.

"Guess what?"

Her friend looked bewildered having no idea what she was babbling on about. So Sharon carried on without waiting for a reply.

"That person I told you would give me a trial."

"Yes."

"Well, it's only a living in job at that big house, used to be a manor or something, and there's some rooms for Denis and me, and he'll still be able to come to this school and…"

"Just a minute Sharon." Lizzie pulled her up. "Stop and think. It all sounds wonderful but do you know enough about it?"

"What do you mean? It'd be rent free. Ok the wages aren't high but there'd be no bills."

A little bit of Danny had rubbed off on Lizzie and she was looking at this from another angle. "And who is this person that's going to employ you?"

"Oh he must be the Lord of the Manor or something."

"You mean the butler."

"Of course not."

"And where did you meet this... this man?"

"What difference does that make?" Sharon thought she was going to get a more positive response but come to think of it, Liz wasn't one for new ideas was she?

"Have you been to the place yet?" Lizzie asked.

"Well no, not yet, I've got to go and sort it out."

"Can I just ask one thing then?"

"S'pose so." Sharon wondered what damper was going to be put on it now.

"You take this job, leave your home and go and live at – wherever it is- and what happens if you don't like it or you don't suit?"

"Liz! Why do you always have to be so bloody gloomy? Can't you even be a bit happy for me?"

"Sorry Sharon," Lizzie smiled at her "of course I do and I hope it all works out for you."

"Oh thanks, I knew you'd see it my way."

"There's just one thing."

Sharon thought to herself "Oh there would be wouldn't there?" but simply said "and that is?"

"Well Bethany and Denis will miss each other."

"Christ we're not going to the North Pole. They'll see each other at school and we can still visit."

The conversation ended on a slightly happier note as the children came out of school but the watching angels picked up on the slip Sharon had made as her tongue ran away with her.

Amity and Symphony, Lizzie's and Margaret's guardians had been made aware of the controls placed in their charges and were ordered to be on high alert at all times, not letting the slightest thing go unnoticed. Having had experience of this kind of placement before, Amity was warning her partner about some of the tricks the evil sources would employ.

"They may appear to have removed the connectors so that our guard is down, but that is pure thought control."

"They are still there?" Symphony asked.

"Very much so, and in those cases, they strengthen them so that they are more powerful and cover a much wider range than before, while all the time we think they have gone."

"Can you detect them?"

"Not on my own power. Although I am fairly high, this takes even higher ones to find them but then they can make me aware."

"So you can feel them now?"

"Think of it like a picture which has something hidden in the artwork, it's been there all the time but it has to be pointed out for you to see it."

"So what form does it take?"

"There is no form."

"So how do you know where it is?" Obviously Symphony was eager to witnesses one of these as she felt vulnerable knowing something was there, but out of her mental reach.

"A feeling, a sense."

"So where is Margaret's?"

"Hover directly over her head and concentrate. Then tell me what you notice."

There was a pause while Symphony carried out the instructions.

"Well?" Amity asked.

"Not sure. Something just feels not quite the same."

"That's a start." Amity knew it would take a long time to acquire this skill but the angel was diligent and would master it one day but would have to ascend to a higher realm first.

Amity knew that Margaret's was placed in her brain so that, with her medical history anything she did would be put down to her having a relapse. But the main reason was to keep her out the way and not interfere when the time came. This was one of the reasons why she was refusing to go the Bethany's birthday tea. Something was stopping her, and to force her against the will of this power could have devastating long term effects.

But Lizzie's was a more serious matter. The main placing was in her brain, but the next was right in the middle of her heart. It was of such a powerful nature that it could be ordered to stop her heart at any given moment. All that Vedron had to do was pick the right time and that would be the start of their new life together. But nothing must obscure or hinder it for he knew he wouldn't get a second chance. He would not attack when those close to her were present which meant he must wait until after the week end. This thought nearly drove him mad with frustration, but he had waited and trained for this so it would be foolish and weak to throw it all away now due to lack of patience.

Beth had decided to do all her baking on Saturday. She would make Denis's cake first so that it would be ready to take round to Sharon's when she or Robert took Bethany. She got up early and as soon as breakfast was finished, cleared the kitchen and got out her equipment and ingredients. Margaret put in an appearance just as she was weighing out the flour.

"Any toast?" she flopped down on one of the chairs, sprawling over the end of the table.

"Oh Margaret, I called up but you didn't answer, and I'm just getting this cake made." Beth was normally very patient but this seemed a bit thoughtless plus the fact she wanted to get as much done before the first 'hot one' hit her, and working in a warm kitchen didn't help.

"Don't bother then." Margaret huffed.

"Well you can see I'm busy. Couldn't you do it, you're quite capable?"

Robert had heard Beth's voice raised and came in quickly.

"What's up?"

"I'm in the way again." Margaret got up and stormed out of the room.

"I only asked her to do her own toast," Beth whispered and indicated she was busy.

He held up his hand to stop her saying any more and followed his daughter into the lounge.

"What was that all about?" he asked rather sharply.

"Ask her."

"And who's 'her'?" He was getting annoyed.

There was a silence and Margaret turned her back on him and folded her arms.

He walked round to face her. "Now you look here young lady, there's no need for this attitude. We let you get up when you like because of your medication, but you could try and fit in with the smooth running of this house. Beth has given up a lot for you and this is how you repay her."

"Oh you'll always stick up for your darling wife won't you. Doesn't matter about me, or how I feel."

"And just how do you feel may I ask?" His eyes flashed in anger at her ingratitude.

"Like I'm always in the way." She shouted till the spit shot out with every word.

"Well let me tell you something Margaret. You are the luckiest girl I know. You could have been locked away but no. We, no Beth" he corrected "has cared for you here, and how do you repay her?"

What more he would have said nobody would know for Beth appeared at the doorway red faced and close to tears.

"Stop it. Enough. We've all been through too much for this. And if you want to know who feels in the way Margaret, it's me because you make me feel I've come between you and your father, so just think on that while you're in your self pity me-me-me mode." She left the room, the tears flowing down her cheeks and flew to the kitchen and buried her face in a towel.

"Thank you very much." Robert hissed at his daughter inches from her face, and for once she looked afraid of him. He ran after Beth took her in his arms and was almost crying with her, it hurt him so much to see her treated this way.

They must have been locked in that position for several minutes until Beth was so hot she was gasping for air and Robert quickly filled a glass with cold water for her.

"I didn't mean to say that." She was barely audible.

"None of us did. But you know the truth is supposed to come out when we lose our temper."

"I'm sorry Mama Beth, I'm sorry Dad." The sound made them turn and the sight of Margaret drained of colour, her eyes staring straight ahead shocked them.

They all sat for a moment to gather their thoughts. Beth was silent from exhaustion and Robert explained that nobody had meant anything they said and it was best to forget it, but made a mental note to ask her doctor to review her medication.

When everything had settled down Margaret asked if she could help but Beth worked better alone and when she didn't answer straight away Robert cut in and said "I could do with some help outside if you wouldn't mind. Is that alright with you dear?" he turned to Beth.

She nodded and whispered "Fine."

Margaret was about to put an arm around her shoulder but thought better of it. But Beth noticed and said quietly "Don't do too much."

"I won't. Um. I'll help wash up in a bit if you like."

"That would be really helpful, thank you." and she raised her hand and patted her on the arm as she passed.

It would have been tempting to stop and make Margaret some toast and tea before she got on with the baking but something told her to leave it as this may have been a good lesson for the future. Even someone as sick as she had been could learn that everything didn't revolve around her and she was a perfectly capable woman.

Hovering evil forces had tried to stir up animosity in the Bradley household for their own satisfaction, but they had been overpowered by the guardians who had ousted them and sent them packing. The visiting fiends couldn't have known of the importance of unity in this family circle just now but when the news reached the upper spiral the question arose as to whether it was of Vedron's doing in an attempt to split the important players in his game and thus lessen their support. He could have been testing the 'connects' to see if they worked, so this had to be taken into consideration.

Watcher was gradually building a picture of Vedron's movements. At first he had thought the evil sex fiend was operating under his own motivation, but the more he studied him, the more he realised he was having to report at almost regular intervals to someone and it obviously had a lot to do with the spiritual cloaking device. As he weighed up his evidence, watcher likened it to earthly drug trafficking, which is often the answer to one's problems at the outset but very difficult to rid yourself of later. The possibility that Vedron could be being used as a 'mule' couldn't be dismissed, but what kind of mule. He certainly had the freedom to flit between worlds both known and unknown, but the kind of entities watcher had encountered in the past didn't deal with trivia. So he had to be carrying something more important than mere information. If the high evil powers realised they had a self opinionated little upstart here, they could feed him any useless facts to get him to do their dirty deeds and he would think they were just helping him to achieve his own ends.

At times like this watcher often put himself in the place of his enemies and now asked the question "What would I use him for?" Laying out all the evidence he had, the main point that stood out made him ask another question. "Why only the northern hemisphere?" There were possible answers. Maybe the evil plotters were only going to attack that part, or they only had control of that area but it had to be considered that they may only be allowing Vedron to use the hemisphere in which his love target was situated. So did they have someone in the southern one doing the same job in the mistaken belief that it was for their profit.

Then there was the time factor. As soon as Vedron had secured Lizzie, what would he do with her? Watcher now realised that her life was in danger, for Vedron would seduce her while he could but would then have to keep her with him until other earth forms could be available for them both. But would that suit the traffickers? In his experience they always demanded value for money, and often they bought the everlasting existence of souls to carry out their dirty work for ever. It was most likely that Vedron had no knowledge of this, and as his whole being was intent on possession, the fool had probably given that side of it little thought.

So watcher had no alternative but to employ one of the secret skills very few had mastered, and enter the lions den alone.

Chapter 8

Robert had offered to drive Lizzie and Bethany to Sharon's for Denis's tea. Armed with a small present, Beth's cake and the results of Lizzie's baking they arrived a few minutes early, and when all had been safely deposited in the house, he said his goodbyes and told them he would pick them up later.

"Just give me a ring when you're ready." he smiled and went back to his car.

Denis was waiting for Bethany eager to show her his present from his mum and when she handed him theirs he took it gently and opened it very carefully.

"That's unusual for a lad," Lizzie smiled, "they generally rip it open don't they?"

Sharon smiled and Lizzie noticed how quiet she seemed. They left the children talking happily and went into the kitchen.

"Are you alright Sharon?"

"Yes, fine, why shouldn't I be?" Sharon still seemed distracted and not her usual self at all.

"You know you can tell me, if anything's bothering you I mean." Lizzie put her hand out but the gesture was ignored.

"No, No, everything's Ok." And Sharon busied about getting plates and dishes from the cupboard but her friend knew everything was not all right.

Trying to change the subject Lizzie said "Where are you going to eat?"

"Hmm? Oh in there. I've got a cloth here somewhere, I'll put everything on the table then they can just help themselves, I mean we can."

"Oh." Lizzie's thoughts of two children of that age not having food put in front of them made her shudder. This wasn't how she had been brought up and she felt a little sorry for Denis as he obviously didn't get the kind of loving surroundings that she had known and had passed on to Bethany. But this wasn't her house and she went along with whatever Sharon said. When the table cloth was on Lizzie realised she was the only one bringing in the food and setting it out as she thought fit, but if Sharon wasn't going to explain what was wrong, she would have to leave it and not spoil the birthday for Denis.

When they had eaten most of the food, Sharon lit the candles on the cake and told Denis to make a wish as he blew them out. He stood at the table in silence looking straight at Bethany, and without changing his gaze slowly blew them all out. Sharon looked from one to another but before she could speak, Bethany ran over to join him and whispered "Now your wish will come true."

"Only if he doesn't tell anybody what it was?" Lizzie laughed but had the strangest feeling her little girl knew without being told.

"You cut it," Sharon pushed a knife into Lizzie's hand, "I always cock it up."

"All right, if you like." Lizzie didn't mind but still felt she was having to take over. Beth's cakes were always delicious and this was no exception and soon they were all enjoying a piece.

"Are you going to thank Lizzie's mum for your cake Denis?" Sharon licked her fingers.

"Of course. I will write her a note." The two mums looked at each other in surprise but said nothing.

"Can we watch my DVD now please?" Denis had used his Gran's money to get something he had wanted for a long time and hoped Bethany would like it.

"Well, if that's alright with everyone else." Sharon seemed distracted again.

"Oh can we?" Bethany was beaming

"Go on then." Sharon turned to Lizzie who was busy clearing the table. "He can do it better than I can. Never know what button to press."

They took the tea things into the kitchen and left the kids to watch the film.

"Um Liz, don't suppose you'd do me a big, big favour?"

"Yes, if I can." Lizzie was always willing to help anyone and she wondered if this was going to throw some light on her friend's unusual behaviour.

"Good. Only, well, you see, um, well ...I've got to pop out for a bit, not long but..."she seemed to be searching for an explanation and Lizzie sensed that all was not well.

"Oh I don't mind staying with the children if that's what's bothering you, but you're sure there's no trouble or anything?"

"No, nothing like that." Sharon seemed relieved that she didn't have to explain further and she checked herself in the mirror, grabbed a jacket and bag and had gone.

"Well, what's that all about?" Lizzie thought as she looked at the pile of washing up. "Oh well, this won't do itself."

Before long she had cleared the kitchen and had to admit it looked rather better than when she had arrived. She slid the remains of the cake onto one of Sharon's plates and washed the one belonging to Beth ready to take it with her. Popping her head round the living room door she was about to ask if they were enjoying the DVD but stopped dead. Denis and Bethany were sitting on the floor as close as it was possible to be. Although neither had their arm around the other, she could sense the extreme closeness between them but if she could have seen what was really going on she would have been lost for words even more.

Doag had located the 'connects' in Bethany and had an instantaneous conference with Denis as he watched the film. They decided to leave them alone, for to intervene now would alert Vedron, and this would foil their plans. They agreed Denis would remain in contact with Bethany for as long as possible and transfer as much protection as he could without being traced. This was one skill both these higher angels had used many times, and one which Vedron had never mastered, for after all he didn't need to protect, only control. Denis had returned to his bodily boy state but knew he had to stay close to his friend, and she didn't seem to mind, but she wouldn't, for Amity was taking an active part in holding her to him. It was convenient that Lizzie was here for she could guard them both.

Not wanting to disturb such a lovely scene, Lizzie went back to the kitchen and decided to make a cup of tea. Sharon shouldn't be long so she put a cup ready for when she returned and began to ponder the strangeness of her actions. Surely she must have known she had to go out, so why not mention it sooner. As her thoughts tried to make sense of it, she seemed to remember Sharon saying there was the chance of a good cleaning job, to live in possibly, so she must have gone there to sort it out, but why not say so?

Sharon had gone to the old manor, but not to sort out any cleaning. It was a place she had disappeared to many times and being positioned the way it was, didn't give cause for any curiosity. The place hadn't been lived it for a few years and although was on one of the main roads leading out of Banbury, was hidden by trees and the drive turned away from sight giving no onlookers any idea of who may be there at any time.

During the day she had the freedom to flit in and out between jobs and caring for Denis, but in the evenings it had become a little more difficult. Her mother was very good at sitting for her but it still tied her down, and she knew the time had come to make this a permanent dwelling. She thought of the idea of saying they had their own rooms so that Denis wouldn't realise the place was unoccupied and her secret would be out. She would make her own area presentable and as long as she didn't have any visitors, nobody would be any the wiser. She would stall Denis if he wanted to have Bethany round to play by saying the owners would forbid it, but he could go to Lizzie's as that would give her a free run.

But she wasn't alone, far from it. This had been the base from which an evil sector had been operating. They liked their workers to be ordinary everyday people that nobody gave a second glance to, but they were some of the most vicious beings of the spirit world. Although under constant scrutiny by the lower spiral, the angels had to keep a distance as the invisible radar operated by these monsters was so highly advanced it could barely be detected and many had fallen into the trap with horrendous consequences.

Jenny and her upper spiral had been aware of the presence and had many thoughts on what the purpose was in using that site. It couldn't be ruled out that it was on Lizzie's doorstep, but why would they be interested in Vedron's sexual reasons unless he had paid the price for their help to achieve his ends. But they wouldn't be there just for that or to collect their rewards. It had to be something bigger, much bigger.

Beth and Robert were relaxing in front of the television, and Margaret had gone up to her room. The air was calm and the earlier episode put from their minds.

"I'm dying to know if they liked the cake." Beth snuggled up to her husband.

He laughed. "You are funny." and gave a loving kiss on the cheek. "Of course they'll like it, who wouldn't, in fact they were lucky to get it all."

"You wouldn't have pinched a slice." She gave him a little thump with her hand.

"Keep going lady and you'll have something to punch me for." That look was in his eyes again, the one that said he was still as much in love with her as ever and would make love to her at any give opportunity. But his urges stemmed from love and not the lustful cravings of Lizzie's predator.

"Perhaps she'll ring." Beth looked at her watch.

"Will you stop fretting and just wait and see." Then in his usual tormenting manner said "Nobody's had food poisoning yet have they?"

"Oh you!" she had to admit she did worry for nothing.

They sat there watching a film but as the evening drew on, even Robert began to get a bit edgy.

"Go on, say I told you so." He got up and went upstairs to the toilet, then he checked on Margaret but she was asleep and looked very happy in whatever dream she was in. As he went back into the lounge Beth asked "What did you mean?"

"Regarding?"

"Why would I have told you so?" but she noticed he was checking the clock and his watch and almost pacing now so added "you're worried too."

"Well it's gone ten o'clock, a bit late for two children to be having a party. You don't suppose…No can't be."

"What?"

"Well, that Lizzie's walked Bethany home and not said."

"She wouldn't do that, she'd not that kind."

"I know, but why not just let us know?" Robert got out his mobile and said "I'm going to ring her. She'll have hers with her won't she?"

Beth nodded also very concerned. "Yes I've told her to always have it in case of ..." her voice trailed off as she heard Robert say "Lizzie, is everything alright?"

The pause seemed to go on for ever then Robert said "Look shall I come over and take Bethany home then come back and wait with you?" Another pause. "Right, see you in a few minutes."

"What's going on?" Beth was standing next to him.

Robert's face had changed to one of anger.

"Well it seems that her friend went off out and left Lizzie to mind the two children. That was a few hours ago and there's been no contact from her since."

"Oh I hope nothing has happened to her. Where did she go?"

Robert shrugged "Didn't ask. But I'll go and take Bethany home. It seems Danny's been ringing her as well because he was concerned."

Picking up on what she had heard Beth said "And then you'll go back and stay with Lizzie and then take her home when Sharon comes back."

They were interrupted by his mobile ringing. "Hello, Yes. Oh thank God. See you in a minute." He turned to his wife "She's back so I can take them both home, could you let Danny know?"

"Of course." As he left the room she called out "Take care."

"I will." And he had gone.

Lizzie wasn't in the best of moods when Sharon walked in as though nothing was wrong.

"Oh Sharon I was so worried. I tried to get Denis to go to bed but he wouldn't and Bethany's long past her bedtime." If she was expecting any sort of apology she was disappointed for her friend just shrugged and mumbled "Just one of those things."

Lizzie got all her things together and helped Bethany on with her coat. She said "Bye" to Denis and said she would see him on Monday at Bethany's birthday tea.

He walked with Bethany to the door as if he didn't want her to go and said he would see her at school Monday morning. She was so tired she nodded and thanked him for a nice time, needing no prompting from her mother.

As soon as they had gone Denis flew upstairs to his room and shut the door but Sharon paid little attention to it. He was in her way somewhat and she would be glad when he was old enough for her to be able to go her own way and not have to bother with him at all. She was another one who was so locked up in her own ways, she was unaware of what was going on around her, but had she opened her eyes, physically and spiritually, she would have been in for one almighty shock. The evil group controlling her were aware of her feisty spirit which must be kept in check or she could jeopardise their plans at just the wrong moment if she was allowed to be self willed.

But now she was tired and didn't even notice how clean and tidy the place was thanks to Lizzie's efforts. She must rest, but unlike Denis and Doag sleep was not the means of communication, it was simply a requirement of the body. Her controllers gave their orders in her waking hours, putting her into a trance to impart her next moves, then withdrawing so no trace of them could be observed. It was not the continual process used by the good angels and therefore had to be approached in a totally different way when trying to combat them.

Although completely dissimilar to the entities controlling Vedron, the group now dominating Sharon was about as vicious and dominating as it was possible to be, and once they had a subject in their grasp, there was no hope of them ever being free from it. The ultimate existence for Sharon would be to become one of their number but of a very low level that she would never rise to give orders, and would be in a perpetual state of anger and hatred which would only fuel her revenge to try and get even. But that would never be.

Many times the high angels had tried to rescue such a soul but with little success. Jenny suspected Zargot of spawning such a group, but in a lot of ways it didn't bare his hallmark. He may have helped certain things along for his own pleasure but he wasn't known for concentrating on one space, but spreading his wings so that all areas could reap the benefit of his evil. But this group wasn't something that could be overlooked and must be monitored even though it was unfortunate that it just happened to be in the Vedron sector. However, Jenny instructed the high levels, that diligence must be applied to all, but to be aware that Vedron seemed about to strike, so they mustn't be caught out or the consequences could be irreversible.

Doag and Denis were soon in conference and knew their placing had been arranged for two reasons. Mainly they had known of the 'group' operating in the area but hadn't located them so when Sharon had kindly led them to the current base it was almost too close for comfort. It is difficult enough to track enemies without them suspecting, but to be on your doorstep requires highly honed skills of deception. But these two were capable of things way above most and could keep watch on their two young charges but also observe the happenings being executed from the manor house.

Watcher had one object in his sights at all times, but was able to observe the vortices even if Vedron was not using them. A strange new pattern was forming. If anything entered a triangle zone and exited from a different one to the east of the original, the being appeared to gather strength from it, but if the opposite occurred, that is they entered one then exited to the west, they lost power. If they came out of the same one they entered, they appeared to be exactly the same in strength but the time factor could have altered one way or the other.

It seemed that Vedron had bought a limited knowledge of these routes as he only seemed to be using two. This could mean either that he hadn't been given permission to use any other or his target lay somehow connected to these. Watcher also considered that it would depend upon what one considered to be east or west. For if Vedron had entered The Bermuda Triangle and tried to exit The Dragon's Triangle it would be to the west facing one way but could also be to the east if the opposite route was taken. Watcher decided therefore it depended on which direction was used. So at least he could narrow his observations to these two as far as Vedron was concerned but would be alert for any activity along the same tropic.

There had been no sign of his quarry at the boarding house for a while and Watcher guessed it had to mean that the final plans were being put into place. Knowing the Vexons, they didn't mess about for long and were not the most patient of any being. Having done his training, this one would be chomping at the bit to get going, not forgetting his primitive urges which by now must be driving him crazy. So Watcher prepared for the final curtain, knowing which one of them would be taking the final bow.

Sharon had been to the manor base for one urgent reason. Her 'connect' had been detected by her rulers and they had called her in to remove it. They didn't want anything around or on her that could be controlled by any outside force, and they soon knew what race had planted this one, much to their amusement. She was operating under their instructions and they didn't care if the Vexon was aware of the removal. It had been done before, and they would do it many times again. They knew he would realise she wasn't responding when the time came, but that was nothing to do with them.

Lizzie apologised to Danny for being so late but he realised she couldn't do much about it. He had talked to her on the phone and was grateful Robert had it in hand.

"It's about time you ditched her as a friend. She's rubbish." Danny said as they got into bed.

"But you don't know her, she's not that bad and it isn't easy being a single mum." Lizzie always saw the good in anyone. "Besides Bethany and Denis are such pals."

"I've heard she's a slag." Danny pulled the duvet up.

"Oh you can't say that. That's not nice Danny."

"Ok. Wonder where she gets her money from then."

Lizzie slid down into the bed with a bit of a huff. "Now that's unkind. I think she works when she can."

After a minute Danny said "When did you say she's coming here?"

"Monday, to have tea, no dinner with us, and Denis of course, so he can see Bethany."

"He's not got her pregnant has he?" He laughed and pulled away knowing what was coming next.

"Danny, how could you?" The steam nearly came out of her ears.

"Gotcha."

"Oh Danny, you shouldn't."

He turned and put his arm over her. "No, perhaps not. Give it a year or two eh?"

"Danny!"

"Only kidding. Lighten up. Oh well I suppose we can cope for one meal. Anyway it's her birthday tomorrow, so let's just cope with that first."

This brightened Lizzie up. "Oh I'm so looking forward to it. Ten, can you believe it?"

"Makes me feel old." He smiled. "Goodnight"

They kissed as usual and both settled down to a good sleep before the birthday girl would wake them up, then it would be all go.

Beth woke up slowly with the secure feeling of Robert's arm over her, but she was hot and gently moved it away so that she could cool down. She seemed to be dripping from head to foot, and when her energy returned couldn't wait to have a refreshing shower. Her husband grunted in his sleep and lay there unaware she was watching him and smiling as she thanked the Lord for their happiness. She eased her way out of the bed trying not to disturb him and made her way onto the landing.

"Margaret!" she jumped with surprise, "What's the matter dear?"

"I – I – had a dream."

Obviously something had upset her and Beth turned her round and they went into her bedroom and sat on the bed.

"You've had a bad dream? Well just try and forget all about it." Beth spoke very quietly to her but as she slipped her arm round Margaret's shoulder she noticed how tense she was.

"I can't. Something's wrong."

Beth was at a loss for words. She didn't know what was going on in the other woman's mind so didn't quite know what advice to give, and also didn't want to sound as if she was interrogating her for she's had enough of that in the past.

"Can I help?" was all she could muster.

"No. Nobody can. Something's wrong."

"Well, what if you tell me about it?"

Again "Something's wrong."

At this time in the morning Beth wasn't really in the mood for playing games and the repetition was beginning to grate even on her nature so she went for the obvious.

"Right. Tell me what is wrong."

Margaret turned her head to face her and Beth noticed how ashen her complexion was, so this wasn't just a whim but something had really scared her. As she didn't reply Beth pushed it further.

"Who was in your dream?"

"Lizzie."

"Anyone else?"

Margaret started to shake "The devil."

At this point Beth realised she had probably had a nightmare which had left her frightened and there was nothing more to it than that. But then something else hit her.

"So you won't want to be going out today then, even to see Lizzie and make sure she's all right?"

The look she got in return was almost hatred.

"Go out? Of course I can't go out. Why would you think I would go out?" Again repetition. Beth got up slowly and said "Well, I'm going to make a cup of tea, are you coming?"

"No."

"Do you want one?"

All she got was a shake of the head and a mumbled "You don't understand."

"Oh I think I do Margaret. See you later then." She left without turning back but left a very bewildered looking person on the bed.

Beth wasn't the sort to be hard or immune to other peoples' problems, quite the opposite in fact but something had woken alarm bells in her and she felt as if Margaret was trying to control her in someway by playing on her good qualities. Had she only known, Symphony, Margaret's guardian had warned Beth's spirit not to be taken in by some of the play acting directed at her. It had been used with Robert as the target but even he seemed to have adopted a shield against it thanks to the guardian's intervention.

So now Margaret sat alone or so she thought. Symphony was anticipating her every mood and plan and realised that, as she wasn't getting the response here, she would be aiming her next move at Lizzie. But that would be difficult as she didn't want to go out she would have to draw Lizzie to her so she sent a signal to Amity to put a block on any sob story that might be used.

When breakfast was over, Beth rang to wish Bethany a happy birthday, and a very excited little girl was telling her what present her parents had bought her.

"Well you'll get some more when we come sweetheart."

"Thank you Gran. Mum wants you now."

The phone was passed over and Lizzie sounded so happy. "Oh Mum can you hear her? She's been like that since she woke up."

"Sounds like she loves that playhouse, she was bubbling."

"Oh she does, and it's got so many bits that go with it. And you put what you want in the rooms so it's changing all the time."

"Into double figures now, bet she feels really grown up."

"Yes she does. You know our neighbour Janet, she's bought her the most lovely hand made doll, and I've told her she must look after it. There's so much work gone into it. You'll see it later."

"How lovely." Then after a pause "Um – Margaret won't be coming Lizzie, I'm sorry, we tried."

"Didn't expect her somehow. Anyway, you can take her a goody bag."

Beth was relieved that Lizzie didn't seem upset by Margaret's absence and thought that maybe she too was just taking it in her stride and not getting uptight about it any more. It would be up to Margaret herself to get her act together, they had done all they could.

As soon as the phone went down, it rang.

"Now what's she forgotten?" Beth laughed. "Oh Hello, yes just a minute." Then handing it to Robert said "It's Bill."

He smiled in thanks and listened for a moment. "Yes of course you can, only we're going out later, my granddaughter's birthday you know, can't miss that."

It pleased Beth to hear him call Bethany that and she smiled as he asked "Ok if Bill pops round this morning?"

She nodded knowing he was going to help Robert with the patio area, and a lot of planning had to be done before they could get started. When he had finished the conversation he said "It should look really good when it's done."

"Of course it will." She smiled.

"Any sign of madam yet?" his eyes flicked to the ceiling.

"No, she had a bad dream. I'm trying not to make too much fuss about it."

"Oh not another!" he sighed. "You did the right thing." and he bent and kissed her.

After a while she thought she had better check on Margaret to be on the safe side. After getting no response from tapping on her door, Beth quietly went in and stopped in amazement. Margaret was fully dressed, was combing her hair and had a few bits of make up laid out ready to apply.

"My word, you do look better."

Margaret looked at Beth by means of the reflection in the mirror. "Well thought I'd better make an effort, after all it is her birthday."

It took Beth a minute to gather her thoughts. Did this mean she was actually going?

"You do look nice Margaret. But we aren't going till later."

"I know that. Just practising." The tone in no way resembled the earlier image that Beth had encountered.

"Well, I'll leave you to it dear." she smiled and slid out of the room as if she had been intruding.

"Guess what?" she hugged Robert in the kitchen. "I think she's coming."

His eyes widened, partly from the news and partly from the closeness of her which always stirred him.

"Margaret? No!"

"I think so. She's having a dress rehearsal up there."

"My God. I don't know whether to be pleased or apprehensive."

"I know just what you mean, but lets take it as it comes and keep our fingers crossed, after all you could nip her home if she does get a bit stressed."

"Good thinking. Ah well," he reluctantly pushed her gently away "I'd better get ready for Bill coming."

"And I'll just make a little list of what I've got to take."

"You and your little lists," he laughed as he went outside.

If Robert and Beth were looking forward to the afternoon, it was a bit different in Sharon's place. She felt as if Denis resented her going out yesterday and there was a distinct atmosphere everywhere, but she knew he would be a different child when he was with his little friend.

"Wish he'd have mates of his own sex." she thought as she messed with her hair wondering if she should wash it. It didn't seem right to her for a lad of his age to only have one friend, and a girl at that. But he'd always been strange and probably always would be and she had more important things to worry about.

Unlike Doag and Denis, Sharon didn't have the ability to shut off her spiritual side at will. She was merely a pawn who did as she was directed, whether or not she knew why. The evil group had homed in on her at one of the lowest points of her life, offering her better things if she used her hidden talents, which was a load of nonsense. But she wanted to believe that she could improve herself and get out of the poor trap, so she had followed instructions not realising there was no return. She believed that her psychic guide could show her the way to wealth and happiness but she must be very strict with herself and others. She never questioned the fact that she had no physical evidence like a letter, email or text message telling her where to go. They had let her think that it was her own inner spiritual side that was instructing her and that proved how gifted she was and sadly, she believed it.

They had told her to move into the manor with her son under the pretence of working as a live-in domestic. Everything would be provided for her in the way of food and everyday essentials, but she must keep to herself and tell no-one. What they didn't tell her was that there would be others there who would be stocking up the store room etc and carrying out other jobs, but with similar instructions to stay alone and not mix with anyone in the house. The evil group would have a small sector of underlings which they could send out at controlled times to do their menial tasks which would lay the basis for the ultimate event. But the few hungry for better things would never find their rewards for they would be disposed of at the end of their useful period. It would be assumed that Sharon and Denis had moved away. But the evil group were unaware of a vital ingredient. One innocent quiet little boy.

Vedron was ready to move. He was now being driven crazy by his unsatisfied lust and knew it had to be now or not at all. The sentinels guarding his exits from the triangles had been in communication with the other ones along both tropics just in case of any change of ability or route. It was just as Vedron emerged and made his way back to the boarding house, an alert ran through all the sentinels that the North Pole vortex was receiving a lot of use and the vibrations were not of the good kind. Jenny immediately ordered more guards to the area but still warned that it could be a decoy. As soon as they scanned the area she had the answer. It was the evil group which she had encountered many times and when they were in presence a disaster was imminent. It worried her that they should be around just when they were about to apprehend Vedron, but it may be coincidence, so for now they would treat the two things as separate tasks until such time that one of the high level angels could prove different.

She knew the evil group would have appointed its temporary work force and just as she was mapping the location, word came in from Sharon's guardian that she had been groomed. This was too much to be happening by chance. There had to be a connection but what was it?

Bill had enjoyed the time spent with Robert and had picked up more information than could be imagined. He had positioned himself at a safe distance from the Worth household and the preparations for the birthday party, but was soaking up every unseen scrap of knowledge from there. Even before he had said "Goodbye for now" to Robert and Beth his data was being analysed by the hierarchy and they knew the exact placing of each 'connect'. From there he visited Sharon. She opened the door with an expression on her face making it clear she hadn't liked to be disturbed.

"Yes?" she snapped.

"Ah Good Morning Madam, now I'm not trying to sell you anything but...."

"That's good, 'cos I don't want anything." She tried to close the door.

"You could just listen to what I have to say."

She eyed him up and down. "Oh you're one of those bible punchers, well I don't need you telling me a pack of lies, so piss off."

He smiled and said very softly "You don't like men do you?"

"Did I say that? No, I don't think I did. Now, if that's all, I'm very busy. Good bye."

"Oh I can see you are very busy." It was Bill's turn to look at her from head to toe. His soft voice was having a soothing effect and for some reason she didn't slam the door as she had been about to do.

"Well then... um, I'd better get on." But she remained still.

"I'm very glad to have met you, and I know there is no point in my telling you that your windows need attention or I could save you money on your electricity bill, so I'll just leave you now." The words had no actual meaning, but his voice had lulled her into such a relaxed state that he had drained all he wanted to know from her spiritual side.

She came to with a jolt to hear him say how nice it had been talking to her and he was sorry to have disturbed her.

"That's Ok." She murmured and as she watched him walk away, she closed the door quietly and stood there wondered what had just happened.

This information didn't just go to the higher levels, along with that collected from Robert and his family, it all went by the secret route to other watchers. Vedron had made one of his mistakes. After using Bill, he had discarded him like an empty can, never bothering to go back and check that he wasn't being used by another source because he considered the man to be too insignificant. This made a perfect host for Watcher to use knowing it would be the last place Vedron would think of looking. He could easily have removed Beth's 'connect' but that would have drawn attention and so he had no option but to leave it. So now he knew the position of all the 'connects' but had also learned of Sharon's involvement with the evil gang and maybe it was time for another watcher to take over that location eventually. It was decided that, until Vedron really started to move, the fewer high entities in presence the better for although they were adept at cloaking individually, several could produce a kind of wall that would be noticed by the bad forces. He returned to the boarding house and again sank into his non descript form to wait for the next move.

There was great excitement now as Bethany waited for the family to arrive.

"What time is it now?" she bubbled.

Danny turned her face to the clock. "What does that say?"

"A quarter to four."

"And what was it two minutes ago when you asked me then?" Bethany looked a little subdued. "Um- nearly a quarter to four."

"Well you can tell the time, so all you have to do is look at the clock." He laughed and gave her a nudge. A noise at the front door sent her scurrying out of the room.

"Gran, Granddad" she screamed.

"Quiet Bethany, the whole street will hear you." Lizzie scolded.

Robert and Beth parted and there just behind was Margaret clutching her present. If Bethany had yelled before it was nothing to the noise she made as she rushed between them and hugged her.

"Auntie Margaret" she was pulling her inside, "come and see what I've got."

Even Margaret had to smile as she was tugged along to the sofa. Beth hugged Lizzie and Danny as usual shook hands with Robert.

"How did you manage it?" he whispered.

Robert shrugged "I didn't. She just decided to come."

"Well Bethany's over the moon, look."

They all followed into the lounge and Beth gave Robert a knowing look of pleasure. His daughter looked better than she had for a long time and to see her with Bethany made up for all the tantrums they had to put up with.

"Here you are darling." Beth handed over her present.

"Oh thank you Gran. And you too Granddad."

Margaret was enjoying this. "Open that then you can have mine." It was almost as if she didn't want the moment to end and was trying to extend it as long as possible.

There were gasps as Bethany looked at all the craft things and she tried to open the little sections.

"I think it would be best to leave them as they are for now Bethany," Lizzie spoke softly not wanting to spoil the enjoyment "if any got lost you'd be so upset."

"Ok Mum." Bethany continued to examine everything. "I love this."

"Are you ready for mine now?" Margaret asked.

"Oh yes please Auntie."

It was such a happy moment that there were tears in Beth's and Lizzie's eyes and Robert blew his nose a bid louder than usual.

Danny was just happy but then he hadn't been through the horror this family had suffered years ago.

Very carefully, Bethany undid the paper to reveal the most beautiful doll dressed in exquisite clothes, and complete with hairbrush, mirror, and a little wardrobe of clothes for all occasions. There was a hush.

"Oh. She's lovely." Bethany couldn't take her eyes off her, then she carefully laid her down, threw her arms round Margaret and whispered in her ear "She's just like you." The moment was so special, that Lizzie beckoned everyone out of the room. She and Beth went into the kitchen and the men wandered outside but the conversations were very similar. It had been thought that Margaret wouldn't be coming and Beth had tried to think up reasons that Bethany would understand, but now it didn't matter.

"Just as long as she doesn't get too tired." she said quietly to Lizzie.

"You shouldn't have spent all that. I know you got the doll."

Beth shrugged. "Well yes, but she told me what she would like although I was a bit wary. She isn't up to date with things girls like these days, so I tried to find something girly."

"Well you certainly did right with that one." Lizzie was getting things together for the tea.

"I'll just have a peek, see they're all right." Beth was always edgy where Margaret was concerned and didn't like to leave her with a child for too long. She needn't have worried. They were both sitting on the floor trying on the different outfits which included shoes, hats, headbands, and just about everything.

"I'm calling her Margaret," Bethany beamed, "you like that don't you Auntie?"

Beth noticed the glaze on Margaret's eyes and said "What a good idea." And gave both of them a loving look.

"Well I've got to get the table set now ladies," Lizzie joined them with a tray of plates and cutlery in her hands. The two on the floor giggled at being called 'ladies' then Bethany said "I want to sit with Auntie."

Lizzie put her head on one side and said "I want?"

"Sorry Mum. May I sit with Auntie please?"

"That's better. Of course you can." Lizzie had been chatting to her mother earlier and agreed they didn't want Margaret to be overwhelmed with too many people suddenly. "Oh Margaret, to save it being a bit cramped, Bethany asked if she could sit at her little table, and as she wants to sit next to you...."

"I'll sit with her if you like." Margaret said quick as a flash.

"Oh thank you. Sure it's not too low?"

"No, I'd like it."

The sigh of relief that came from Beth was almost audible and Robert's face showed relief. It was the little things that had to be thought through but made all the difference where she was concerned, things most people wouldn't have considered important but they made for the smoother running of everyday life. This was the biggest event Margaret had had to cope with in a long time, so anything that helped was welcome.

There were no pregnant pauses during tea, as everyone seemed to have something to say and the 'girls' at the little table seemed to be in a world of their own.

Bethany was never at a loss for words and was telling Margaret about Denis and the fact that he was coming the next day with his mum.

"So I might get another present, but it won't be as good as yours and Grans, or Mum and Dad's." She never wanted to leave anyone out and if they'd had a cat, then that would have been included as well.

It was time for the cake. Bethany had to stand up to be able to blow out the candles.

"All in one big puff," Danny said, "no cheating now."

They all sang 'Happy Birthday' as she drew a deep breath and blew. The smoke from the ten candles seemed to cover the cake and a stillness engulfed the room.

Robert was the first to move. "What in God's name was that?"

"Look." Lizzie pointed to the candles. They were burned down half way whereas they should have been almost full length as they had only been lit for a couple of seconds. Beth just sat with her mouth open and Danny was shaking his head in amazement. Bethany thought she had done something to cause it and started to cry but Lizzie assured her it wasn't any of her doing. As she comforted her,

her gaze rested upon Margaret who was sitting bolt upright, her face ashen. For a split second Lizzie felt that she must have had something to do with it, or something else had, but she put the feeling from her mind as it seemed too outrageous. Instead she looked straight at her mum and indicated to Margaret. Beth was very quick to realise something was wrong and gently went over to her.

"Don't worry, she's all right, something wrong with the candles." Beth had mastered the knack of drawing the attention to something else, thus letting Margaret know it had nothing to do with her and it seemed to be working,.

"What was it?" she whispered "is Bethany Ok?"

"She's fine. We'll be taking those candles back I can tell you and the shop can have a piece of my mind."

Robert had quickly removed the offending items and Danny said "There we are, everything's under control. Now how about a bit of cake each?"

This seemed to bring everything back to normal and before long they were all enjoying the special cake Beth had made.

"I hope I'm as good as you one day Mum" Lizzie said as she swallowed her last mouthful."

"So do I." Danny piped up then ducked before his wife could throw something at him. This lightened the mood and the episode was soon forgotten. Margaret appeared to have returned to normal and Bethany asked if she could take her up to her room. Nobody saw much of them after that and Lizzie almost apologised.

"Oh please," Beth said "I know it's her birthday, but this was the best present we could have had isn't it dear?"

"Rather." Robert was quick to agree. "Haven't seen her so good since, well I can't remember. Bethany's done more for her than any of those so called doctors or shrinks."

"Well we won't push anything," Lizzie added "but if she goes on like this, she could get back to normal one day."

A general hum of agreement went round the room, but then Robert said "I think we'd better not spoil a good thing. Best be off I think."

"Who wants the job of splitting them up then?" Lizzie laughed and cast a look to the ceiling.

"I'll go." Danny said and made his way out of the door only to return a minute later.

"What's up?" Everyone turned to ask.

"Well you can try if you like. I'm not going to be the one to get told off."

Beth and Lizzie were on their feet immediately and gently poked their heads round the bedroom door.

"Will you look at that!" Lizzie hissed.

"Robert's got to see this." Beth had turned to go and fetch her husband but Danny had already told him. However he knew that Beth wouldn't rest until he had gone up. There they were, both of them squashed onto Bethany's bed fast asleep.

It was thought it best to let them both rest for a while, after all they must have been happy and relaxed, but both needed to sleep. So they all agreed to leave them for about an hour and then think about it.

Vedron was very satisfied. He had been taught to always do a test run before executing a major plan, although unbeknown to him, the evil teachers knew this could be his down fall by exposing his hand too soon. However, regardless of this his scheme had worked. He had the family in one place, and at the crucial moment had made the candles smoke, then put all the players into a time freeze, hence when they came out of it, the candles had burned down, but the players not realising they had all lost those minutes. All it really proved was that the 'connects' were working and he had complete control so there would be nothing in his way in the capture of Lizzie. He was so full of himself that he didn't realise the whole scene had been witnessed by more than one entity. All he knew was that he could take her at any time and as long as only those with 'connects' were present, there was nothing to stop him. The time was now.

Most predators on such a mission would have weighed up various angles and then selected the best move. There were those watching him from a very unsavoury source who would have adopted ways of making Lizzie come willingly, not by sheer force or control. Some would have used Bethany as lure, for if a child was to die, the mother, in her grief often wanted to join them and then she would be a pushover. But Vedron had already considered that and discarded the idea because Lizzie would hold him responsible and hate him even more for what he had done, so he opted to take her alone and knew that in time she would succumb. He didn't even spare a thought for the fact that her family and those protecting them would give him no eternal peace and he would be hunted like an animal until his judgement day. But that couldn't happen to him. Everyone would see just how superior he was and he would be feared, but that was secondary to his obsession which was at boiling point.

If it had only been a case of his own future existence, the good forces would have been happy to let him get on with it and learn from his own downfall, but there were innocent souls involved and they must be protected at all costs. Knowing Vedron, he wouldn't be waiting around much longer, and the vibrations indicated an imminent move, so everyone connected was on high alert, and warned to be watchful, even to the smallest change.

Doag had managed to contact Denis during his waking period to warn him to get nearer to Bethany. Unfortunately, in human form he wasn't due to see her until the next day so they agreed that in the event of an attack they would both move in regardless of being exposed as their higher level selves. Instructions were given to the temporary sentinels to send out a warning the moment they noticed anything threatening, or similar to the event at the party. These lower guards would have known an evil presence was there but would not have been able to identify it, so it was up to them to report any visitor whether they thought they knew it or not. It was essential to let Vedron think the coast was clear and that he wasn't walking into a trap, so for now the present guards must be left where they were.

Denis had also discussed with his partner Sharon's involvement at the manor house. At this moment it didn't seem to have any connection, but could pull Denis away from Bethany just when he was needed. But Doag had been working during Denis's day hours and had realised the evil group had only taken over the place since Vedron's presence had been noticed. Although only conjecture at this stage he had put it to the upper spiral that if these were the ones who had been coaching Vedron and he owed them, what better site for a temporary base than one right on the doorstep. This meant that he couldn't just grab the spoils and run as he had planned, but they would be waiting there ready to claim his soul. Time for him to pay up.

Jenny was now tying up various reports she had received. After Sharon's slip regarding the North Pole, scouts had been sent to observe recent happenings. As a CCTV can record and play back any movement, the same effect can be monitored with the air disturbances, especially in the spirit sector. Her remark "we're not going to the North Pole" proved she hadn't the capability to perform such travel, therefore she was merely a means to an end. But this caused concern. It could be a coincidence that she had been taken into the fold. Yes, they did rake up the lost, down on their luck, desperate mortals with the promise of better things, but she was Denis's Mother and although the high levels knew of Denis's status, none of the lower ones would ever detect it. So if he was the connection, it meant the evil group were also of a high level.

But was Vedron so important? Only in his own estimation. She was turning this over with Graham and Matthew but neither could think why any high force would bother with him.

"Unless!" Jenny had a new idea.

"I think I know." Graham was already on the same wavelength.

"Which is?" Matthew queried.

"He is the lead." Jenny announced.

"You mean they don't need him for himself, but he will take them to a higher source?" Matthew asked.

Graham said "May I?"

"Please do." Jenny indicated.

"Well, from past happenings, and I may be wrong, but I think for some reason they are after Zargot."

"Of course. They're going to the top. But no one can oust him, he is the Almighty Evil Lord. He controls everything." Matthew turned to Jenny. "Is he right?"

"I think he is spot on."

Nobody communicated for a moment then Graham said "And Lizzie?"

"That's what I'm afraid of. She could be drawn along in this when he tries to take her." Jenny was deadly serious.

Nobody said "never to return" but they all knew the threat was more than a possibility.

"We've just got to be successful in the abortion of this attempt of his and I think I know how we can do it." But she knew they would have no second chance, they had to get it right first time.

They continued in conference then, in a second had gone.

Chapter 9

If the earthly beings had enjoyed a peaceful night, it was just the opposite in the spiritual world. There was much covert activity around the vortices, watcher had been on Vedron's tail and there was a constant check on all of Lizzie's family.

Margaret had eventually roused enough to be helped to the car and driven home, and Bethany could reclaim her bed. Everyone seemed to have put the candle incident to the back of their minds and the general success of the party had left them all in a lovely euphoric state.

Sharon had only been to the manor for a quick visit to prepare her living area, as she called it, but as her mother couldn't have Denis for long, she had been forced to return to her rented home. But she would be back there as soon as Denis was at school and then she could carry on her usual activities.

The day dawned with flowers appearing everywhere. The trees were full of blossom and although people complained of the mess the petals made, the children loved playing with them. It was hard to realise the unseen threats that hovered over the world, and thankfully most would be blissfully unaware of most of them. But the evil that was festering in many places was gathering more and more bored people into its net, promising better things like wealth and happiness in return for a few favours. But for the likes of Sharon, they were signing their warrant to eternal misery, and once under control had no hope of escape.

Denis had homed in on this part of her during their sleeping hours even before her guardians had sent out the warning signals, but he had to keep back for now and leave it to other high level operators. His task, along with Doag was to protect Lizzie and her close family and that had to be his priority, but he was still aware that other forces could be coming in from other routes so kept his senses honed at all times.

Bethany was bouncing around as usual which for most children would have been unusual, but she was still on a high from Sunday and was looking forward to Denis coming after school.

"Don't forget his mum is coming too." Lizzie reminded her.

"Oh yes." It didn't bother Bethany, as long as Denis was there.

They set off for school and as soon as she saw her friend she pulled at Lizzie's hand.

"Yes, I can see him." Lizzie laughed "Go on then but stay on the pavement."

Sharon joined her. "Happy aren't they?"

"Very." Lizzie wasn't very chatty after Saturday night and it was noticeable.

"Look I'm sorry, about the other night, I mean, only this job means a lot and I had to go and sort some things out."

"Well it's done with now," Lizzie said but thought, "until that time of night?" She hoped there wouldn't be a repeat of it tonight and said "Um, you are all right for dinner aren't you. You haven't got to dash off again?"

There was nothing that Sharon would have liked more than to go to the manor, but she would be spending enough time there during the day so would have to leave it for once.

"Oh no. Not tonight."

Lizzie was relieved. Much as she would gladly cook for them both, she didn't like the idea that some of it could be wasted because Sharon didn't stay.

"Oh good." Then to change the subject she told her of the party but left out the candle business.

"And Margaret came after all then? Must be feeling better."

Before Lizzie could reply Sharon looked at her watch and said "Must dash, see you later." There wasn't even time for a good bye and Lizzie noticed that she hadn't even said 'Bye' to Denis. Fortunately he was in deep conversation with Bethany, when he could get a word in, and didn't notice. Lizzie being the kind of person she was couldn't leave it there and called out "Denis, your mum said 'Bye'. He just raised his hand in acknowledgement and Lizzie couldn't help noticing it was a very grown up gesture for a lad of his age.

"Oh well, I suppose they're all growing up fast" she said to herself and after waving to Bethany went home to make her shopping list for later.

"I think I'll do a bit of shopping with Lizzie." Beth smiled at Robert.

"Anything in particular?" He glanced up from the morning paper.

"Well, do you know I seem to have got the baking bug again and I saw some lovely things the other day and we were concentrating on getting Bethany's present so I left it, but I wouldn't mind another look."

"Do I get to do the sampling?"

"Of course, and if you're a good boy I might let you lick the bowl out." She burst into her special tinkling laughter.

"Ugh. Did we really do that as kids?"

"We did, and it still goes on you know."

He got up, "Think I'll stick to the grown up version." His arms slipped round her and that was all it took for them to be locked in an embrace almost as if they were afraid to loose each other.

"Oh not again, these wretched things." Beth was boiling and Robert could feel the heat coming out of her.

"My God, you could be a generator," he said, then seriously, "they really are getting to you aren't they?"

"Oh it'll pass, it always does. Someone told me to just give in and not fight it and it goes quicker."

"And does that work?"

"Oh I don't know. Perhaps. Trouble is, they always catch me out when I'm doing something."

Robert gave a little laugh "That, my darling is because you are always doing something or other." He tilted his head and gave her the questioning look parents give when they know their child might be fibbing.

"Stop being right all the time." She turned and went to the kitchen and got a glass of water from the fridge jug. He followed her and waited until she cooled down.

"Need some money?"

"Um, I think I'll be all right, but some of the things were dearer than I thought so I may get what I think is worth the money."

He smiled, took out his wallet and gave her a £20 note. "My thrifty little wife as always." Then "Will that be enough?"

"Oh more than, thank you."

"Well, much as I'd like to stay and cuddle you, I'd better get to work," he glanced at his watch, gathered up his things and after giving her his usual intimate goodbye was gone, leaving a very contented lady to enjoy her day.

Beth glanced at her watch. She would give Lizzie time to get sorted when she got back from the school and ring her then. Just as she was finishing her glass of water Margaret appeared looking a bit tousled but with a rather happy look on her face.

"Did I sleep a long time?"

Beth laughed "Just a bit, but do you feel better for it?"

"Yes, I do. Had a funny dream though."

"Oh" Beth was a little concerned at first for she knew what kind of dreams Margaret normally had. "When you say funny...um.. would that be funny haha or funny peculiar?"

"Well, it was strange. " She went over to the kettle.

"I'll make you a cup of tea dear, do you want to tell me about it?"

Margaret's hand went up "I can do it." And she pressed the switch down and reached for a mug. Beth hoped there was enough water in the kettle but she didn't want to interfere and she never left it empty so turned back to the dream.

"What was it like?"

"What was what like?" It was almost as if Margaret had forgotten it already and Beth thought it might be better to leave it that way but she was still curious.

"Oh nothing, it's just that you said you had a funny dream."

"Oh that. Well we were all at the party," then as if she was reliving it "it was good wasn't it, I really enjoyed it, anyway you know the cake, well we were all the candles and there was a big puff as if someone was going to blow us out."

"And did they? Blow us out I mean." Beth felt a little uneasy at what might be coming next and took a deep breath in readiness.

"Well that's where it was strange because only Lizzie got blown out and the rest of us just flickered for a bit then came back to life. Now that's funny isn't it?"

Beth didn't find it a bit funny but felt forced to agree with Margaret for the sake of her sanity. The last thing she wanted was for her to regress after such good improvement recently.

"Well it certainly sounded strange, but they say dreams just clear out our thoughts so it's gone now." Beth hoped she sounded more sincere than she felt

Symphony had been on extra alert during Margaret's long sleep for she knew that was when any evil entities would try to get into the relaxed mind. As she sensed a force trying to programme her charge she had alerted her higher levels. It was as if something was feeding Margaret with thoughts they hoped she would interpret as bad omens. While she was on a 'high' since the party they used the chance to play their games, but Symphony knew that Margaret had not been affected in any way when the candles smoked, because she would have been if any evil had been strong enough to involve her. So either a lesser evil had been having fun, or a low level had been employed to stir things up around Lizzie, or a more powerful one had simply come planted the evil seed and left before anyone, in the spiritual zone was any the wiser. This was something the higher levels were taking into consideration when looking at the overall picture.

Sharon had arrived at the manor house and felt herself being pushed into a large room which had been used for parties by previous owners. In its heyday it must have looked very ornate but now it seemed sad almost as though it missed the happy days. There was a table in the middle of the room and Sharon was pushed to a seat. The place was very dark and she wanted to go and open the curtains to see who was with her. As her eyes grew accustomed to the dim light she could make out figures sitting round the table but was unable to see their faces. All had dark loose fitting clothing and she wondered if they were some sort of sect and hoped they weren't the sort to go in for sacrifices. The one facing her seemed to be bigger than the rest and a feeling of power seemed to be emitting from it.

It was now, for the first time that Sharon wished she hadn't got into this. She had thought she was being offered a job, then found out she was merely required to be in the place while they worked from there for a while, then when the promises of good things were made, she thought it was an easy picking. But everything has its price.

Although the light didn't change, she thought her eyes were growing accustomed to the light because everything was becoming very different. She felt the nails of the one holding her pressing into her neck and wondered if this could be a woman. Up to now she had imagined they were all men. The one who had made the first contact had certainly been a man, and quite a dishy one at that, and on her previous visits, she had seen one or two different men, still rather attractive, and that was what had helped her to make up her mind to take this position. There was always the chance one of them might have been attracted to her, then who would know where that could lead.

But now it didn't feel the same. She let her gaze travel a little either side of the leader but without moving her head. They were all very good looking people, but she couldn't tell if they were male or female. Her attention rested back on the leader. This was certainly a female and the dark clothing had been replaced with a figure hugging all in one outfit.

"I've been bloody abducted!" she panicked.

The humour was felt in the room although not a sound was heard. The leader remained motionless. Sharon began to fidget.

"Well whatever it is, could you get on with it please?"

Immediately the air trembled and she knew she had overstepped the mark. "Oh I'm…s..sorry…I didn't mean to….." her voice trailed off as she felt the intense pressure around her, but as she sat there it eased and a soft euphoric feeling came over her. She was never sure if the leader had actually spoken, or if she just heard the words in her head, but it didn't matter, the message was passed to her.

"Don't be afraid. We aren't going to hurt you. You will soon be one of us and then everything will be good for you. You will have no more worries."

"Oh that's all right then." It was a nervous reply followed by an equally nervous laugh.

"Now," the leader had risen up to an enormous height and as her arms outstretch the rest of the assembly rose with her including the one holding Sharon in the chair "let yourself float, give your being to us. We will protect you. Nothing can harm you."

Sharon felt her soul being pulled from her body and soon she was floating with her companions who were gradually merging with her until the whole mass hovered as one with the leader in the centre. They resembled a spiral galaxy which would have made the leader the black hole which one day would draw them all into her and there would be no escape.

How long this lasted Sharon had no idea but when she found herself back in her own body, she was completely alone. Her first sense was that of fear, but then the wave of the contact seemed to be part of her now, she knew she couldn't be harmed, as long as she did their bidding. But if everything was going to be good it may be a small price to pay. She didn't consider what tasks she may be ordered to carry out, and another feeling seemed to have been implanted in her. Somehow she knew she was one of many under the control of this group. As she made her way back home she still wondered as to the sex of the rest of them which was strange because she could never remember ever having trouble working it out before in her encounters.

She reached her front door and another instruction was given to her. They had moved to the next stage and there was no need for her to move into the house. They had never wanted the extra burden of a child around but had to let her think that to get her to this stage. The explanation to her friends was that she would go there to clean but remain in her own home. Things would be provided for her so there would be no question of how she had a job but no money. So now she was the latest victim of their harvest of 'get rich quick hopefuls' but it was a trap from which there was never any chance of escape.

Bethany had a job concentrating on her school work that day, as she was still in the after joy of her birthday and was looking forward to Denis coming to her home. When playtime came she rushed outside to talk to him but the strange thing was, that he always seemed to be there waiting for her although she hadn't been aware of him passing her on the way out. It was the same at dinner time and the afternoon break. There he was looking straight at her. If she hadn't liked him so much she may have found it rather intimidating but he had planted the sense of trust in her as she slept so he never appeared to be any kind of threat. Also he had placed a kind of spiritual magnet in her so that she would feel drawn to him of her own choice.

"Are you coming home straight from school?" she was keen to be sharing his presence as soon as possible.

"No, Mum says I'm to go home and get washed and changed, then we're coming."

The temporary guardians watching Bethany thought this was a sweet little exchange, little guessing her real angel was there facing her at that very moment.

Beth and Lizzie had enjoyed a happy mother/daughter session at the shops and were enjoying a well earned cup of coffee at Beth's when Margaret appeared and stopped dead her face ashen.

"Lizzie." was all she whispered.

"What is it dear?" Beth was on her feet in an instance.

Margaret was steered to a chair but her gaze never left Lizzie. Beth immediately recalled the dream but had hoped that she had forgotten it but it was obviously not so.

"Margaret" she said very softly "it's all right, Lizzie's fine, look."

"What's going on?" Lizzie felt she had been left out of something and wanted to know what it was.

Beth was in two minds as to whether she should mention the dream just in case it wasn't that which was now bothering Margaret but before she could make up her mind Margaret said "I thought I'd lost you."

"What on earth made you think a thing like that?" Lizzie gave a little false laugh to try and lighten the atmosphere but she was feeling quite different inside.

"You were gone" The eyes were far away now as if she was somewhere else.

Beth and Lizzie exchanged worried looks and sat for a moment to try and decide how best to deal with her. After a moment Lizzie held both her hands and looked straight at her

"Margaret."

Silence.

"Margaret, look at me."

The head lifted a fraction.

Again "Margaret, you can see me. You can feel me. So I am here, I haven't gone anywhere now have I?"
There was no response.
Lizzie was almost shouting now "Margaret, tell me you know I am here."
This was too much for Beth who put her arms round Lizzie's shoulders and drew her away.
"Leave her for now, let her settle."
"But what's going on Mum? She was so good yesterday and now…"
Beth took a deep breath and beckoned her daughter into the lounge.
"She seemed to have had a bad dream and it's still with her. That's all."
"That's all?" Lizzie almost shouted. "Look at her Mum. I know you're used to her but look." This was the proverbial 'look' as they were out of sight of her but Beth knew what she meant.
"I know what you're saying." She sighed. "Just when you have an up moment, it's followed by a down." Then thoughtfully, almost to herself, "but this seems different."
Lizzie too had calmed a little. "It's almost as if something was telling her I was going somewhere, but how do I convince her I'm not, ever?"
"You can't. None of us can."
"It's locked away inside her isn't it?"
"I'm afraid so."
They hugged for a moment gathering strength from each other then went back into the kitchen not expecting to see Margaret wiping down the draining board as if her life depended upon it.

Symphony had been fighting the force that was trying to destroy Margaret's inner self and had managed to restore her to a stable level and was trying to erase the planted images from her. She realised this was nothing to do with any threat to Lizzie but one of those meddlesome entities that thrived on playing on the minds of the mentally ill. When her thought reports reached the upper spiral, they didn't dismiss it so lightly, as nothing could be ignored in such a delicate situation. But this guardian was very experienced, and although she knew there had been another presence at the party, it wasn't the same one that had stirred up the dream and Margaret's mind had combined the two. But now she seemed to have settled, much to the other two ladies' relief and the conversation moved to other things and the incident was put behind them.

Vedron was making his final plans. He was so sure that nothing could go wrong, and having thought it all through very carefully left it at that. Many in his position would have checked and rechecked, but he imagined that, with his new powers, and the time spent arranging it, nothing could go against him. These people didn't know what they were up against now. He was invincible.

It almost amused Watcher as he trailed the fiend, for if only Vedron would ask his opinion, he would blow holes right through the plan. Therefore Watcher already knew of all the weak spots, and although it may appear to be working at first, Vedron would soon hit the first pothole and then they would have him. What the higher levels did with him then was not Watcher's concern, for he would have done his part of the job and would disappear to reappear in another form for his next job. Such was his work pattern.

Sharon was getting some strange feelings now. She would be going to do something, then somehow she did something completely different.

"I must be going round the bleeding twist," she muttered as she grabbed her bag and made her way to the local post office. It was only a small place but one which also packed its limited space with sweets, papers etc and although the prices were dear, it was often handy to pop in for odd items, rather than go to the supermarket. But shopping wasn't her reason well not exactly.

On entering she picked up a packet of biscuits but by the time she had gone round to the till there were numerous other items concealed about her person. At every blind spot or when the assistant was serving, something went into her pocket or into her handbag. She had kept the biscuits on full view when in line with the camera and after looking around as if checking she didn't need anything she went and paid at the till and left. She didn't hurry to attract any suspicion and when she reached the end of the road, knew she had pulled it off.

"Greedy bastards, they can afford it," she thought but then realised "so this is what they meant by 'everything will be provided', well why not?"

She got home and emptied her spoils onto the worktop. Not bad for the price of a packet of biscuits. But this was an advance deposit on what she would be doing for her overlords, or ladies, whatever they were. When the job was complete, she would be sent out to 'find' cash to pay her bills. This probably wasn't what she expected but if it worked, so be it. Did she really think they would just lay a pile of money in her hand? She was already learning it didn't work that way.

Everything in the spiritual existence was on high alert in the area. Vedron had appeared to be concentrating on one particular vortex and Watcher was monitoring every slightest movement, even the wakes being left behind when he had gone. A special team had been placed to try and ascertain the purpose of the evil group at the manor leaving the personal guardians around Lizzie's family to concentrate solely on their charges. Symphony and Amity would remain throughout due to their high status but the temporary ones looking after Bethany would be immediately removed when the time came and Doag would replace them. Denis would then join Amity. This left Sharon's guardian who couldn't be replaced at the moment as that would draw attention to the evil group, but there was one standing by of a higher level to be placed if the need arose.

The problem when anything is brewing in the unseen world, is that it draws unwanted attention from other malevolent species and can often hamper an operation, rather like a road collision where some other drivers cause more chaos by slowing to have a look and often create more smashes. The mischievous spirits like to join in and it can soon become a party, wrecking all the years and even decades of work in preparation. Fortunately the high levels have a certain way of toning down their activities just as Denis and Doag are at present mixing with the lower powers undetected. Once exposed they never again take on that image except in extreme circumstances and are never traceable. The watchers will flit from one form to another constantly and are above detection.

"We couldn't have got it wrong by any chance?"

Graham had voiced his concern and Jenny pulled her nearest workers to her.

"I had considered the option," she admitted "and there may be other angles to this but on the whole we can't turn our backs or we will be caught out." Then to Graham "What in particular alerted you?"

"A feeling that there is something bigger lurking that we may have missed."

"Are you thinking of the evil group's attempt to usurp Zargot?"

Graham hesitated. "No, we know about that one, but I feel there is something else. But what?"

Matthew cut in "The unusual activity in the vortices?"

Jenny didn't seem to think that was it. "We've had that many times before, and although it's been a recurring thing, they are now so well monitored, there's little that can escape us."

Graham said "I wish I could narrow it down. But it's strange. It's almost as though it's right under our noses. It's there looking at us and we can't see it." He was referring to the spiritual sense but it didn't answer the question.

"Well," Jenny said "keep concentrating Graham, something may just hit you." then addressed her next remark to the assembled company "Diligence always."

Lizzie had everything in hand for the meal and despite the usual little hiccup that always pokes its nose in, everything had gone pretty well. Danny had done a couple of hours overtime in the last week and it was agreed he would come home at five o'clock today. He knew the company liked that as they didn't have to part with some of their precious cash. Of everyone at the meal, he was the one least looking forward to it, but he kept up a front for Lizzie and Bethany's sake knowing how much it meant to them. He decided he would keep out of Sharon's way as much as possible. Since the cleaning job idea he had her tagged as a 'user' and hoped his wife wouldn't get too involved with her in any way and if Lizzie did get the job at the hospital, that would take care of that side of things. What Sharon did didn't concern him as long as his family weren't involved. If he only knew what she was really up to, he would have been horrified and banned her and her child from the house.

Bethany was so excited as she rushed out of school she nearly fell over.

"Be careful." Lizzie warned. "You don't want to go getting another graze on your yourself."

"Denis is going home to have a wash." Her voice wasn't quiet and everyone round here found this very amusing. Some of the parents tried to hide their mirth, but the kids whooped on it and began chanting "Denis is having a wa-ash, Denis is having a wa-ash." This brought Bethany close to tears and she looked around for him but he seemed to have gone. Lizzie too, looked for him and Sharon but there seemed to be no sign of either. She was tempted to get Bethany out of this situation by hurrying her home but stopped as she saw Sharon running towards the school.

"Oh Christ, I'm late. Where is he?" She was absolutely out of puff and gasped the words.

This started the kids chanting again but Lizzie shouted "Be quiet. Has anyone seen Denis please?"

"He's gone to have a wash." One of the older lads yelled and his little gang guffawed in amusement.

"There he is" one of the mums pointed to the school.

All heads turned. Denis was standing stock still at the doorway staring at them. The laughter hushed until there was no sound as he slowly took very precise steps towards his mother. The look he cast at the mocking lads seemed to have an uncanny effect, for they shrank back and made their exit as quickly as possible. Even Sharon was, to quote her expression 'gobsmacked'. A little murmur ran round the parents and the odd sentence was audible.

"Told you he was weird."

"Strange one, that."

"Well he can keep away from my kids."

Denis gave a little smile as he said quietly "I already do."

Sharon seemed to shake herself and went to grab his arm to lead him away but froze as she saw the look on his face. It was as though she was looking at someone she didn't know.

"Um, we best be going, you don't want to be late."

As they walked home he chatted normally and she began to wonder how much of the scene had actually happened and whether she had imagined it. Her mind wandered to the manor folk as she called them and she decided that she must try and get out of their clutches as they seemed to be doing things to her mind. But she stood no chance, for when they had you, you never walked away.

Lizzie was rather quiet as they made their way home, but Bethany was still full of beans and didn't seem to notice.

"I hope he isn't like that when they come back." Lizzie thought. The episode had unsettled her a bit and she wondered what had caused Denis's strange behaviour. The idea came into her mind that maybe Sharon could be the cause as she never seemed close to the lad and always had her mind on something else, whereas Lizzie lived for her family and put them first, as her mother had always done. Perhaps Denis was left to his own devices. The fact that he didn't mix much with the other children didn't seem important as he was quite deep and was probably very bright and people like that could appear to separate themselves from the silly ones who looked on learning as a bore. But Bethany adored him and children often have a sense in these things.

"Mum." She was jolted out of her reverie.

"What? Oh sorry Bethany, what did you say?"

"Where are you going? We're here."

They had reached the house but Lizzie couldn't have recounted any of the short journey.

"Oh, sorry, I was miles away." They went in and Bethany foraged in her bag and pulled out several pieces of crumpled paper which she thrust into her mum's hand.

"Look what some of the girls did in art today. The teacher said they could make birthday cards for me if they wanted, and some said it wasn't my birthday so they didn't. That wasn't very kind of them, was it Mum?"

"Certainly not. You wouldn't have been so rude." Lizzie started to look through the papers then said "Shall we put them up?"

"I could put them in my room?"

"If you like," Lizzie smiled, grateful for the suggestion as the fridge and freezer were both rather overcrowded already. "Go and have a wash. I've put your favourite dress on your bed."

"Thank you Mum." Bethany grabbed the papers and was about to fly out of the room when Lizzie pointed to her bag still lying on the floor. "Oh sorry." She grabbed it and ran up the stairs.

"It doesn't take anything to dampen her spirits." Lizzie thought as she checked on the dinner and took a strawberry gateau out to thaw.

There was slight consternation as Watcher sent his coded message via the unknown route. Vedron was not using VVB or VVD triangles and there had been no trace of him for some time. A scan of the North Pole also showed no signs of movement by him and he was not in body at the boarding house. In simple terms he had lost him. In Watcher's experience any entity left some sort of trail so what was happening that was different now? There was only one possibility. He had a sweeper. These spirits were used to clear the wake of any particular passing spirit but leave others in tact. It had started as a tool to be used in emergency situations but like most good ideas had become poached by unscrupulous beings who had destroyed many a good trail. But when one side outsmarts the other, it isn't long before a counter attack is employed and there was a force of experts who could perform the equivalent of examining a hard drive on a computer. In this case they could hover over a given suspected area, then shrink to infinite proportions and pick up the tiniest scrap of residue left which would be overlooked by lesser competent spirits.

Some of these now examined the vortices but still came up with nothing, therefore Vedron must be either hitching a ride under cover of another party, or using his cloaking device which must be now linked to another zone. An order went out for the manor house to be searched but that came back with nothing. The evil group had left no trace and there was no atmosphere of any presence.

Jenny was in receipt of all the facts and now called another gathering to try and plan the fiend's next move. He had to be somewhere and if there was no evidence of him on this planet, then they must search beyond but that would mean depleting her much needed forces, so she called on her old friends the Schynings who had helped her in the past, and asked if they would search the solar system to which they readily agreed. In physical terms this would be an impossibility due to the vastness, but they could cover light years with no problem and would soon locate Vedron wherever he was.

There was nothing else to do but wait until their reply came, as all earthly locations had been vetted with no result.

Margaret was shaking her hand then sucking her finger.
"What on earth are you doing?" Beth laughed.
"Trying to get this thorn out?"
Beth moved closer to have a look. "But you haven't been near any thorns dear. Let me get the magnifying glass and see if I can find anything".
Unbeknown to both of them, Symphony had already detected the cause of the problem and the message had gone back.
"She's carrying."
This had only one meaning to the higher angels. Margaret had an unwelcome passenger on board. Something was hitching a ride or trying to hide. But as soon as the alert had gone out, the invader had departed.
"Oh it's gone, must have sucked it out." Margaret said while Beth ran her eyes over the finger.
"Well, you must be right, can't see anything."
They both forgot the incident within minutes, but Vedron hadn't. He thought this would be the last place any one would look while they were scurrying about checking the main areas but he hadn't bargained on Symphony's expertise. He had forsaken the triangles now and wanted to be as close to his target as possible which proved his lack of professionalism. The well trained entities could lie low anywhere and yet home in on their prey from any distance or location but this was another small detail his trainers had omitted to impart. So now he must find another host and another and even another until he swooped, but it would have to be soon or he would be detected then all his preparation would have been in vain. In his ignorance he believed he could keep flitting between numerous people and not be caught, but again he slipped up. He would leave a more impressionable wake by moving at speed than one who crawls or remains still for a while. But for now he must home in on some unsuspecting mortal but stay alert.

The evil group were now monitoring his progress with much amusement and thought how nice it would be to give him a sanctuary for a while. As the manor had already been checked it seemed a safe place to put him for now, so one of their drones beckoned to him and pulled him into her grasp. If he hadn't been so obsessed with Lizzie, his urges would certainly have been on full power for she was stunning. As soon as she had made close contact, he was instantly in place in the manor surrounded by many more of her appearance. For a moment his guard was down and he was very tempted by the menu. He couldn't tell how many of these beautiful creatures were with him but to some males they would have thought they were in heaven.

After a moment they all moved in against him and if he had been on an aircraft, he certainly would have been in the upright position! But they were closing in, pressing, squeezing all over his being until the whole mass suddenly shrank to nothing. Any passing scout would never have detected them, unless they had special skills like Watcher, who now had him in his sights.

It was now obvious to Jenny that the evil group had to be Vedron's instructors which proved he would be helped along in his task, which he would need because of his incompetence, arranged or otherwise, but then he would have to settle his account with them. What that would be only the evil would know, but it wouldn't be something simple, probably the total annihilation of his being. But the most likely possibility was that he would have to spend the rest of his eternal existence under their control, and obeying their every command.

Chapter 10

When Danny arrived home he was met with a very happy atmosphere. The children were laughing at a book of jokes Sharon had given Bethany and she was clutching a small fluffy cat from Denis. They were both stretched out on the lounge floor looking as relaxed as one could wish, leaving the mums to chat in the kitchen. Lizzie welcomed him with her usual kiss and he gave Sharon a polite "Hello" then went to get out of his supermarket uniform.

"Dinner's ready" Lizzie called after him.

"Two minutes." came the reply.

Lizzie laughed "That'll be ten unless we're very lucky." She was used to his disregard for time but it didn't matter.

"When are we having dinner Mum? I'm starving." Bethany had homed in on anything to do with food.

"Just as soon as your Dad gets back down here."

As the dining area was part of the kitchen, Lizzie soon laid the table and thought carefully about where they should sit. The children could sit one side, but if she sat at the end it meant Sharon and Danny would be next to each other and that may not be a good idea, so she would put Danny at the end and she would sit next to him with Sharon on the other side. She was still aware that he wasn't very happy at being in her presence and didn't want any unpleasantness.

It never occurred to her that, had the role been reversed, she would have asked if she could be of help, but Sharon had made it clear on Saturday that she didn't do anything if she didn't have to, and she'd had no qualms about leaving her friend to wash up and clear the place.

"Here I am then. Where is it?" Danny looked fresh and clean.

Lizzie laughed and pretended to hit him with a towel. "Sit down there and behave yourself." Then called out "Come on you two, dinner."

Sharon was about to sit next to Danny when Lizzie said "Oh you go there Sharon, I have to be near to the oven."

"Oh you'll be fine." and she sat down.

Lizzie opened her mouth to speak but Danny was there before her. "I think it's more difficult getting out from that seat, so I think we had best do as she asks." Then after a slight pause. "Don't you?"

Sharon had no option without making a fuss and she miserably slid along. Lizzie turned away to hide a smile. Danny could be quite masterful when he needed and she hadn't liked the way Sharon had eyed him up when he came in. Perhaps he had noticed and was aware of her tactics. The children seemed to be in a world of their own and were chatting away happily. Denis, being the little gentleman had let Bethany go first to the seat on his left, which meant he had Danny on his right and Lizzie opposite. Perfect planning by Doag. Denis was now in close contact with the three that mattered but there was a flaw. Doag had observed a difference in Sharon which had tied up with the information circulated regarding her manor visits. Denis was now picking up his vibes and although he didn't know why in his child form, something alerted him to be aware.

Lizzie had cooked everyone's favourite to perfection.

"I love lasagne," Bethany said to Denis.

"And me. We don't have it very often do we mum?"

"Not unless it's out of a packet!" Sharon laughed. "Too much faff."

Denis's eyes had homed in on the garlic bread.

"Help yourself Denis" Lizzie said quietly.

"Thank you." He smiled back with quite a knowing look in his eyes and Lizzie was taken back to the incident at school.

"I love garlic bread don't you?" Bethany couldn't eat quickly enough.

"Bethany don't talk with your mouth full, and don't gobble, you'll have indigestion."

"Oh wind, I get that something chronic I can tell you." Sharon announced as if she'd just won a prize.

Danny was about to thank her for sharing that when he caught the glance from Lizzie and got on with his dinner.

When they had finished the first course, Sharon proved her point and gave a rather dirty belch.

"Oh mind my manners." she said before the next one came.

Bethany giggled then noticed the stern look from her mother so nudged Denis who nudged her back. As it was getting stronger with each push Danny said quietly "That's enough." While he could understand their amusement, he wasn't impressed with this woman and the sooner she left the better for him. The fact that she never even offered to help clear the table was noted. All right she was a guest but he was so used to Beth and Lizzie and now sometimes Margaret, all mucking in that it had become the norm.

"Idle slut" he thought.

Lizzie returned with the strawberry gateau much to everyone's delight.

"I want the first piece." Bethany chimed up.

"Manners." Lizzie looked up.

Bethany was on the ball "to go to Denis." She smirked knowing she had scored this time.

"Hmm..." Lizzie wasn't sure if she'd just been hoodwinked.

When everyone had been served their slice, Lizzie returned with some fresh cream and little was heard until all the dishes were cleared.

Sharon stifled another burp and covered it with "Not bad that Liz, not bad at all."

Before Lizzie had chance to answer Denis said "I think that was the nicest meal I've ever had. Thank you Mrs Worth."

There was a stunned silence, then Sharon broke it by saying "Don't know where he gets it from I don't, all that fancy talk. Not from me I can tell you."

As Danny's mouth opened, he felt a sharp kick under the table and closed it again.

"Well I'll just clear up and then we'll have a coffee, or tea if you like."

"Can we watch my DVD now please?" Bethany was rearing to go.

"Yes, but don't have the sound too loud."

"We won't. Thanks Mum."

She and Denis went off into the lounge and Danny offered to help her with the washing up.

"No I'll be fine, you go and sit down." Lizzie assured him but she knew he would rather be with her than Sharon if she decided to follow him to join the kids.

"Yes you come and sit down Danny and tell me all about yourself." Sharon beckoned to the seat Lizzie had vacated. Alarm bells went off.

The thought was like a kick in the stomach "She's after Danny." Lizzie's back was up and she did something unusual for her.

"Tell you what Sharon, why don't you come and lend a hand, Danny's been working all day."

"No I'm Ok here ta. Don't want to be in the way."

"You are in the way," Danny and Lizzie thought together but neither voiced their displeasure. Without speaking, Danny went into the lounge and like a shot she was after him. He quickly sat in an armchair so that she couldn't sit near him but she sat on the arm and draped herself over his shoulder, Fortunately the children were now engrossed in the DVD to notice anything but he didn't want to make a scene on his daughter's birthday meal especially as she was so happy with Denis.

"There's more room over there." He pointed to the sofa.

"Oh I know, but it's cosier here." Her one hand was now stroking his chest down to his waist while the other was caressing his neck and ears. He tried to get up without making any commotion but somehow she was holding him down with such a force he couldn't move. Panic grabbed him. What if Lizzie was to walk in and what about the kids if they should look round?

Doag had been observing this and pulled Danny's guardian in close but he had no power against the force which was driving Sharon. Not wanting to blow their cover yet, Doag couldn't alert Denis, but they had a ploy which was only used in this kind of situation. He drew back and sent a message by an alternative route but it was in Denis's mind instantly. No onlooker would have realised its source for the operation was only known to a few of the higher levels.

Denis turned and looked straight at Danny. "Have you seen this one?"

Sharon immediately felt herself being dragged to the sofa by some unseen force, but there seemed to be another pushing her back.

"No I haven't. Is it good?" Danny was relieved at being released from this viper.

"Very. I think you'd like it."

"Well I will have a look then." He leaned forward in his chair which brought him slightly nearer the children but put Sharon out of his line of vision. Not to be outdone she moved to the other end of the sofa where she fixed him with such a look, he felt himself being drawn to look back at her. But the tussle on his behalf was too strong and Doag kept Danny's attention focused on the television.

"This is a good bit isn't it?" Bethany grabbed Denis and sat there with her arm through his. Most boys would have pulled away but this one knew he had to stay close to her for some reason and he cast a glance at Danny as if to see if he was enjoying it.

Lizzie came in with drinks for the children and tea for the adults. Sharon took hers with barely a "Thank you" and as she handed Danny his, Lizzie felt as though she had missed something.

"Everything all right dear?" she whispered.

"'Tis now," he murmured.

She said no more but knew she would be asking questions later.

"We'll have to go soon Denis." Sharon was quite abrupt.

"Probably needs a fix," Danny muttered to himself.

The atmosphere proved there was no love lost between these two, but thankfully the children were oblivious to it.

"Oh they're watching the video," Lizzie cut in "be a shame not to see it now."

"DVD." Bethany corrected without turning her head.

Sharon was decidedly edgy and kept looking at her watch.

"Didn't think you had to go anywhere tonight Sharon."

"I told you, I still have to go and do that woman's place."

"Oh yes, sorry I had forgotten." With the excitement of the weekend, it had been the last thing on her mind.

They drank their tea and as soon as Sharon had finished she said "Well thanks for the meal Liz. Denis say 'Thank you.'"

He looked up in surprise, "But you said we wouldn't be..."

"Are you going to do as you are told?" she cut him off, and started to get up. As she passed Danny's chair her hand slid across his shoulder and he flinched. "We must do it again sometime," she whispered in his ear.

As he stood up it was a wonder he didn't knock her sideways, and with a "See you again Denis" he went upstairs in a fury.

"Do you mind telling me what that was about?" Lizzie could feel her temper rising.

Sharon shrugged and gave a sickly smile. "Don't ask me Liz. Some blokes don't know when something's being handed to them on a plate."

If the children hadn't been there, Lizzie would have slapped her, but instead said through her teeth "Well this one does. Ok?"

The battle that was going on around them could almost be felt. Sharon was being programmed to stir up as much distrust between the couple but the undercover forces were using Denis as a block, but it was done in such a clever way that the evil group would think it was Amity's skill. Sharon's good guardian had been removed for now as the risk was too great and it could have been pulled into the evil's control, so for safety reasons it was held off while full surveillance was put into operation by a high force.

Vedron was just about at bursting point. Of all the skills he had acquired, being in control of his urges wasn't one of them, and they continued to rule him as before. The long wait hadn't deflated them, in fact just the opposite so it had to be now or he would explode. He could tell Lizzie wasn't alone and that only a few people were in presence but when he realised that two of the party were about to leave, he decided to wait until they had gone, giving him an almost clear run. The dopey husband and a child would be no opposition. His coast would be clear.

Danny called down the stairs offering to walk Denis home when he had watched the film, but Sharon said she had to get him to her mum.

"Then I'll take him there. Where does she live?"

"She's expecting him."

"Then ring her." Lizzie joined in.

There was a stalemate until Denis turned round. "Oh yes please Mum. Can I?"

Bethany was starting to pout and put the film on hold. "You promised we could watch it together. I've been waiting all day to see it with Denis."

"Oh keep him till I get home for all I care." Sharon made for the door.

"Hang on just a minute." Lizzie's hand slapped on the door preventing her from opening it. "And what time will that be?"

"How the hell should I know? When I've finished of course."

Danny had reappeared and said very calmly now "Just give us your mother's address and phone number, we will ring her and tell her he's watching a film and that I will bring him round when it's finished."

Sharon looked from one to the other then to Denis then back to Lizzie.

"Got a pen?"

Lizzie got a pad and pencil from beside the phone and handed it to her in silence. She scribbled the details and pushed the pad back.

"There, you've got it." then turning to Bethany snapped "So you can stop snivelling now." Everyone breathed a sigh of relief as she went and Lizzie put her arm round Bethany and told her to ignore that last remark.

"That's very kind of you." Denis said and Danny looked at him in amazement.

"You're very welcome." he said, then to cheer the pair up added "now then, where were we?" and sat down on the sofa pulling Lizzie with him.

Vedron wasn't too worried about the lad being there, after all what could he do? Jenny was thankful that Denis could be so adept at keeping his identity well hidden and hadn't needed to expose it just yet, because the trap was about to close.

The evil group were satisfied that Sharon had carried out her instructions thus making it easier for Vedron to home in without hindrance. She had made physical contact with Danny to boost his 'connect' thus rendering him helpless when he was needed most, but had been told to leave Lizzie completely alone and let Vedron think he had a free run. The children were no threat, but now it had been arranged that Danny would take Denis out of the picture, plans were being rearranged for the attack to take place then.

Vedron was flitting to and from the manor in readiness, but still in his reduced size and surrounded by his bodyguard, so no one apart from Watcher was tracking him but other watchers had been alerted. The evil informed him that Sharon had left but to wait a short while longer. This didn't go down very well as he was now like a coiled spring and his surrounding companions were having a job to keep him, literally, down to size. He wanted to burst out and get back to his normal state which was very different to the man at the boarding house. He had formed his image into one of irresistible attraction so that Lizzie wouldn't recognise him immediately and be drawn under his spell by his enticing charm. But his frustration was turning into anger and the evil group were aware this could be jeopardising the whole operation, for the agreement was, they would see that he carried it off without obstruction, but then he would have to return the favour. But with his ego, he thought he could outsmart them, and after using them for his own ends, he would simply disappear and the debt would never be paid. But where did he think he could go? With his limitations he was confined to the earth area where he could always be traced by one source or another.

Although he had been hidden from the good forces for so long, he had been under the close scrutiny of his trainers who were the most sadistic sect in the spiritual world and even hated by other evil forces. It was their modus operandi to hook onto some one else's operation and either destroy it or take the spoils for themselves, the spoils being souls of unsuspecting victims. Vedron was no match for this group and they considered that if he thought he could just walk away, he was a bigger fool than they had imagined and so they would be eager to bring on the fun at his expense.

As soon as Danny had left with Denis, Lizzie started to tidy up.

"Come on now Bethany, bed."

"Oh Mum," the face dropped.

"Look, you've had a lovely evening with Denis, and we can do it again soon, but you've got school tomorrow so chop chop." Lizzie always clapped her hands at this order the way her mother had when she was little.

"Ok."

As many children do when they are forced to do something against their will because they don't want the moment to end, she obeyed but very slowly, dragging her feet along the floor as she went.

"I'll be up in a minute to say 'Goodnight'. Don't forget to brush your teeth."

"I won't." she stopped on the stairs. "Will Daddy come up to kiss me goodnight when he comes back?"

"Of course he will, now off with you."

Denis had been handed over to his Gran who took him in and politely thanked Danny for looking after him but it was clear she felt a bit put out.

"I'm sorry it's later than you thought".

"Oh that's all right lad, not your fault, good of you. It's that daughter of mine." Then checking that Denis was out of earshot whispered "Should never have had kids you know."

"Oh, right." Danny didn't quite know what to say but smiled and made his exit before he could be pulled into any family problems.

The Gran had kept the spare room for Denis so that, if Sharon was working late, he could sleep over and not have to be up beyond his bedtime, then she would collect him in the morning and take him to school. She had tried to get her mother to take him, but Gran had drawn the line at that, knowing it was probably the thin edge of the wedge and the woman would put on her even more.

With a quick 'Night Gran' Denis had taken refuge in this room now as Doag alerted his true self to the imminent danger. Immediately a stand in spirit was placed in Denis's child body to allow him to function without raising suspicion in the human world, and would be guided as how to act and speak, hence the low profile Denis had kept up to now had been geared for this purpose.

It was time for Doag and Denis to assume their natural roles but they had to keep out of range for the moment to still avoid detection but the temporary guardians at the house would be withdrawn by the higher levels at the precise moment for them to take command.

The evil group slowly restored Vedron to his normal size and he seemed to unfold like a butterfly, almost preening himself and admiring his stunning appearance. He viewed his 'assistants' who appeared to be all female expecting them to show some sign of approval of what was before them. Some decided they would enjoy the fun and appeared to be in awe of him but their leader knew by this that his concentration could easily be detracted due to his own self esteem, and that was the precise time an enemy would strike. He would always be a weak link, but they could use him for their own ends, after all, he owed them a debt which would never end.

He stood tall, every sense pulsating as he was about to strike.

"You will assist, but do not interfere when I take what is mine."

The mirth was suppressed. Who did this creature think he was? But let the fun continue.

"Of course my lord." The nearest female bowed to him.

"Anything you say."

"Your wish is our command."

Although the leader found this amusing she quickly summoned them back to attention, but of course without Vedron being aware. Time to go.

Watcher was sending out secret messages to the chosen few but was ready on the front line as this was his operation. He knew the objective and had noticed the high level backup which was ready to act although he would make no contact with them. Jenny and her upper spiral were watching every move but had to rely on the operating spirits to do their jobs without interference. The question had arisen as to why so much attention was being paid to such an unimportant target but Graham and Matthew had pointed out that it wasn't always the obvious that was the threat, and often there was more going on than was apparent. Due to their past experience, they took nothing at face value but gave no further details.

Lizzie had tucked Bethany up in bed and as she went downstairs her mind returned to Sharon and a feeling of jealousy ran through her veins.

"Is that what she was after?" she thought but knew that Danny would never be tempted with someone like that. There had been a suggestion once that he liked a fellow worker, but there had been no proof and he assured Lizzie she was the only one for him.

She went into the kitchen and everything went a grey colour but there were streaks of bright light attacking from all directions, then the grey became black and she felt herself being lifted at great speed with a controlling force encircling her. Any attempt to free herself was in vain for she had no energy or power to resist and was being carried along like a vast moving current in a river. Who it was that had her in their grasp she didn't know but had no option but to go with it.

As Vedron took the unexpected opportunity to seize her while she was alone, Denis and Doag came in from opposite directions, one trying to divert Vedron whilst the other tried to pull Lizzie under his own care. They expected some sort of back up on his behalf but the attack took them by surprise. From every possible angle the evil group swooped until the two were thrown off course. As quickly as they came, they disappeared, but so had Lizzie's soul, her empty body lying on the floor.

Doag tried to follow but Vedron and his support seemed to have been transported from the area and there was no wake to follow. But Denis had noticed something important and called his friend back to follow a new lead.

Vedron had attacked like an eagle swooping down and grabbing its prey in its talons then taking it back to its nest. He had Lizzie, now all he had to do was use one of his skills to take her from the clutches of the evil group. He held her so tightly so that no one could ever take her from him but the anger he felt when he realised he had been miniaturised again exploded around him. How dare they?

"How else do you think we would get you out?" The leader didn't sound friendly.

"Put me back". He roared.

"Put yourself back, if you're so clever." was the reply.

He turned his attention to the cargo in his possession. At least he had what he came for, but something was wrong. Slowly his perception homed in on what he held so tightly.

"What are you?" The horror exceeded the anger now.

Slowly a being unfurled itself until Vedron was faced with the most hideous creature he had ever seen. He tried to recoil but it seemed to be attached to him.

"What are you? Where is Lizzie?" he screamed

"You seem to have made a mistake." The echoing laughter was driving him insane.

"No, I had her. What have you done with her?"

By reply an image appeared in front of him.

"Is this what you're looking for?" The mocking tone ate into him.

"Lizzie!"

Nothing happened and Vedron waited, wondering what was going on. Was this Lizzie or not?

"Give her to me."

"Oh we will, in good time."

"You evil bastards! You tricked me." His temper was now at its pitch and he would have killed any physical being in his sights, but these were not physical and his frustration was clouding his ability to work out the next move.

"You will get her, when you have paid your dues."

"I need her now." he shrieked.

The silence was eerie. There was no more conversation and how ever many times he called, shouted or blasphemed there was no reply.

Jenny was very concerned. Having witnessed the attack they couldn't believe that Lizzie had been taken by the evil group after such careful planning. But certain facts are not always divulged during an operation as delicate as this and would have to remain secret for now. Lizzie's guardian, Amity was blaming herself for not hampering the attack and even though Graham tried to assure her she would have had no chance, it still left her deflated and guilty.

"We need you even more. We are putting you in charge of Bethany along with the temporary guards. It doesn't matter about the obvious strength of presence now, it will be expected." The order gave her a bit of a boost as she knew they hadn't blamed her and this was something even bigger than she had imagined.

Denis and Doag were examining a mark on Lizzie that they had seen somewhere before.

"So that's it." Denis was stunned.

"Think you're right." His friend agreed.

Danny came in the front door as quietly as possible so that he didn't disturb Bethany. He was a thoughtful lad and always did this if he was working late. When he saw Lizzie wasn't in the lounge he went through into the kitchen and as he saw her lying on the floor his first instinct was panic. Had she fallen, passed out, what had happened? He flew to her and raised her head slightly.

"Lizzie. Lizzie can you hear me?"

There was no response and her head felt so heavy in its limp state.

"Check for breathing." he told himself. He had been through a first aid course at work and now pulled on all he had learned, trying desperately to get it right. It seemed so different when it was your wife rather than a practice dummy. His blood ran cold as he realised she wasn't breathing and he couldn't find a pulse. He was almost on automatic now as he grabbed his mobile and pressed the quick dial for Robert and Beth then put the phone on the floor while he started to try and revive Lizzie. Every few seconds he would call out to the phone but still carry on with the resuscitation,

"Get an ambulance." Then "Lizzie isn't breathing." "Help me."

As Robert heard the desperation in his voice he handed the phone to Beth and said keep calling out to him, I'll ring for an ambulance. "Lizzie isn't breathing." After giving them the details he dashed upstairs and told Margaret that he and Beth had to go to Lizzie as she wasn't very well but they would be in touch.

"Let me know how she is Dad." Margaret looked concerned.

"I will. As soon as I know anything. Must go." and he kissed her lightly on the cheek.

Beth was in tears as he rejoined her "What's happened?"

"Don't know yet. Here's your coat" he helped her on with hers then got his.

"Come on, we're going, I've told Margaret Lizzie isn't well, that's all. Keep on that phone."

They hurried out of the door and were soon in the car on their way. It wasn't far but to Beth it seemed miles.

"Come on." Robert felt he had to motivate her as she was crumbling. The door was locked so he used his own key and they dashed into the kitchen. The relief on Danny's face spoke for itself.

"I can't get her to breathe" he was crying now.

"I'll take over. Put the phone off now Beth."

As he got down on the floor Beth and Danny hugged each other unable to take in what they were seeing. Danny was gabbling but Beth got the gist of the fact that he had taken Denis and came back to find her like this.

"What's happening Daddy?"

The little voice made them all freeze. Bethany stood on the bottom step of the stairs, her new doll in one hand. Beth rushed to her and took her up in her arms.

"It's all right sweetheart. Mum's had a fall."

At that moment the siren stopped outside the house and Danny flew to the door.

"Quick my wife's not breathing." He almost dragged the crew in.

"Where is she?"

"In the kitchen. I couldn't get her to breathe and now Dad's trying and..."

"Ok son, let's have a look. "The older man gently moved him to one side as his mate went straight to Lizzie.

"Is Ok sir, we'll take over now." The paramedic said quietly but firmly.

Robert got up and moved to give them room but realised they would need all the space available so went to join Beth.

"Why not take her upstairs." He indicated to Bethany.

"I can't, I need to be here, she's my daughter." Beth couldn't hold back the tears and Danny took Bethany, who was now very distressed at all that was going on and sat cuddling her. He too couldn't go far from Lizzie, and he couldn't leave Bethany on her own upstairs so this seemed to be the only option.

The older paramedic said very gently, "We need to put her in the ambulance to give her some treatment, that's where the equipment is so if you could um..." he glanced at the child "give us a bit of room to take her there," he was choosing his words carefully but they knew he wanted them to leave the room. Robert knew he had to be the strongest here and said "How about if we take Bethany upstairs Danny?" After a quick nod in reply they left and Lizzie was soon carried out to the ambulance.

"I want to stay with her," Danny was following closely.

"Just give us a few minutes son, we need to get her on this machine."

Danny turned but couldn't bring himself to go back indoors so sat on the step with his head in his hands. Neighbours had been looking out of their windows and a few were now filtering into the streets. Robert had left Beth looking after Bethany and now joined Danny.

"What's happened?" Someone called to him.

"Oh, um, Lizzie's not very well. They're just checking her over," he called back.

"He doesn't look too bright either." Another said.

Robert glanced at Danny then whispered "Don't worry I'll get rid of them." He walked to the onlookers and addressed them all.

"Probably nothing but best to be on the safe side. Just checking her out, so you can all go home now. Oh and thank you for your concern."

"Well that's told us." One muttered as they left reluctantly but the words fell on deaf ears.

One of the paramedics got out of the back of the ambulance and went over to Danny. "We think we have a faint heartbeat. Need to get her to hospital ASAP. You coming with her?"

Danny looked up at Robert who nodded. "You go, we'll stay with Bethany."

"Oh thanks, I'll let you know when."

"Take your coat and your mobile."

"Oh yes." Danny grabbed the items and dashed out.

As soon as he was on board and belted, the other para took off on blues, and at every opportunity used the siren.

Everything seemed to be in a haze from then on. The crew ran with Lizzie to a waiting team who whisked her off to resus while they were given all the relevant details on the way. Danny was left to sit and wait until someone came to gather more information as to the cause. He would always remember this as one of the worse things anybody could endure, the 'not knowing' period.

Doag and Denis had witnessed the scene but their attention was in a totally different area. The tiny mark on Lizzie's chest was the only physical sign and would be missed unless examined under a microscope, but it was merely a signpost to what lay beneath, in the very soul. This changed everything. While Denis remained with Lizzie, Doag paid Margaret a visit and did a quick examination of her, looking for a similar mark. His experience told him that such a thing had been in situ but it had been erased. In other words, she may have once been a selected target but had been discarded.

Denis was performing his remote surveillance. He wasn't actually near the body of Lizzie but was in tune with everything spiritual and although he didn't understand exactly what was taking place knew he had to stay close for the duration. On Doag's return they went over the facts. Both young ladies had been implanted with something for future use and identification, but while Lizzie's was still active and giving out signals, Margaret's had been deactivated. The only entity that had been in a position to plant these was Vedron, and it could be a possibility that he would only choose one for himself. These were nothing like the 'connects' which were used for a short term operation to bring people under his control if necessary. They were placed, as he had done to be able to hold back any opposition when he struck, and if they hadn't been needed, they eventually disappeared. No, this was something of a far more sinister nature.

"But why did he also plant a 'connect' when this was already here?" Denis wondered.

"You're trying to understand Vedron's mind." Doag mused. "It's something we've often done, but not always come up with the answers.

"There's always the red herring factor. It might appear strange that he didn't connect her when he'd fixed her family. Then he would be afraid that we would look further and find what we just have."

Doag agreed but was still musing.

"What's eating at you?" Denis was curious and wanted to get to the bottom of this.

"Think. Knowing what we know, when the ladies were raped. Would Vedron have had the knowledge or skill to plant this homing cell?"

Denis was digging into the files of his memory. "I don't think so, not then."

"Was anyone from the evil group involved then?"

Again Denis had to answer in the negative.

Doag was studying him now. "Rewind. To when Lizzie was in hospital."

"I don't think I was there at that point."

"But I was." Doag now transferred the following to Denis who could now see what his companion had realised.

(The Spiral - final page)
At least the emotions planted by Jenny and her team were working. But wasn't that the weapon which had scored? Love, not fear. The forces from Eden had helped these good people overcome the most powerful evil known, and they had won, so for now right had triumphed again.
But it was the final sentence that hit Denis.
Zargot hovered momentarily over Lizzie's hospital bed before returning to Zargon, his thought trail hitting Eden as it passed.
"It isn't over yet."

There was no communication for a moment while the truth sank in.
"So Vedron wasn't working alone, apart from the evil group?" Denis was musing.
Doag reminded him "We still don't know the origin of this group."
"You mean Zargot could be behind them. Using them for his ends."
"Not necessarily. They could be another upstart bunch, they pop up all over the place for a while but get crushed in the end. But we can't be sure of anything. Yes, he could have put them into play, but also he could just be sitting back watching all the fools knock each other out, then come in for the kill."
Denis had to be sure. "But why does he want Lizzie?"
"Don't think he does."
"Then..."
"Means to an end. She's a pawn, and an easy picking."
Their attention was drawn to the resus room. It had been decided that the team should stop and everything was halted. Lizzie had gone. As no life was detected in her body, her ideal (soul) should have remained in presence for a while. This was the moment they had waited for.

With all Vedron's so called skills, he had been fooled into thinking he had captured Lizzie, but all he had in his grasp was a 'stand in' spirit, very clever at imitating any character, thus leaving Lizzie to be transferred to a safe place shortly. The group weren't bothered whether they had the goods or not for they could produce any image to keep Vedron happy in order to get him to obey their demands. They didn't need the real thing, as they could rustle up one of their own for as long as they needed. The stand in had evaporated as soon as Vedron was in the group's clutches which gave them even more amusement. Now they could play him at will.

But it was important to keep Lizzie hidden from all sources and when the stand in had departed a cloak was placed over Lizzie and a different image portrayed. Now that her death had been certified she must be removed and a look alike placed to prevent any suspicion.

This was split second timing but it was now in place and Lizzie was drifting in safe hands. Since the attack she had been in a strange place, unknown but pleasant almost as if she was floating in and out of a dream. She had heard Danny's voice but didn't know why he was calling her. But something told her she was safe and everything was going to be alright.

It was a sad time in A and E. Danny had been taken to a room and told they had tried everything but Lizzie had gone. Gently they broke the news that there would have to be a post mortem which drained the last drop of energy from him. After all the necessary details had been taken he phoned Robert who said he would be there immediately to take him home. He didn't know how to face Bethany or Beth and was silent for most of the journey. Robert didn't try to get him into conversation and he too felt the stinging of the tears in the back of his eyes but he was going to have to be even stronger now for everyone for they would all be upset in their own way and he would have to put his own grief on one side for now. The big question everyone would be asking was how? She didn't seem to be ill and had been in good spirits lately so how could she be dead?

Fortunately Bethany had gone to sleep from tiredness and Beth was waiting for them in the lounge. No words were spoken for a long time as they consoled each other then Danny said the inevitable.

"What do I tell Bethany? How do I tell Bethany?"

"Tell her Mummy was ill and has gone to Jesus, and he will look after her." Beth whispered the words but didn't really believe what had happened.

They all sat united in the pain that everyone who has been in this situation knows only too well, but which words cannot describe.

If they had been privy to all that was going on in the spirit world they would have been hanging on to the hope that everything would come to a happy conclusion soon, but that kind of information would have destroyed the outcome and must be kept secret for now.

Time was of the essence. Lizzie couldn't be kept in this state for long as her physical body would soon be under investigation, so a little help was needed from specialist forces. A time delay may have to be used in order to keep her body ready for repossession. The tenant would occupy the position for her indefinitely, but they were up against the doctors and medical examiners who would be eager to shed light on this sudden 'death'.

Chapter 11

Graham and Matthew knew better than to raise any questions with Jenny when she appeared to be apart from them in thought, and also from experience were aware that it was one of the times when they shouldn't speculate too deeply. There were always prying entities trying to home in on the slightest thought wave and these two advanced spirits appreciated they too must wipe their ideas in case they had hit upon the truth and Jenny's plans would be in immediate jeopardy. But they would be ready for any command and execute it without question,

Jenny had never been at peace since the Burford episode and had received many warnings from her Father who reminded her that love had conquered and she must not harbour any revenge in her soul. But she knew the world was constantly changing. In all areas there were new ways of dealing with tyranny and dictatorship but when she looked at the planet as a whole she often wondered how far it had really advanced in the ways of mankind. Surveying many areas, she knew the human race had not progressed and was still behaving like savages, killing, torturing, robbing, the list was endless.

"And I have to fight the evil to nurture the good." she pondered.

Although still under her Father's will she felt it needed more than pure faith to overcome the persistent battle and often wished he would look at the world from an updated aspect. His basic creed was good and she followed it, but over the years all mankind should have learned from it but the craving for possession and power was rife.

She looked at the moon, the only physical thing of any size between Eden and Earth.

"People are buying pieces of it." She mused. "But they don't own it. They don't own any part of the earth even though they call themselves landowners. When will they realise that they have been given the privilege to live on it for the length of their existence? It is part of everything but it won't be there for ever."

At times like this she did wonder as to the point of it all, but hastily put the thoughts from her and got on with the many tasks in hand. She quickly scanned the hospital concentrating on the mortuary, including her two trusty operatives knowing the situation would be handled perfectly. She also visited Lizzie's house and skimmed over the manor. At this time she dare not delegate and had to reap her own information, but no one could beat her on speed or covertness and used her 'switch' method to advantage. Had she been in the flesh, nobody would have even known she had left the room, such was her skill. For now she had all the information she needed and she put it to the back of her mental file, out of the reach of onlookers. She had to appear to even the high spiral, that she didn't know all that was going on, but this was a necessary ploy on her part.

Vedron's anger had reached its zenith and his captors knew it. If he had been ready to explode from sexual frustration before, it was nothing to the growing revenge he was festering against them as a result of being tricked during his own operation. They were supposed to be helping him in return for later favours, but this changed everything. Even the evil group hadn't quite expected this turn of events as they thought he would just be the same as previous little conquests, but Vedron wasn't run of the mill. The image of Lizzie was haunting him and driving him crazy. They had her and she was his, not theirs. How dare they?

He may not have acquired perfection in the many skills he had been learning but the power of anger together with revenge can produce such a force of energy and can lead to unexpected results. If a person is lying injured they may say they can't move, but under very severe circumstances, if they think something is coming towards them and is about to crush them and they will die, they will move.

Although Vedron was being held in the miniaturised spiritual state, the power emitting from his being could be felt by any nearby power high enough to recognise it. Watcher was there, waiting, willing him to erupt.

The explosion sent out a shockwave which rocked not only the surrounding spiritual zones, but could be felt on the earthly level.

"Bloody hell, was than an earth tremor?" one gardener asked his friend.

"Gave my taters a shaking I can tell you." was the reply.

"But you ain't planted any." Then noticed his mate adjusting his crotch as though he was putting everything back into its right place. "Oh got you .Haha."

"Wasn't funny. Didn't it shake yours?"

"'Ad a funny feeling up me arse but thought it must be the piles jumping around again."

As there was no follow up, they got on with their gardening and soon forgot their peculiar sensations.

But the evil group found no humour in it and couldn't ignore the possibility that this creature could make trouble and lots of it. His immediate captors had been sucked back to normal size as Vedron erupted and he towered above them screaming "Give me what is mine. Give me Lizzie."

Even if they had any intention of doing so, it was an impossibility for they hadn't got her and knew they must play for time. His temper was violent now and even the group, as strong as they might be, were showing signs of the effect.

"Summon up the image." The command ran through them and a likeness of Lizzie was portrayed above them.

Vedron swooped but stopped suddenly, eyed up the image and slowly approached it until he was a hair's breadth away. With his spirit arm extended, he reached out and as he passed through something equal to a hologram his temper was refuelled and he rose roaring with such a force, the evil group doubted if they would ever regain power over him. The leader tried something in desperation. The whole group adopted their Amazon women mode and tried to surround him and bring him back, stroking his form, caressing him all over and using every trick in the book to seduce him. But the longing for Lizzie was driving him, and if she wasn't here he had to find her, and soon.

Even the leader couldn't have verified which direction he went, but the stillness after the storm sent cold shivers through them all. But they weren't allowed to speculate for an even greater power appeared over them crushing them until they were all reduced to specks of spiritual dust.

"You failed!" The scream of wrath rose as if coming from an angry warlord. "You are less than dirt and that's how you will exist from now on."

The evil gang, now redundant were left in this useless state until they may be used again, but certainly not by this high evil power. Let some small fry use their incompetence.

Now free from their clutches, Vedron went in his search of Lizzie. Watcher had passed the message and everything was on high alert now. The instructions had taken the roundabout route in a millisecond and Doag and Denis knew they hadn't much time to execute the next stage, but their orders were very clear. Lizzie must be returned to body at a precisely given moment, for now there was more than one predator, one being much deadlier than the other. Denis would be in charge of removing the temporary tenant, and as soon as Lizzie was passed back into their territory, Doag would reposition her. But these two operations had to be done at exactly the same moment so that her body wasn't completely empty at any time. They had performed this kind of operation before so weren't novices, but they sensed this had far reaching implications so every sense must be honed. The autopsy may be scheduled for the following day and as midnight approached there was almost a spiritual count down clock ticking away the seconds.

Lizzie was in an induced state of spiritual coma. To save her fretting and thus attract unwanted attention, she had been tuned down so that only the faintest trace of existence was evident. She couldn't be in a safer hiding place, but any whisper of it being picked up by one particular evil entity it could result in a terror power reign which may never end. Jenny knew that this was what it was all about and she couldn't afford to let that happen. So a decoy plan had to be put in place to draw off the predators so that Lizzie could be replaced after her ideal (soul) had been cleansed and wiped of any homing device or evil interference. Then and only then would she have the chance of leading a happy contented life, and ultimately a worthy place in the levels of permanent existence doing what she did best, being one of the spiritual helpers, drawing on the knowledge and experience she had gained. Sadly there was the possibility that Lizzie would be a casualty in this, not only by not returning to her bodily form, but to spend her future existence in a horrible place, away from those she loved and doing the bidding of one so powerful he could not be disobeyed. The place most people refer to as hell.

Again Jenny knew that Lizzie was only a minor part of this and not the main objective. She prayed none of the upper or lower spirals had worked out the truth, for that in itself would have ruined everything. Until the final orders went out, she must bear the weight alone.

Sharon had phoned her mother to check that it was all right to leave Denis there for the night and then went home. Her thoughts went to the manor and she was almost tempted to go there, but the thought of entering the grounds on her own at that time of night brought a cold chill over her so she decided to leave it until the morning. Denis had left his child body with a caretaker spirit on board and was well aware that the Gran would be waking him for school the next morning, but he would deal with that event as it happened, for now there was something much more pressing.

Vedron was hovering over Lizzie's house surveying the scene in disbelief. She was the only one not there, and everyone else was in a state of shock and crying. He searched the entire place but there was only the trace of her earlier movements. He noticed a soul had been removed from the house with Danny but to his knowledge it wasn't Lizzie. At this time she was cloaked with a different image being projected, but Vedron guessed this must be a ploy and checked back in the house. The child was upstairs, and Danny and the parents were downstairs, so who else could it have been?

He knew of these tricks so, ignoring the anonymity of the person he guessed they had gone to the hospital and decided to follow Danny's wake instead. This led him straight to A and E and the resus room. There she was, or rather her body lay there lifeless and was being placed onto a trolley.

His mind now tried to calculate the happenings.

He had been tricked into taking another soul which he thought was Lizzie.

His attack had resulted in her physical death as he had planned but why was another soul planted in her.

She was now physically dead so who was still in her body until the seventy two hours was up.

He placed himself on top of her almost merging with her and got his answer. This must be the decoy.

So where was Lizzie?

The careful planning had worked. Vedron would never have understood the intricacies needed. He assumed a decoy was used from the start and Lizzie had been removed at the time, whereas she was almost under his nose being cloaked from his perception, therefore, her body was the last place he would have rechecked and so he went off on his search. Knowing she was not in the hospital area he now had to rethink where to look next which didn't do anything to calm his frustration. He felt he was almost back to square one, no worse than that, as before he knew her location and now she could be anywhere. Little did he guess that while Lizzie was the bait to wind him in, he in turn was the larger bait to tempt the evil that had just destroyed the group, the one who was in charge of the whole nasty scheme with an underlying plan which would have massive disastrous consequences.

He made his way back to the house and hovered over the sad scene trying to work out the strategy. When Lizzie was removed from her body she could have been transported, not only away but upwards, even off the planet. Suddenly his attention was pulled to the neighbours' house and the realisation hit him. Of course, she could have been moved but not far, and she was in the same building but not in her own home.

This stroke of realisation made him pat himself on the back not realising he was falling straight into the trap. Watcher was observing all this knowing full well Lizzie was elsewhere, although he didn't know the location. But he guessed what sort of trick was being played and knew Vedron would fall for it. Sure enough he merged into the atmosphere of one of the bedrooms and there on the bed lay his beloved. It was the body of a young man but the ideal it contained was definitely Lizzie and that's all he wanted. As he gently lowered himself down onto the sleeping form, Lizzie's image rose and as she was now above him. A look of horror was on her face and she tried to float off away from him but he was too quick and he engulfed her squeezing her to him.

"Got you at last," he pushed the words into her, "you won't escape me this time."

"Leave me" she tried to fight but his strength was greater and although his anger had abated, his sexual possession was at its height. He was so busy concentrating on holding her to him, he hadn't noticed they had floated way above the houses and were above the highest flight paths. She started struggling and they began to twist until they were in a spin above the North Pole vortex and were slowly being lowered into it. She twisted again and suddenly he was alone but in the still of the night air above the Atlantic. Trying to get his bearings he noticed something wispy moving in front of him and as he made his way towards it, it seemed to be moving farther away. Something was making him follow whatever it was and as it seemed to be moving just quickly enough for him to keep it in his sights. As it turned, he knew it was Lizzie so he followed as quickly as he could but something seemed to be holding him.

"Lizzie" the call echoed across the distance.

It seemed to be that she was waiting for him, so with a frantic effort he pushed himself towards her but this time he was being propelled against his will. They both suddenly changed direction and were now over the South Pole vortex, but something was very different here. Vedron noticed a drastic thinning of the earth's magnetic field and thought he was witness to a natural phenomenon but there was something else there. Above the area was an unseen presence of enormous size, a blackness that was emitting a power which was destroying the field which was the earth's protection.

Why was he being shown this? He couldn't see Lizzie now and his attention was fixed on this strange apparition.

"Who are you? What are you doing?"

Panic took over as he was drawn upwards to the power who guided him to a position where he could see the effect the thinning was having.

"But you will destroy the earth."

A horrible roll of uncanny laughter hit him. "No. You will destroy it."

"Never. I need it to live with my Lizzie."

"Your Lizzie! She was never your Lizzie. Now you will go to the North vortex and start the thinning there."

"I won't, I need the earth."

"You no longer have any say. Now use the paltry little powers you have learned and transport yourself there now."

Vedron was about to argue but the evil force that hit him made him realise that they had used Lizzie's image to get him to do their dirty work. But another fact remained.

"If I can't have Lizzie, then I don't want to exist."

"And if you do not obey, she will live the rest of her spiritual existence under my power, starting from now."

This was too much for Vedron. It was one thing to have her taken from him, but to cause her everlasting existence with this evil was more than he could bear. So he came up with an idea.

"All right. I'll go, but against my will."

"You will be monitored, so don't come up with any stupid tricks, or...well you know the consequences."

In an instant he had gone, but had more than one tail on him as the evil lord knew he would try something to outwit him.

Jenny was surveying the whole area and knew the time had come for the operation to move up a notch. She warned everyone to be ready and only move when ordered. She had been in conference with her Father and stated that this was not a time for pure love as that would not stop the kind of foe they were up against.

"We have to be ahead of them, and we have to be stronger." she had emphasised.

"But again you are playing with innocent souls, and you know I don't approve."

He knew the enemy had to be checked and had no option but to let her handle it her own way, even if there were casualties.

"I will do all I can to protect them Father."

The meeting was over and it was time for her to take the driving seat.

Watcher had reported and his work was almost done. When he and Vedron didn't appear at the boarding house, there would be no questions asked and the rooms would be re let. Such was the way of thing in those establishments. But for now he hadn't quite finished and set about tying up the loose ends. Firstly he made secret contact with the spirit group who went about undoing the carnage left in the wake of disasters and the like. Sometimes things could be pieced back together and although would always still show the cracks, would function as before. Now he alerted them to the magnetic field and requested a repair job but that could only be done when the source had been removed. Jenny knew this wasn't going to happen without a struggle but it was the only way.

Up to now things had worked. Lizzie had led Vedron to the evil one who was going to destroy the earth but there was more to it than that. The final target was Eden and her in particular. Without the earth, the moon would be affected and behind the moon lay the space area Eden, the base for the Almighty one, Jenny and the upper and lower spirals. Obviously this evil knew Jenny would do all in her power to protect Lizzie, so had used her to get Vedron and many more like him under their power to carry out his plan. Whether he actually destroyed the earth at this time was immaterial, as long as he destroyed Eden and all on it. Then with the good forces eliminated he could control the earth, if it was still there, or move to another area without their interference. And so he would keep up the path of destruction until he would control everything in the universe. He would be God, but an evil God. And there was only one entity to fit this description, Zargot.

"Time to return Lizzie, he can't hurt her now." Jenny ordered. "Everyone stand by."

Denis and Doag were ready, and at the given time Jenny handed Lizzie over to Doag while Denis removed the stand in.

It was mid morning and the medical examiner was just deciding which body to take next, the young mother or the elderly gentleman.

"Come along," he looked at the tag on her toe "Lizzie, let's be having you." The mortician moved the stainless steel tray containing her body onto the rollers and soon she was in place on the base.

"Doesn't look dead does she?" he said as he pulled the cover back.

The examiner raised his scalpel and smiled, but the smile soon faded as Lizzie opened her eyes. Quickly he checked and found a faint heartbeat. To say there was panic in the mortuary was an understatement as the mortician grabbed the phone and almost shouted to A and E that they had a live one. Two porters ran with the trolley and the emergency crew were waiting with the door open as she was rushed back into resus. Everyone was working like mad to get all her vital signs monitored and soon she asked where she was.

"In hospital sweetheart," one of the nurses answered with tears in her eyes for this woman reminded her so much of her own daughter and she would have loved to have taken her in her arms and told her everything was going to be all right.

When they knew she was stable, the doctor thanked everyone and asked that her husband be brought back to the hospital to be informed.

Denis and Doag remained in presence for they knew this could be a volatile time and didn't trust that Vedron wouldn't try again.

Robert had taken the day off work and was at home to break the news to Margaret. Danny's phone rang and he sounded surprised. After a few words, he almost dropped the phone and turned to Beth with tears in his eyes.

"They said they want me to go back to the hospital, and when I asked why they said Lizzie's come round."

Beth went white as a sheet. "Oh Danny are you sure?" then burst into tears.

He rang Robert and repeated the conversation but Robert was a bit hesitant.

"Are you sure it was the hospital?"

"Why?" Danny couldn't understand why he wasn't overjoyed.

"It's just, well…some people like to play sick jokes, and we couldn't stand it …wait. Tell you what. I'll ring them and check just to be sure."

It seemed to take an age before he rang back.

"It's right. She came round in the mortuary and is now recovering in resus. They are going to put her in a side ward soon but only you can go at the moment."

"I want to see her." Beth sobbed when Danny told her.

"You will, just as soon as you are allowed. But at least she's alive."

"Bethany!" they both said together.

Although she had been in the room, she was curled up on the sofa in her own little world crying and had not heard what had been said. She looked up at the sound of her name.

"You can tell her." Danny motioned to Beth as he thought it would be a small consolation for not being able to go and see Lizzie.

There were so many tears of happiness just then and when the little voice said "I want to see my Mum," it took all of Beth's strength to explain that they would when she was a little better but for now only Daddy could go.

"Robert's coming to take me."

"Oh good." Beth didn't know what emotions she had and realised she was trembling from head to foot.

When he arrived Beth asked how Margaret had taken it.

"Pretty well really. Strange though."

Danny thought that Margaret was always strange and went off to the toilet.

"How do you mean?" Beth asked.

"Well when I told her first thing that ... well you know.." he couldn't bring himself to use the words, she said "No she isn't" So I left it at that for the time and thought I'd have a go later. But then we heard that Lizzie was back she said "Told you. How could she be gone, she was with me?"

"Probably dreaming dear. You know she does."

"Anyway, she's fine. Now my lad," he said to Danny on his return "let's get you off to see your missus."

But Margaret hadn't been dreaming. For the later part of the time Lizzie's ideal had been hidden in with Margaret, and Jenny knew that if anything was said it would be put down to her mental state. Where Lizzie had been before that was only for the very higher levels to know, suffice to say that she had enjoyed a meeting with a very kind man who exuded goodness and purity in every way and someone she would never forget in whatever state of existence she was in.

Chapter 12

With the safety of Lizzie being under guard, Jenny's main objective was to work out Zargot's next move and thwart any chance he had of carrying out his objective. In astronomical terms, the earth would not be around for ever and was about half way through its possible life, but that wasn't the problem. Of course it would cause untold distress and horror in its demise and all living organisms including man would be casualties, but this was something completely different.

When a star dies, even when the elements are redistributed, the spiritual levels continue to operate, and reposition to accommodate the new sun and its planets and moons forming a continual balance in all that exists. But the dilemma facing the good forces now would alter everything. Zargot would obliterate what most people refer to as Heaven in his attempt to wipe out the good power but he wouldn't stop there. He most likely had similar operations in force in other solar systems. Jenny's Father the Almighty Good One had his base on Eden for the reason that it was nearest to the planet with the most life forms in this solar system, but his reign stretched out into the Milky Way until it connected with a neighbouring territory. Likewise Zargot, the most evil power could only operate in the same area, thus creating the balance. It would be the same in every other space area in every galaxy, every cluster in the whole universe, and as the whole thing is supposed to be expanding, both forces would be expanding with it.

This proved that Zargot's sights weren't only set upon this tiny area but extended to infinity. The realisation of the effect wouldn't bear even considering. As Jenny mulled this over with her nearest high spirits she began to consider, not the largest aspect, but the smallest.

"We can't even try to fight the outcome," she said "we have to start with the beginnings."

"But we don't know his planning." Matthew had also been pondering on how to stop this evil.

"We know something." Graham answered.

The others in the group were keen to know his thoughts.

"Think of how he uses people."

Jenny was glad he was on the right track. "Look at the proof so far. Lizzie was only a tiny part, but there were millions being used in exactly the same way."

"But if their earthly existences were halted, what would that achieve, because they would still be in spirit?" one asked.

"Move up a notch," Graham cut in.

Jenny said "I had better explain. Although passings of this kind cause distress and sorrow to relatives, it means nothing to the evil powers, merely necessary to the end result. Now, let's take Graham's comment." She paused to let them gather their thoughts.

"He uses the small fry to pull the next stage into his control."

"Vedron and his level." Matthew said.

"Exactly. But they all had to be those with a score to settle. The Vexons are highly sexually driven and won't give up until they have their prey, but look at all the others, many driven by greed, power, revenge, the list is endless. These are all very powerful emotions."

"So then he gets them into such a position they owe him and he then controls them?" one of the group asked.

Graham offered "Can I speculate?"

"Please do" Jenny said.

"Well, judging by the way Vedron behaved I would say that help is offered to give them more powers in order to achieve their goal, but of course they pay highly for it."

"Bit like a loan." Matthew understood what was being said. "People are desperate to pay someone so they borrow but then they have to pay the lender."

Graham added "Except in this case, they never pay back. They can't."

"Because the interest is too high." was the general comment followed by "selling their souls."

"Exactly," Jenny agreed "he takes complete control over them from then on."

"Does he only want the ones seeking power?" Matthew asked.

"In a way. The small fry are usually the insignificant people, just going about their lives not making any waves. No, the ones he needs are the ones with fight in them, because they will be used to cause the destruction."

"One question." Graham cut in.

"Go ahead." Jenny was open to all thoughts.

"Surely he doesn't stop at that level. How high will he go in his enlistment?"

There was silence for a moment then Jenny said very calmly "Very high."

"So the Vedron's in this are merely the first step on the ladder?" Graham's question froze the surrounding air.

Again, Jenny gave time for the facts to sink in. "I believe so."

"But what about the magnetic field around earth, hasn't he already started on destroying that?" another asked.

"Yes, but he can't do it alone. And while he is positioning his soldiers to thin it, we in turn are rebuilding, so we do have some time on our side."

Lots of questions were arising now.

"Who are the ones on the next level that he will employ and what will be their purpose?"

"Is he using human form and has been operating under our noses without our knowledge?"

"How do we stop him before it gets out of control?"

Jenny assured them that they would be kept informed of every detail as it came to fruition, but knew that extra help was needed. It was time to send a communication to another little known group.

Unlike the watchers who excelled in their skill but simply did just that, they watched and were never tracked, there was an elite sector that didn't need to observe. They received the information sent by the secret routes and they acted in ways no one would have dreamed of, but they always succeeded. Unlike watchers, they never took physical form but acted solely on the spiritual planes. Their methods were known only to themselves which was essential and would not have been approved by the Almighty and their existence was denied. They didn't fight with love which went against what the good spiritual followers stood for, but there were times when the alternative was needed. When any reference was required they were simply the 'Unknown'.

Amity was guarding Lizzie, and Doag took over the general control of the guardians of the rest of her family as the threat to them appeared to have subsided for now, leaving Denis free to reoccupy his body for the time being. The temporary tenant was dispatched and all appeared normal to the outside world. It was dinner time before Sharon learned of the events surrounding Lizzie.

"But she's Ok now then?"

Danny didn't want to speak to her and had asked Beth to make the call.

"Well as far as we know she is. But I haven't seen her, only Danny can go today."

"Must have been something she ate." Sharon didn't sound as concerned as would have been expected. "Oh did you ring before only I've been out?"

"Well yes, I did, a few times, but I thought you might be at work." Beth was getting very tired and somewhat disappointed in this so called friend.

"Well you know how it is."

Beth didn't quite know what she meant and said a quick farewell.

Sharon put down the phone, checked the time and left the house. She was soon walking up the drive to the manor but once out of sight appeared to be in the house in no time.

Denis was standing in the playground alone today as Bethany had been kept at home. He was no longer just the quiet little boy, but his own self, acting out the child part but taking in, not only his surroundings but the vibes he was picking up in the area. So that was it! Doag's suspicions had been right and it was time for him to act.

The bell went and the children filed into school but there was one missing.

"Where's Denis?" the teacher called out.

"Not seen him miss."

"Who saw him last?"

There were general shrugs around the room and the teacher told them to get out their reading books and left them with a teaching assistant while she went to alert the headmaster.

Denis was outside the door of the manor house. He realised that if he knew Sharon was inside, she or someone else would almost certainly be aware of his presence. He had to do something and fast.

"Mum." He called cloaking his true identity.

Silence. He knocked at the door and it opened slightly with a creak.

"Mum, are you there?"

"What the hell are you doing here?" The scream made him jump as Sharon stood there fuming.

"I didn't feel well and you weren't at home so I came here."

She looked a bit relieved and said, "Oh well come in, now you're here."

He knew instinctively he was walking into a trap but was relying on the fact that someone was monitoring him at this moment.

"So what made you come here?" her voice was changing and in the gloom her form seemed to be disintegrating.

"Where else would I have gone?"

"Depends on what you were looking for."

They were in the hall way and she turned round to face him. The words appeared like hot embers on his face.

"Well, well, clever little bastard aren't we?"

"I don't understand." He was still trying to keep the little boy image to the fore but he felt it being slowly stripped from him.

"You don't fool me." Whatever was facing him now bore no resemblance to the one who had been masquerading as his mother all these years.

Denis stood his ground facing this new foe and hoped back-up would arrive soon as he knew he was no match for this evil.

"So, you are not so forward now are you?" The mocking cut through him and although he had experienced many foes in the past, this one outdid them all. He was facing pure evil in its most powerful form and it was just a matter of time before it overcame him.

It all happened very quickly. The Unknown swept through the hall, one taking Denis's spirit while the other attacked the evil warlord, finishing him off in seconds and leaving a mere wisp of smoke behind. Denis's body was disintegrated and he would go on the list of 'missing persons'. Bethany would be devastated but she was young enough to get over it and it was one of the many prices that had to be paid in this kind of operation.

Instantly Jenny was receiving the report. Sharon had always been one of the lower evil workers, placed many years ago to get a foothold in an area but not having many spiritual talents. She had been the butt of amusement from her seniors and would be disposed of when she was of no more use.

But the big question being asked was "Who had been using her recently?" She had left Lizzie's leaving Denis to be taken home by Danny, and that meant the way was clear for Vedron. But Vedron wasn't in the area at the moment and the thought had occurred to Jenny that Zargot himself was using her body as a cover. They knew it was a big risk to use Denis to flush him out but he was the obvious choice. He had been in placement since his physical birth to keep an eye on his 'mother' so they soon worked out what her purpose was.

But now it was confirmed that the fiend just destroyed wasn't Zargot but definitely one of a higher level than Vedron, it proved the offensive was being moved up as Jenny had expected. But she couldn't help feeling that they had given it a push and whether that was a good thing, they would have to wait and find out.

The case of the missing mother and child soon hit the national newspapers and everyone who knew them was questioned. The doctor attending Lizzie requested that she was not interviewed until she was stronger and the detectives agreed reluctantly wondering if she knew something connected with the disappearance. Everyone had said that she and Sharon were friends and that their children were close friends too, so they weren't going to leave it until they were satisfied. The guardian spirits had to let this run its course, but knew it wouldn't have any long term effect on the family. Hopefully Lizzie wouldn't be put through the mill too much, but there were ways of dealing with that if it got to be more than she could cope with.

Vedron found himself with others in the Arctic area. At first they seemed to be hanging around doing nothing, and as they all shared his impatient nature, the air became charged with combined anger. Zargot's henchmen tried to shepherd them into one place to concentrate their energy towards the magnetic field. This was the first weak link in the chain, for if Vedron felt rebellious it was nothing to some of the others. In gathering some of the most hateful, vengeful entities together, instead of fighting each other which they would have done normally in order to gain supremacy, they formed an alliance and turned on the ones who were trying to force them to work. In one mass they charged, destroying all the henchmen in one go, then immediately freeing themselves they were gone.

Zargot's anger was unbelievable. Not only had he lost control of his carefully amassed army, but now he had to train new henchmen. He couldn't rebuild the casualties for their souls were shredded and cast to the elements, never to be reformed. But his main emotion was shame. He was the God of all evil, this should never have happened, so what went wrong?

Jenny praised the Unknown for she knew they had intercepted but didn't ask questions. You never did where they were concerned, you just accepted the results gratefully. Graham and Matthew, remembering their last stint on earth joked "Bet they have to put the report in triplicate." Although the humour was apt, they were reminded that they were far from bringing this to a positive conclusion and the threat was there even more now, for Zargot wouldn't admit defeat.

For safety reasons, Denis had been removed from the task completely. Whatever level of evil had been facing him in the manor, although destroyed, would attract the attentions of that level or even above, and this was something else that would upset Zargot's little plans.

At Banbury, the next days were spent trying to put Lizzie's episode behind them so that the family could function as normally as possible. For Danny to get back to work, Beth offered to see that Bethany got to school and back and was surprised when Margaret offered to help as well. When Lizzie was due to be discharged Bethany wanted a party but Beth explained that her mummy would be very tired and they had to let her rest.

"When Denis comes back, I shall ask her if he can come to tea again."

Beth was at a loss for words. She hoped that he and Sharon would turn up soon, even if they had moved away, at least they would know they were all right. It seemed strange though, to go off just when Lizzie had been so ill, but she had no answers and her granddaughter had to be her main concern. She just prayed that no harm had come to either of them.

"Of course dear, but we have to look after Mummy first." was all she could say.

Doag was ordered to stay in place for the time being and keep his senses alert as Jenny still wasn't sure what Vedron might still try. But all attention on the upper spiral was now concentrating on Zargot and the protection of Eden.

Robert had just got home from work and was surprised to see Margaret was busy making a cottage pie.

"My that looks good," he beamed and playfully pretended to poke his finger in the mashed potato she was spreading over the top.

"Get off!" Margaret went to stab him with the fork.

"Is it all for us?" Robert wished his beloved Beth could spend more time at home but knew she had to support Danny and Bethany for now.

"Yes. Mama Beth brought the meat earlier and we started it then, and I've just finished it."

"Think I'll go and see her later, you coming?"

"It's all right, I want to watch a film. Anyway she's coming here tonight. Whoops."

"What did you say?"

"Oh, I'm not supposed to have said, it's a surprise."

Robert was grinning "She's coming home to sleep?"

"Yes, she says Danny and Bethany are all right 'cos Lizzie's coming home soon and she wants to come back here."

"But she'll have to go back in the morning?" Robert asked.

"Not tomorrow, Danny's working a later shift."

Not wishing to offend her Robert thought, "Well we got there in the end."

"You won't tell her I let the cat out of the bag?" Margaret looked a bit downcast.

"Course not. Our secret."

She beamed at that and put the pie in the oven.

They had just started their meal when there was a knock at the door.

"Forgotten her key I expect." Robert got up and went to the open it.

"Hello Robert, hope you didn't mind my calling."

It wasn't Beth who faced him but Bill. This took him completely by surprise and he stood mouth open for a moment.

"Oh sorry, I was expecting Beth, do come in."

"Um, I'm not stopping, just wanted to give you this little note of thanks from the charity."

Something made Robert's hair stand on end. He had seen the man during the day so why bother to come round with something which he could have given him earlier, or even tomorrow. As he took it Bill asked "And how's your daughter?"

"Which one?" Robert was on the defensive now.

"Well the one that was poorly of course."

"Doing very nicely, thank you, now if you will excuse me..."

"Oh, home now is she?" Bill's eyes were fixed in a stare as though he was searching Robert's brain.

"Well it's early days."

"I hope she's better soon, must be a worry for you."

Margaret appeared at Robert's side. "What do you want?" the emphasis on the 'you'.

In normal circumstances Robert would have told her not to be rude, but he was almost relieved that she had picked up that something wasn't right here.

"Well, I'd better be going, lots to do." Bill, giving Margaret a very hard look turned and went.

They both went into the lounge and Robert gave his daughter a hug. "You didn't feel comfortable with him did you?"

"Well I wouldn't would I? It was him again."

"Just a minute. Him?"

"Yes, the one who I keep dreaming about."

"But that was Bill." then after a moment "wasn't it?"

"Bill? No Dad, not a bit like him."

Robert was tempted to ring Bill at his home to see if he was there, but that would sound as though he had lost his marbles completely, and of course he couldn't explain why. Not wanting to alarm Margaret too much he said "Oh some weirdo I expect, probably wanted money for drugs. Hang on, where's the note he brought?" He seemed to remember taking it from the man but couldn't think what he had done with it afterwards. Although they both searched the place, there was no sign of it whatsoever.

While they were eating their meal, Robert gently touched on the man in Margaret's dream but she didn't seem very keen to talk about it so he thought it better to leave it for now but would try and find out what the connection was at another time.

Beth had tucked Bethany up in bed and made sure everything was clean and tidy before saying goodnight to Danny. She could have asked Robert to fetch her but fancied the walk and she still thought she was surprising him by suddenly turning up. The air was chilly but the skies were clear and she filled her lungs with the oxygen. Although she was still looking very drawn from the recent events, her eyes held hope for Lizzie's complete recovery and she still wondered just what had been the cause of her sudden collapse.

About half way home, she felt that someone was following her and quickened her step. Being on the outskirts of the town the houses she passed had small front gardens and there was no waste land so the route was fairly safe. It occurred to her to turn into one of the gardens as if she lived there or was visiting, but what would she do then? She would still have to come out and whoever it was may be waiting. Taking a deep breath she crossed the road and listened to see if the footsteps followed. There was no sound and she quickly glanced over her shoulder across the road. It was completely empty. With relief she turned back to walk on and bumped straight into a woman which made her cry out in surprise.

"Are you Ok?" the woman was holding her by the shoulders. "Sorry, did I startle you?"

"No, no, I was just surprised that's all, I didn't think anyone was there." She gave a nervous laugh.

"Would you like me to walk with you? It isn't nice being out on your own is it?" without any confirmation the woman took Beth's arm and started to march her along the pavement.

"Just a minute." Beth stopped suddenly. "Now, I don't want to be rude, but I am perfectly all right on my own thank you, now, if you would be so kind...."

"Oh quite the lady aren't we?" the tone was mocking "can see where your girl get's it from."

"You know my daughter?" Beth's back was up now. Who was this person, and how did she know them?

"Look over there." The woman pointed and Beth followed the direction of her hand.

"What? I don't see..." but as she turned back the woman had gone.

She didn't know how long it took her to complete the rest of the journey and she felt she ran most of the way, but by the time she reached her front door she was shaking so much she could barely get the key in the door. Robert heard the noise and rushed to let her in. She almost fell into his arms and as he guided her into the room he beckoned to Margaret to get her a drink.

It all sounded silly as she related the incident but Robert was comparing it with the visit from 'Bill'. It must have happened after his visit, but why? Margaret seemed the calmest of them all but what she said next brought a chill to the room.

"Well he did say he'd be back."

Doag had contacted the upper spiral following these two strange incidents and immediately Jenny was involved.

"Oh no not that game again!" then to Graham "Tell Doag to watch Danny, closely, and then Bethany, in that order."

"What's going on?" Matthew asked.

"The oldest trick in the book I'm afraid." Jenny knew that only the most experienced levels would recognise this approach. Quickly she explained "Vedron knew Lizzie's trail had gone cold when she 'passed'. You see while she had a body he could home in on her and her spirit, but without it he wouldn't know where to search, he was going up dead ends."

"But just a minute, one of the spiral queried, "she's come back, she does have a body." There was a murmur of agreement throughout the assembly.

"So why hasn't he homed in on her?"

Everyone present knew by the pause that Jenny had something special to impart.

"Because he doesn't know she is there."

"How?" Matthew was trying to piece this together.

Graham answered with a question "You've cloaked her again?"

Jenny knew he would be the first to work it out. "Had to. Couldn't have left her for him to seize again."

"Alright, but please explain why he, if it is Vedron has visited Robert and Beth and now you think it will be Danny?" Matthew asked.

"Well they always assume that through grief, the vibrations go from the bereaved to try and stay in contact with the departed and quite often they are successful as you know. From there they piece together a spiritual trail in the hopes of finding their objective. It's worked before."

"Can you update us on the Zargot/Vedron situation please?" Matthew asked.

"Yes, things didn't go according to plan there did they? After Zargot got all his evil soldiers together, they turned on him and really messed things up. But that was only on the level of Vedron, he won't let that get in the way. He must already be working with higher levels of evil and even we don't know how that will work out."

"So he is still after Eden?"

"Even more so now. He won't want to loose face, but his main aim is control and that's what is driving him."

Graham was very solemn. "He will let nothing stand in his way now until he reigns over everything."

Matthew although taking all this in had been musing, and now said. "I know this is going back to Lizzie, but why was Robert the first to be approached? I'd have thought Beth would have been first choice."

Jenny's reply left them all to ponder. "He wasn't. It was Margaret."

Jenny was right in one way. Zargot was already working with higher levels but he had been all along. He wasn't just moving up in steps as the upper spiral imagined but sending his workers through all planes of existence from the start. His plan was to cause disruption, mistrust, grief and terror everywhere regardless of the realm. There were many more like Lizzie with predators on their tails, millions of Vexons chasing fulfilment of their lust and stalkers concentrating on one particular person, up to terrorists who felt no remorse at murdering thousands of innocent people. He had been playing the latter like puppets for years and as soon as one horrific attack had been perpetrated, many more were already in progress.

He didn't confine his activities solely to the planet earth. He interfered with various rocket launches and space programmes and had more control on the moon than could ever have been imagined. The weapons previously noticed on the surface led down into an underground maze manned by creatures unknown to man. When the moon was eventually destroyed, they would go with it, but there was no sentiment in his evil mind.

With the recent escalation of his activities, Jenny knew they were getting near to a final showdown, for if he was allowed to perpetrate this horrible disaster, there was no hope for the universe. But she was aware of one important fact. Yes, he could take them all out and try and control everything, but there was one enemy he seemed to have forgotten completely in his lust for power. The universe itself. This was a hostile place and even Zargot wouldn't know all the hidden dangers and if there was one shred of consolation, it was that it would fight back and it would win.

Robert was so concerned with Beth's experience, he almost forgot that 'Bill' had been. They were lying in bed quietly caressing and his mind slipped back to what Margaret had said. He would have liked to have asked her again what she meant but she seemed to have shut off and didn't want to speak about it. He certainly didn't want to discuss it with Beth at this time as she seemed to have settled down. But something was niggling at him and he knew that somehow he had got to get his daughter to open up to him. She seemed to be living a double life, one here and one somewhere else. But as he tossed it around in his mind he realised where the other place was. It was her inner self and it was still as sick as ever. He wondered if she could separate the two but what was more important was the question of what entities shared her inner world. Although keeping things to herself she seemed to take it as matter of fact that certain ones were there and part of her life. Robert wondered if they would ever know.

In the next room Margaret lay on her back, her eyes wide open, but even if it had been light she wouldn't have seen anything for she was far away in the world nobody understood. She didn't always like the people here, but she couldn't do anything about it. But there was one that was always welcome. He was always there when she needed him and soothed her in times of trouble. Symphony was aware of his presence and had alerted Jenny, but he had planted roots so firmly that he couldn't be removed easily. At first he seemed to be a playful spirit and could raise her moods to make her appear normal for a while, but then he could sew seeds of doubt so that she didn't trust herself or anyone near to her. She could never remember when he had first appeared as he had been with her for such a long time, but he had helped her through her 'nasty' time as she called the Burford happenings, so he must be good. Jenny had ordered a check to be run on him to determine his origins but there appeared to be no trace of him anywhere.

Symphony was hovering now as the visitor seemed to be lulling Margaret into a trance like state, and acting on impulse inserted her being between them. She wasn't prepared for what happened next. The spirit rose and pressed himself against Symphony pushing her backwards and out of Margaret's body, but retaining his hold on her.

"Who are you? What are you?" Symphony's question ran through him.

"Nothing to do with you. Get out."

The force of the order pushed her back but she had many skills and now was the time to use her favourite. Her whole being split into fragments and reassembled inside Margaret acting as a barrier. Frantically he banged against her trying to regain his position. The fight that went on inside the poor woman lying there was so frantic, her body was jolted as if she had been given an electric shock.

The warning message went out to the higher levels and within seconds reinforcements had ousted the evil and it had been taken to a place to be dealt with, permanently.

"What was that?" Symphony asked the remaining powers.

"One of many that have been using her as open house since her trauma. Seems she's like a beacon that attracts all the unwanted scum."

"Then it wasn't Vedron?"

"Oh he is a regular, when it suits, but he just uses her as a port in the storm. Evil attracts evil, so where there is a gathering, any passing spirit uses it, often as a cover."

"Ah that would explain a lot."

Satisfied that all was taken care of, the helpers left Symphony with a calmer Margaret for now but knew that in the circumstances there would be others coming along for the ride.

This seemingly innocent little incident didn't escape the notice of the upper spiral and Jenny felt it somehow fitted into the general plan so they would be on the watch for other similar events to try and piece the jigsaw together. There appeared to be many aspects to this and the smallest details may just hold the key.

The latest news regarding the magnetic field seemed positive, for although Zargot was using teams of evil to thin it, the good forces seemed stronger in replacing it and the earth was still safe. But then news came in that rocked the whole area of Eden.

The vortices were all super active including the north and south poles. This was having a tremendous effect on everything concerning the earth. Reports were coming in by the minute of aircraft disappearing from radar, ships being way off course, extreme weather conditions all over the globe including earthquakes, tsunamis, and tornadoes with severity never having been seen before.

Jenny began to wonder if all the minor events were simply decoys to mask the real attack, and they had missed important clues. But everything everywhere had been closely monitored so that shouldn't have been the case. But then something triggered and she called her spirals for conference.

"What have I been saying all along?" she didn't wait for an answer "The little things. Of course."

Everyone waited for an explanation but she quickly sent sentinels out to check certain facts before confirming her suspicions. It only took moments.

"He has been planning this for a long time." she began. "Placing his players into position for many years until the right time came to act."

Everyone waited, there had to be more to it than this, and they were eager to know what she had surmised.

"He has used every wicked emotion to plant his seeds, from the tiniest thing imaginable, through animals, plants, people, maybe even inanimate objects, and even the structure of the earth itself."

"How do you mean used?" was asked.

"Take Vedron as an example. Everything, everyone he has touched has had something left in them."

"What?" the unanimous exclamation almost exploded the air.

"Exactly, and how many Vexons, and all the other evil forms have done the same?"

Graham asked "So taking Vedron again, Lizzie, Margaret and all their family would be carrying the deposit, or whatever it is?"

"And anyone they came into contact with."

"How?" Matthew was confused as he thought Vedron would have to make contact personally.

"Because it is like a virus. Once placed it can be passed on."

"So is anyone, or anything safe from it?" another asked.

Jenny's silence was the answer. Then Graham very slowly said "So he has made the earth destroy itself, or rather the occupants do his dirty work for him."

It took a while for this awful fact to sink in.

"Can you explain how please?" One of the group needed more evidence.

Jenny said "He has activated the deposits, and the electrical power for a start was tremendous, but he has other strong powers and the combination is what is taking effect now."

"But he was trying to thin the magnetic field. Why do that as well?" Matthew said.

"Probably leaving nothing to chance."

All now wondered what action was being taken to combat this disaster.

"We have to put ourselves into the hands of the Unknown," as Jenny said it she knew that this was yet another example of not being able to use the power of love alone as that would never have worked against such a powerful evil force.

As the Unknown calmed the vortices, other super powers were removing all the minute deposits from every living being. Zargot knew there had been a sudden intervention but would never know by whom. Frantically he tried to rebuild all the work which was being destroyed all over the planet but the Unknown were making it impossible for him. As he called on his underlings, they were gradually failing to respond as their deposits were evaporated and many were crushed in the terrific power being used against them. The war raged without the knowledge of most humans, but there were those who were in tune with higher spiritual levels and experienced some of the ferocity of the elements.

With the magnetic field back in tact, attention was now paid to the moon. The under ground cell was completely demolished and the beings sadly had to be disposed of, but that was a small price to pay. Certain equipment was placed to give early warnings of any future invasion of the moon

Zargot realised he hadn't won this battle and had retreated for now, but was already making plans for his next offensive. Then the good forces would realise who they were dealing with, and the victory would be his.

As with all major events, things don't return to normal immediately, and although the Unknown had performed to their usual high standard, it was left to the usual spirits to sweep up and remove many traces of evil intervention. But this was where the tremendous power of love came into its own as can be proven in everyday life on earth. When one hears the comment "I don't know how she copes with it" or "How did he come through that with such a positive attitude?" there lies the proof for it is the love of someone, or even of life itself that fuels the determination to overcome the most awful situation. Yes, it leaves scars, but they add to the experience which is then passed on to others and in turn helps them. It has often been likened to something being dropped into water and the ripples that are produced are like the love and the good reaching out to others who then hopefully do the same, ad infinitum.

There were many ripples being employed at this time and if mortals and lower spirits could have been seen through the eyes of the upper spiral, the whole earth appeared to be covered in connecting ripples until the entire surface was engulfed in the waves of love.

Jenny hoped her Father would be satisfied with the outcome. She didn't expect him to be pleased as he would never have condoned the Unknown intervention, but this would be something on which they would never agree. He didn't like the idea of using innocent souls as bait against such evil forces, but Jenny knew the success had been due to the participation of the faithful watchers, and even others who must not be mentioned or even given a name. As long as this cat and mouse game continued, her support would continue to grow until the power of her Father's love was totally supreme, but when that would be was, in itself the biggest mystery.

Chapter 13

Just over a year had passed since the threat of the destruction of Eden, and although there had been many other attempts at evil supremacy, everything paled into insignificance compared to it. The spirals had been forever busy with the normal kind of activities and the moon watchers had reported nothing unusual from outside forces. Mankind was still observing it constantly and monitoring its increasing distance from earth, but the main interest now seemed to be sending probes to the edge of the solar system and beyond.

Robert and Beth were as much in love as ever. They had their new decking area which had added enchantment to the house as it had a see through roof with hanging baskets and various wooden tubs filled with flowers. Margaret had taken quite an interest in the gardening side of it and had picked the colour scheme which was admired by all. She was now planning a different look for the coming season and often sat browsing through the gardening catalogues for new ideas. The home had never known such peace and Beth prayed constantly that it would remain untouched for always.

It was on a Saturday in May that they had all shared a very busy day clearing out a lot of unwanted foliage and Margaret had been walking around with her plans in her hand, deciding which plants would be put into which pots or tubs. They were all pretty exhausted at the end of it and to save Beth cooking had opted for fish and chips for their evening meal.

"I must be getting old," Robert yawned and patted his full stomach "I never used to feel this tired after a bit of gardening."

"It's all that fresh air Dad, you vegetate inside." Margaret laughed as she cleared away the plates.

Beth leaned over and patted his arm "You'll never be old, not too me."

"Woah, look at you, smoochy as ever. You're like a couple of love birds sitting on the nest cooing to each other." Her mood was so different now and was a welcome change to the two now gazing into each other's eyes. But her dad was quick to pick up what she had said.

"We are hardly on the nest, and if we were you would still be an egg."

This caused such a laugh that Margaret nearly dropped all the things she was carrying to the kitchen. Beth followed and started to fill the bowl with water for the washing up. She had never wanted a dishwasher and was quite happy with the old fashioned way.

"You two are so funny." she laughed.

Margaret gave her a saucy look "I could have said a lot more, but you'd have said I was being mucky."

Even that brought the two women close to tears of merriment then Margaret put her arms round Beth's shoulders and said "I hope I find someone someday that will make me feel like you do with Dad."

Beth turned and hugged her in return "Oh so do I my darling because you deserve it so much, but don't be in too much of a hurry to find it."

"Well you and Dad married later and look how happy you are."

Beth gave a wry smile "Yes, but we have to be honest, we had actually fallen in love a long time before but we couldn't admit it. He was married, and I wouldn't have done anything to interfere."

"I don't remember Lizzie's dad." Margaret looked thoughtful.

"Oh he was a good man," then after a pause "in some ways."

"But not like Dad."

Beth was trying to be careful with her answers. "No, not a bit like your dad."

"Anyway, that's in the past, I don't like dwelling on things that were, well, not so nice."

"Did he hit you?"

Beth was visibly shaken now and Margaret said "Oh I'm sorry, I shouldn't have pushed it."

"No. No it's probably better that you know everything then it can be put out of our minds for good."

Margaret felt guilty "Look if you'd rather not."

"Let me tell you. Yes he did hit me and I was afraid for the baby, Lizzie of course. He had seemed so lovely but he turned after we were married and everyone was saying 'I told you' but I tried to make it work. Only…one day he …pulled a knife on me and I knew I couldn't take any more."

"Oh Mama Beth I never guessed." Margaret was close to tears.

"Well, to cut a long story short I left with Lizzie and he would come after me and… oh, it was terrifying. In the end he was arrested and went to court and then I found out that it wasn't only me. He had been violent to many others, and I can't tell you how many charges there were against him."

"So did he go to prison?"

Beth's lip was trembling now. "It didn't get that far."

"What do you mean, didn't get that far?"

There was a long silence and Margaret looked at Beth, waiting.

"Well, someone took the law into their own hands."

"What?"

"Well, the police thought it may have been someone connected to one of the other women."

"And what did they do?"

"There was no proof you understand, of who it was I mean, we don't know who's car it was."

Margaret was afraid to ask, but was still burning to know. She knew she must be patient if she was to learn the truth.

Beth took a deep breath. "He was coming round to where we were living you see, I didn't want him to but he wanted to bring something for Lizzie but he never got there."

Margaret nodded, urging her to continue.

Beth was visibly shaken now. "I didn't see it, but I heard a scream and when I went out he was lying there in the road. A neighbour said the car had come from nowhere, hit him straight on and raced off."

"And nobody knew who it was?"

"It was all too quick, and no one else was in the street it seems."

"And was he… you know…dead?"

Beth nodded. "It hit all the papers of course and you wouldn't believe how people changed. Margaret, you never know what people can be like. I always try and see the best in them but, oh dear. Some cut me dead. Some pretended to sympathise then ran off and spread what I had told them, only they changed it to their satisfaction. But there was one person who was my rock, and on whom I leaned through it all."

"You're going to say it was Dad, aren't you?"

"Yes, he helped me to hold my head up and face the world, after all I was the victim, not that you'd have known it."

"Ooo if I'd been there I'd have told them what I thought of them. The bitches".

Beth had to laugh now "I guess you would too."

Robert entered the kitchen at that moment and asked what all the frivolity was about and in chorus the two said "Girl's talk." then laughed as they threw tea towels at him saying that he would have known if he had been there doing the drying up. The mood was of family unity as they all went to bed.

Robert may have felt tired but as soon as he felt Beth's body against him he was anything but in the limp state. Having just been reminded of her former husband, she now appreciated more than ever being married to the man of her dreams and responded immediately to his caresses. It wasn't long before they were both in the throws of lovemaking, the gentle rhythm stirring up the feelings they had come to crave. Robert erupted like a giant wave crashing on the shore taking Beth with him and they became one being with nothing separating them as their physical liquids merged and their souls seemed to fly off to a place where they were alone and entwined in their emotional love.

It took a while for them to 'come down' and get their breath back. Robert reached for the tissue box which was always very conveniently to hand and was about to get out of bed when the door burst open with such a force it nearly came off its hinges.

"You filthy animals. You do this to torment me." The screech must have been heard streets away and Beth and Robert looked on in horror. The tirade continued "You can't leave me in peace, you enjoy your sex to punish me. You don't want me, but I'm here. Now!"

Beth was nearest the door and was looking at the figure in front of her. She couldn't believe what she was seeing for facing her with venom coming out of her mouth was Madge. Her eyes were like coals and her arms seemed to be extending towards them the fingers growing with the nails reaching out to slice into her. Robert tried to turn round but his movements seemed frozen. The horrible scream that emitted was enough to chill the most hardened and they both felt the utter evil hatred being projected at them.

The alert had gone up from Symphony and in an instant Graham and three others were there.

"Think of your love, build it, concentrate." he fired at Robert and Beth. Then he and his team surrounded Madge's image and slowly drew together until she was encased in the power of them. They slowly started to lift as a whole until they had left the house and were now taking her away for 'cleansing'.

Symphony was draped over Margaret's body which was in a heap on the floor and coaxing her back to her own self. The words 'it's gone..it's gone..it's gone..it's gone..' were being repeated in a flow through her brain.

Beth was the first to move and ran to her, while Robert saying he would be back rushed off to the toilet. When he returned, making sure he was decent in front of his daughter, found she was coming round slowly.

"It's all right." Beth was repeating and almost rocking her in her arms, tears streaming down her face.

They both had a flash back to Burford and knew that the spirit of Madge, or something emulating her had been in the room but had used Margaret to vent their anger. There was no explanation for why they had suddenly used the power of love because the thought had seemed to just come to them.

"Where is she?" Margaret whispered.

"Gone. Gone for good darling." They were both hugging her.

"I had a terrible dream."

"Try to put it out of your mind." Robert said, thinking that if she could forget it now she may never have to recall it again, as long as Madge had gone for ever.

"Why am I on the floor?" she looked round "and what am I doing in here?"

Beth helped her up. "Probably just sleep walking, lots of people do it."

"Did I do anything silly?"

"What you? Never." Robert was still trying to get over the horrible shock so decided to make himself useful. "Tell you what, don't know about you ladies, but I could do with a cup of tea."

"Oh that sounds good." Beth agreed and while Robert went downstairs to mull over the apparition, the ladies sat on the bed and slowly returned to normal.

Jenny had witnessed the scene and had been assured that the spirit of Madge was well out of the way and could not return. Although it had been a serious and delicate operation there was a slight ripple of mirth when Graham referred to her as now being in the 'drying out zone'."

Lizzie had come through her experience pretty well, and before being discharged from the hospital had made friends there. So when she had recovered and applied for a job as a domestic, she was taken on straight away. It wasn't long before she fitted in as her likeable ways endeared her to many. One of the supervisors noticed her natural communication skills and now she was working on the wards where she often brightened the patient's days with her simple friendliness and caring nature.

"It's almost like being back in the home." she thought as she busied about the geriatric unit but remembered to watch out for some of the fruity old men as they could be very naughty boys. One of the ladies who was very frail said that she liked her so much as she wasn't patronising like some she could mention. Lizzie never got involved with gossip or opinions about staff as the odd chance comment could be altered into something completely different.

Danny was amazed at the change in her recently and knew she was doing what was close to her heart, caring for others. She was the perfect wife and mother, but Bethany was moving up to another school and would be away longer, and he had his steady job in the supermarket so he realised she needed fulfilment. Plus the money was very useful and meant they didn't have to watch the pennies quite so much. He worked with a few flighty young girls who would tease him or even try to come on to him, and although he would cast an approving eye over some, it was merely window shopping and Lizzie was his only true love. Luckily he knew she felt the same, and while he saw other women, and married ones at that, flitting from man to man he knew she would never be tempted into that area and they would remain a perfect family unit.

Lizzie had finished her shift and was making her way along one of the long corridors to clock off. Many parts of these passages were glass from floor to ceiling and at certain intervals they was a small garden area where staff could sit to take a break or just get away for a moment after a particularly traumatic incident. As she passed one of these little havens she noticed one of the male nurses sitting on one of the benches, his head in his hands. Her caring side came straight to the fore. Gently opening the door she went out and carefully shut it behind her. She quietly walked to the bench and sat down, not close but at the side of him.

"Hello." she almost whispered.

He raised his head slowly and she noticed how tired he looked, but his eyes were beautiful and she couldn't remember when she had ever seen such lovely ones.

"Oh hello."

Her heart fluttered. Not only had he got the most drop dead gorgeous eyes but his voice. It purred.

"Hope I didn't disturb you." She whispered.

"No it's Ok, just catching my breath." The words seemed to float on the air and she felt she needed to hear more.

"Have you been on a long shift?" she didn't know quite what to say but he looked tired and it was the best she could muster.

"Pretty much."

"Well I don't want to be in the way," she went to get up.

"No, please stay." he looked at her name badge "Lizzie."

"Oh yes, that's me." She gave a nervous laugh but didn't need a second invitation to remain where she was, but noticed he seemed to have pulled slightly closer to her. Being at a loss for words she looked at his badge and said "Keiron, that's a nice name, but I didn't know it was spelt like that."

"It's a variation of Keiran."

"Oh I see. I don't suppose you know what it means do you, only I like to know what names mean."

"It's Gaelic, and means dark or black."

"Oh.

"And what does Lizzie mean?" His eyes were searching her and she felt as though she was falling under his charm.

"Well mainly it means 'Oath of God' but can mean 'God is Satisfaction'."

"Interesting." Was all he said but gave her a smile which made her feel uncomfortable, as though he was reaching into her very existence.

"Um, my little girl is named after the village near Jerusalem." She said nervously feeling she ought to leave but something was holding her there. If he had made love to her there and then she wouldn't have refused but immediately felt the guilt of having such thoughts when she was in love with her husband.

"As a matter of fact, I don't use this name at home."

Now she felt a little more at ease. "Why? It's such a nice name."

"Well the family call me Dev, same as my father."

"Oh I don't like that so much, can I call you Keiron?"

"Why not, everyone else does."

She didn't expect what happened next for he turned full on and said "Thank you so much, you've made me feel better. Only I've just had two people die you see, and I just like to gather my thoughts before I go and speak to the relatives."

This brought out her caring side to the full and all thought of embarrassment or awkwardness disappeared.

"Oh I'm so sorry. I expect you have that a lot." Her hand instinctively went out and touched his arm.

"Well sometimes." he said as he placed his over hers.

The contact sent waves of electrical impulses through her whole body and she knew she had to see this man again. Even his touch was magic and she had never experienced such a beautiful euphoric feeling as this, and she didn't want it to end. Slowly he removed his hand and she almost came to with a start.

"I had better go, my daughter will be home soon and I must be there when she gets there."

"Of course. Till next time."

They moved towards the corridor and suddenly he was in front of her, only inches from her his eyes melting with emotion. She was longing for him to kiss her but knew she had to tear herself from his gaze.

"You mustn't be late for Bethany," he whispered.

"No I mustn't. Bye" and with a little wave she hurried past him and had to force herself to hurry towards the exit.

It was only when she was sitting on the bus she realised he had used her daughter's name, but she hadn't told him what it was, but then she realised he would have worked it out from the description she had given him, and so her mind was at rest. If she had been one to play around with words, she may have pieced a few letters together. Yes his name did end in RON, but he said he was called DEV, reversed to VED made Vedron.

No one would see him standing in the garden for he was only visible to her. He now felt very smug. This time he had got her. She had made the first move. She had touched him first. She wanted him, and by God he knew she would have him. Vedron had played his trump card by using the very thing that had been his enemy. He had resorted to the power of love.

But his satisfaction was short lived for he had made a huge mistake. He had forgotten to keep his protective guard around him and in the next instant he had evaporated and the only spiritual proof he had been in presence was a small puff of dust which was being carried in numerous directions by the breeze.

The instigating power reigned with satisfaction but its source was not of this earth.

It will never be

THE END

as long as good and evil are in conflict

About the Author

Tabbie Browne grew up in the Cotswolds in central England which is where she gets the inspiration for her novels. Her father had very strong spiritual beliefs and she feels he guides her but always with a warning to stay in control of your own mind.

Her earliest recollection of writing was at primary school and it has seemed to play a part at significant times during her life. She thinks it is only when we are forced to take step back and unclutter our minds for a while we realise our potential. This point was proved when she slipped a disc, and being very immobile had to write in pencil as the ink would not flow upwards! At this time she wrote many comical poems which, when able again, performed to many audiences. Comedy is very difficult but you know if you are a success with a live audience.

In 1991 as a collector of novelty salt and pepper shakers, she realised there was no book in the UK devoted entirely to the subject. So she wrote one. Which meant she achieved the fact that it was the first of its kind in the country and it sold well to like collectors not only in the UK but in the USA.

Another large upheaval came when she was diagnosed with breast cancer, and due to the extreme energy draining, found it difficult to work for an employer. So she took a freelance journalist course and was pleased to have articles accepted, her main joy being the piece about her father and his life in the village. Again the inspiration area.

But the novels were eating away inside and drawing on her experience at stamp and coin fairs she wrote *'A Fair Collection'* which she serialised in the magazine 'Squirrels' for people who hoard things.

When she wrote *'White Noise Is Heavenly Blue'* and its sequel *'The Spiral'* she sat at the keyboard and the titles just came to her, as did the content of the books. There is no way she could write the plot first as she never knew what was coming next, almost as if somebody was dictating, and for that reason she could never change anything.

Loves:
Animals,
Also performing in live theatre and working as a tv supporting artiste.

Hates:
Bad manners,
Insincere people.

Printed in Great Britain
by Amazon